Emily Brugman grew up in Broulee, on the far south coast of NSW, on the lands of the Yuin people. Her writing has previously appeared in literary journals, magazines and anthologies, including *Tracks*, the *UTS Writers Anthology* and *Lines to the Horizon: Australian surf writing*. She currently lives in Mullumbimby, on Bundjalung country, and works at Byron Writers Festival. *The Islands*, her first novel, is inspired by her family's experiences living and working on the Abrolhos Islands between 1959 and 1972.

'There is an other-worldly quality about the Abrolhos which is beyond the reach of ordinary storytelling. Emily Brugman has captured them, staked them to the page in all their isolation and aridity and scoured indifference, because her storytelling is extraordinary.'

Jock Serong, bestselling author of *Preservation*

'A beautiful breathtaking salty book about finding home on the far reaches of the continental shelf.'

Marele Day, author of bestselling *Lambs of God*

THE ISLANDS

EMILY BRUGMAN

ALLEN&UNWIN
SYDNEY・MELBOURNE・AUCKLAND・LONDON

First published in 2022

Allen & Unwin
83 Alexander Street
Crows Nest NSW 2065
Australia
Phone: (61 2) 8425 0100
Email: info@allenandunwin.com
Web: www.allenandunwin.com

 A catalogue record for this book is available from the National Library of Australia

ISBN 978 1 76087 858 0

Internal design by Simon Paterson, Bookhouse
Maps by flatEARTHmapping
Set in 12/18.25 pt Janson Text LT Pro Roman by Bookhouse, Sydney
Printed and bound in Australia by Griffin Press, part of Ovato

10 9 8 7 6 5 4 3 2 1

Silloin seppo Ilmarinen
itse tuon sanoiksi virkki
Saattanen takoa Sammon,
kirjokannen kalkutella
joutsenen kynän nenästä,
maholehmän maitosesta,
ohran pienestä jyvästä,
kesäuuhen untuvasta.

These the words of Ilmarinen
I will forge for thee the Sampo,
hammer thee the lid in colours
from the tips of white-swan feathers,
from the milk of greatest virtue,
from a single grain of barley,
from the finest wool of lambkins.

For Mummu and Pappa (Maila and Auno 'Herman' Talviharju) and the Finns of Little Rat

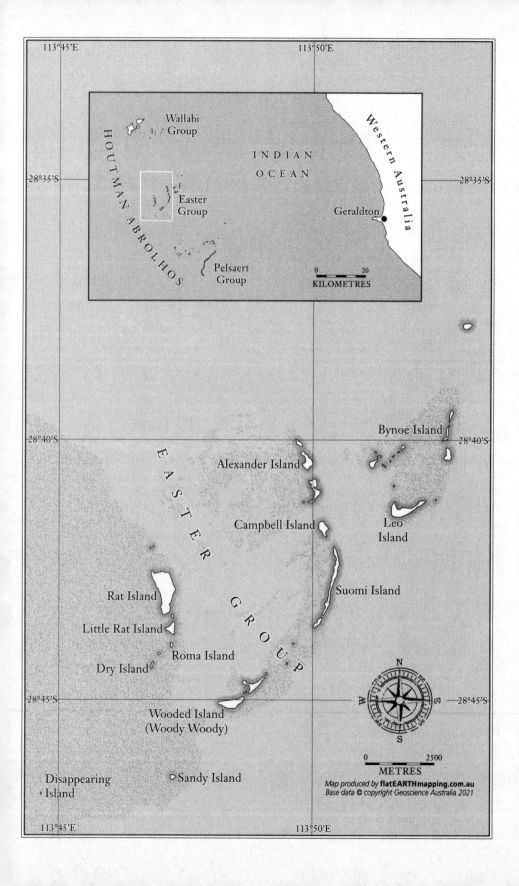

PART 1

WEST

Crayfish (white)

THE ISLANDS WERE A DAY'S boat ride west of the mainland. There was a point halfway across, the fishermen said, like an imaginary line drawn in water, where you left it all behind. Sparse weatherboard suburbia. The dusty rhythm of mainland life. The port, with its towering silos, its tugboats and ocean liners. Halfway across the deep trough you entered another universe. A few more hours of travelling and the welcome sliver of an island would come into view, then another. Landscapes built of bleached coral rubble, of saltbush and seabird droppings.

Onni Saari had sensed it on previous crossings, that vaguely magical feeling, as though freedom was waiting for you just over the horizon. But on this occasion he could not conjure it.

There was nothing good about this particular boat ride.

In the aftermath of the storm the sea was flat and still, its energy all but spent in the deluge. As the carrier boat neared the mooring at Little Rat Island, Onni took a deep breath and found the stone face he needed.

Sulo Koskinen, a seasoned fisherman, met him with a sombre and meaningful handshake. Sulo stood with his legs apart and was solid as rock.

'He was last seen motoring out towards Disappearing Island to collect his craypots.'

It was now Onni's turn to speak. He shifted his weight from one foot to the other.

'When he didn't come back,' continued Sulo, Onni having remained silent, 'there was nothing we could do. The swell was on the up, son. We've been out looking early this morning. No luck. We'll head out again soon.'

Onni coughed, like a motor spluttering to life. 'I'd like to go with you.'

The message had been sent by short-wave radio two days prior:
Nalle Saari lost at sea. Contact brother.

It was the Northampton constable who had delivered it. They were taking their lunch outside the miner's humpy, seated on empty dynamite boxes. After the policeman left, Onni let Alva unfurl his tightly clasped hand and take it in her own, but ignored her suggestion to let the morning blasting be. The boat wouldn't be going out until the sea settled, he told her, and it wouldn't be right to leave the work for others. It was the covering of the earth that he longed for. Out there, in the wide open country, he felt exposed. So he had gone down into the hole and shovelled dirt furiously, his heart pounding from the labour, and from the not-knowing. Sweat marked the high planes of his cheekbones, and he was grateful for the solitude afforded by the dark narrow

4

tunnel. Onni made the drill holes in which he would lay the dynamite, each one the length of a body. When it was time to blast the new section of the lead mine, he welcomed the rumble of dynamite in his bones. His body trembled with each explosion, and that helped a little.

The next day Onni drove from Northampton to Geraldton. He could scarcely focus on the road ahead, nor on the countryside around him. He would have followed the red-dirt track leading out of the mine site into yellow wheat country. He would have passed by several river red gums, bent over the Chapman, before rattling his way into town and down to the port.

Nalle Saari lost at sea. Contact brother.

The words returned to him over and over, but he could not settle on them. They didn't sound like any language he knew.

'Good luck, mate,' a man from the fishermen's co-op said, shaking his hand with a firmer grip than usual. 'Hope you find him.'

Onni had looked at him with his lake-water eyes, and the man could not hold his gaze. Onni did not want his pity. Besides, it wasn't over yet, was it? He refused to count the hours. He didn't want to know how long his brother had been out there. It was possible he had been swept a long way in a squall and even now was navigating his way back to the islands, laughing at his good fortune. It was possible.

The search party was made up of six men, including Onni. The others were all Nalle's good mates. Onni knew them a little, from his few, brief visits to the islands, and from the stories Nalle would tell him when they came together during the off-season. Sulo, Esko, Tall Tommi, Risto and Latvian Igor. They'd come out to the islands almost ten years back, around 1950, on hearing that a kind of gold could be found in the waters here. Come with a map and compass and little else. In Sulo's cray boat, they now circled the perimeter of Disappearing Island with Onni, keeping an eye out for the strewn debris of a boat and, far less likely, a man clinging to it. Gulls cawed, and the stale odour of dead fish, emanating from the vessel, entered his nostrils. Onni scanned the water, willing Nalle to turn up, for some miracle to come to pass.

'Why do you call it Disappearing, then?' Onni asked, head down.

After a moment, Sulo's gruff voice: 'Comes and goes, this island, with the movement of the water.'

So it was not some gyre that swallowed lone fishermen.

The men were quiet, and Onni wondered if they, too, were thinking about water. How it could shift great swathes of sand. A melancholy feeling settled down in the boat, until the man with one eye passed wind, and someone laughed.

For Onni, time became elastic, the hours warping, bending, with no beginning and no end. He tried not to blink, lest he missed something. A mere shadow below the water. Some remnant of Nalle's boat. His equipment. A craypot. Anything at all. Evidence that he had been here, that he existed. The water, glistening in the sunlight, reflected nothing but calmness. Onni couldn't equate this blissful aquamarine with the sort of violence that might drown a man.

Upwind from him, Sulo began to chant under his breath—a half-song, half-poem, his voice low and rumbling. At first Onni clung to an irrational hope: was this some siren call to bring his brother back? Then the song took shape in his memory, like a figure moving into the light. The rhythm was old, of pagan origin: *The Kalevala*. The story of the forging of the fabled Sampo. All the men knew the folktale, but they didn't have the words, or the metre, like Sulo did.

> *Siitä seppo Ilmarinen*
> *takoja iän-ikuinen,*
> *takoa taputtelevi*
> *lyöä lynnähyttelevi.*
> *Takoi Sammon taitavasti*
> *laitahan on jauhomyllyn,*
> *toisehen on suolamyllyn*
> *rahamyllyn kolmantehen.*
>
> *Siitä jauhoi uusi Sampo*
> *kirjokansi kiikutteli;*
> *jauhoi purnun puhtehessa—*
> *yhen purnun syötäviä*
> *toisen jauhoi myötäviä*
> *kolmannen kotipitoja.*

> Quick the artist of Wainola
> forges with the tongs and anvil,

> knocking with a heavy hammer,
> forges skilfully the Sampo.
> On one side the flour is grinding,
> on another salt is making,
> on a third is money forging,
> and the lid is many-coloured.
>
> Well the Sampo grinds when finished,
> To and fro the lid in rocking;
> grinds one measure at the daybreak—
> grinds a measure fit for eating,
> grinds a second for the market,
> grinds a third one for the storehouse.

The quiet chant had the quality of a salve, somehow soothing them. Onni allowed his mind to drift back to the homeland. To the old, old Finland, which he knew only through myth and rhyme. His thoughts circled the mysterious Sampo. What was it? A mill that ground out corn and salt and money, and anything its owner wished for? He remembered that in a later canto, the Sampo was lost at sea.

His trance was broken when Sulo paused to let out a husky hawking, followed by a tobacco-laced gob over the side of the boat. Onni was aware again of his surroundings—of the sound the keel made as it sliced the clean skin of the water; the plop of a coral trout as it fluttered on the sea's rippled surface—aware that his brother was likely drowned.

When the sun dipped in the western sky, Onni felt the resolve in the boat slip away.

Risto took out his rod. 'Might as well see if we can get some dinner while we're out here.'

The mention of dinner pierced Onni with a pinprick of sorrow. The world would continue to turn on its axis.

When it came up, the baldchin groper had a gouge in its side. The men noticed the fleshy sinew of the fish, torn and untidy, and looked away. But Onni caught Sulo's hurried glance to Risto, the movement of his lips: '*Tiikeri hai.*' Tiger shark.

Later, alone at last in Nalle's camp, Onni sat on the edge of his brother's cot with his head in his hands, pressing his palms into his eye sockets. He had lit the kerosene lamp, its humble light casting shadows on the tin walls. There was little in the camp in the way of furniture and possessions: it was a bachelor's sleep-out. The cot, sagging in the middle, and a small primus burner. A hand-carved wooden spoon, half finished, lay on the small square table. Onni remembered whittling wood with his brother as a youngster. How they'd made spoons then, too. He had shaved the birch wood away carefully, working on it for days. When he'd finished with it, his spoon was straight up and down like a ruler. Nalle, on the other hand, had carved his in one sitting: a rutted, off-kilter thing but, in the end, somehow better and more interesting than Onni's. This spoon would have had life in it too, thought Onni.

The table was littered with things that Nalle had touched just days earlier. An enamel mug with a sad puddle of black coffee at the bottom. A fishing manual. An ashtray, the stub of his last smoke still there.

All around, Onni felt the presence of that vast dark ocean. Finally, his choked cries came, the sound of some wretched animal. He was grateful for the night breeze that had picked up on dusk and now rattled through the cracks in the hut, muting the sound.

The search was launched again the following day, and again the sea offered up nothing.

In the evening, Onni looked out the kitchen window and noticed a dim light in the small lean-to by the jetty.

Brother.

Inside his chest, a moth beat its wings. Of course, there was no logic to it. He remembered then that he had been out by the jetty at dusk with the tilley lamp. Must've left it behind. But he couldn't shake that feeling. That here, Nalle was just around the corner.

On the third morning, Onni waited again at Sulo's boat. He noted the slow habitual movements of the island folk. He saw fishermen sculling out to their moorings. Cray boats being loaded with gear. The distant sound of motors grumbling to life, a skipper calling to his deckhand. Onni understood that the fishermen were returning to their work. As he waited by Sulo's boat, he felt like a forgotten child.

Some time passed before Sulo turned up, his hands in his pockets, an apologetic look on his corrugated face.

The search was over.

And as the sun moved over the sky, and Onni allowed himself to calculate the days since Nalle had gone missing, he understood that all this searching business, those long stretches adrift on the boat, were likely for his sake more than Nalle's.

That night Onni sat with four of the fishermen around a fire in front of his brother's hut. The silent Latvian did not join them this time. There was a touch of ceremony in their movements, in the low hum of their voices, in their decision to sit at the lost man's camp. They talked about the early days on the islands, about the building of the *kivi kämppä*, the stone camp. Again Onni had the sense that this was a performance of sorts. Their own, clumsy version of a eulogy. They spoke in the mother tongue, an English word thrown in mid-sentence, modified to fit the Finnish sound.

'There was just one *kämppä* on Little Rat when we came out,' said Sulo. 'Then us Finns turn up in our skiff with nothing but the clothes on our backs and a bit of vodka.'

Five of them had come in that skiff. One-eyed Esko, the best dart player on the island; Tall Tommi; Sulo; Risto; and a bloke named Jussi, who had since moved on to pearl farming. Most had gone looking for copper in the mines of Mount Isa before heading to the west coast, where they'd heard there was fishing going on. Letters home told of good money and endless sun, and soon other Finns followed, like Onni, taking a similar migratory route to end up here. Back in Finland, before coming out to Australia himself, Onni had spoken proudly of his brother. *He's a pioneer*, Onni told his friends. *He doesn't give a damn about comfort or fine things. He goes where the money is. He'll end up a rich man.*

Onni remembered his first visit out to the islands, maybe a year back. To see it with his own eyes, this landscape that Nalle had described. Islands as flat as pancakes that sat at the edge of the continental shelf. His brother gave him the full tour, motoring between the many atolls, describing the geological formations. Some of the islands Nalle had shown him were mere sandbanks that came and went with the falling and rising of the seas. Like Disappearing Island, Onni thought now. Others were a touch sturdier: the roots of squat shrubs acted like fibres, knitting the sand and coral together, making them one organism. Once upon a time the area would have been connected to the mainland, Nalle guessed, before sea levels rose. Had blackfellas walked across? wondered Onni. Had they reached down into holes and pulled up crayfish, way back then when the land looked different?

Beside him, Sulo's large, gnarled hands expertly worked a wad of tobacco into a rollie paper. He stood up and held it into the fire before taking a long drag.

'There was nothing here then,' Sulo said. 'Little Rat was an abandoned mine site. You know they came out here in the 1920s, digging for *paska*?'

Onni nodded, yes. Fishing wasn't the only lure of the islands. The guano miners were digging for something different altogether. Bird shit. Thousands of years' worth of seabird droppings had helped to build the island up from its limestone base, but it was mostly gone now. Little Rat had been mined to the core and left in a rocky shambles. The black rats had already arrived by then, colonising both Big Rat and Little Rat and providing their names. Nobody knew how they'd got there. Some ship-wreck or other. Numerous wrecks littered the craggy reef beds of the Abrolhos Islands, but there was one in particular that stuck in the mind: the *Batavia* was thought to have run aground somewhere near the Southern Group. It was difficult to accept that just over there, some three hundred years earlier, men had wielded axes and women were strangled in the night, because for these men from the cold north country, these islands were surely some version of Eden.

Sulo stoked the fire with a bowed stick. 'Nothing here then,' he repeated. 'So we built a stone wall; a windbreak. That's all it was. When it blew from the north, we bunkered down on the southern side of the wall, and when it blew from the south, we slept on the north side.'

'Perkele, oltiin kurjia kuin kerjäläiset,' said Risto. Goddamn, we were as rough as beggars.

'As time passed we built a second wall, and a third and a fourth,' said Sulo.

One-eyed Esko slugged *pontikka* from a tall brown bottle. 'Not ideal in a downpour.'

The homemade moonshine was passed Onni's way. It burned as it went down.

'Didn't have the money to buy the tin to build a roof,' said Sulo. 'One day the carrier boat turns up and the boys tell us they've got this corri for us Finns. We say nope, that's not our corri! *Perkele!* We don't have the money for it! They tell us, "That bloke up the end bought it for you." That was Bobby Dunn, the Aussie bloke, sneaky bastard. He said we could pay him back by and by, as the cray money trickled in.'

The stones of the *kivi kämppä* were stacked one on top of the last with mud and newspaper stuffed in between as mortar. The north-west wall stood four stones thick, taking the brunt of the cyclonic northerly winds. Boulders lined the edges of the roof, keeping the tin weighed down in bad weather.

'We slept in that camp, the five of us, that first year,' said Risto. '*Pontikka* every night, scales stuck to our skin and in our hair, smelling of fish guts all season long.'

'Farting, burping and snoring,' added Tall Tommi solemnly. In the firelight you could see the beginnings of wrinkles at the corners of his gently sloping eyes, fanning out in rays from a decade of squinting. 'Rats nibbling on our toes as we slept.'

'Your brother,' said Sulo to Onni, shaking his head, 'he seemed to have no fear of the sea, even when he first arrived. He never bothered with the easy spots, did he?'

An affirmative murmur rose from the circle.

'*Oli kyllä uhkarohkea poika*,' said Tall Tommi, who, with the *pontikka*, had found his voice. He sure was a threat-brave boy.

Onni thought now about a summer dance of his youth, when Nalle had pulled a knife on the blacksmith's son. It was no surprise that a scuffle had broken out—there was always a scuffle at the village dance—but it was the look of thrill in his brother's eyes that had stayed with Onni. His easy, carefree movements as he wielded the knife. The air of indestructibility.

From across the fire, Onni quietly studied the faces of the four men. They were sun-hardened, their eyes bloodshot from wind, water and booze. They were seamen through and through. He felt they knew something about life that he didn't yet know. Onni shifted in his chair, mirroring Sulo's posture.

Esko drained his bottle and opened another. 'Wouldn't see a woman for months in them days,' he said. 'Send a bloke insane, if the island hadn't done it to you yet.'

The others nodded.

'Later on, we all agreed we had to get the women out here,' said Sulo. 'But we couldn't have them sleeping in the *kivi kämppä* with the lot of us.'

Twenty-one corrugated-iron camps now lined the island's eastern flank, from which a series of topsy-turvy jetties extended like fractured finger bones. It resembled a small, ramshackle village. During the fishing season, for almost six months every year, it became a small bustling community, way out here at the verge of the Indian Ocean. For the other half of the year, when most of the fishermen and their families moved back to the mainland, it was a floating ghost town. There were only a few solitary types, like Latvian Igor, who remained on the island year round.

As the embers in the fire began to fade, the men staggered off one by one to their own camps.

Risto thumped Onni on the back as he passed. 'Can't blame him for going out to Disappearing,' he said. 'The crays are like a small battalion down there.'

Onni gave an awkward nod, his face tight with restrained emotion.

Sulo remained, and the two of them sat in silence for a while, watching the dying fire.

'You going to take over the camp?' asked Sulo at last.

Onni nodded uncertainly. *'Ehkä niinkin.'* Perhaps so.

He had no loyalty to the lead mine. In Northampton he spent whole days underground, and the upkeep of the shaft was dodgy as all hell. There'd been a small cave-in a few weeks back.

'I've just about had my fill of flies and dust and heat,' he said. 'Get out before the thing collapses on me.'

Onni knew, even as he said this, that there was more to it than the mine, and the dust and heat and flies. He couldn't abandon the cray lease. Not after all of Nalle's hard work. All of the nights spent sleeping out in the elements. And now, the tin hut complete and nobody here to shelter in it.

'Think hard on it, Onni,' Sulo advised. 'Your mother's lost one son already. You lot, you're farm boys. Nalle was a good mate, but he was reckless. He went out no matter how bad the weather was. I used to say to him: *Nalle, you let those pots soak another day.* But he wouldn't listen. You got to grow into her. Takes a long time. *Tyvestä puuhun noustaan.*' A tree is climbed from its base.

It was true, Onni and Nalle Saari came from central Finland, from undulating hills and flat cow paddocks, from dense forests of spruce, pine and birch. The water lived in the people there too, but in narrow stretches traversed in rowboats. In the summer months, before the lakes and rivers froze over again, they'd drop small nets and pull up *ahven* to salt or smoke or char on the sauna rocks.

A scene came to him. A gentle midnight light. Nalle calling to him from the rowboat, having defiantly taken it out alone. A dropped oar. And Onni diving in, stroking towards the older boy, pulling the rowboat back to shore.

Imagine that. His brother, the fisherman, couldn't swim.

'How long you been on the water, Sulo?'

'Since I was a boy. I was a deckhand when I was fifteen. Worked the merchant ships on the Gulf of Finland. They were logging the spruce forests in the south-east at that time. Used to float the logs down river.'

A few feet away the water lapped quietly, black and syrupy in the moonlight.

'These crays,' said Sulo, 'they're like our Sampo. Some gizmo that could make you a rich man. Nalle thought he'd found it out there on the reef.'

Onni sat on the carrier boat tracking back towards the mainland. In his hands he held a book. It was Nalle's crayfishing manual. He'd laboured through the first pages in the dim glow of the kero lamp, learning about the life cycle of crayfish. How they moulted many times throughout their development. During the migratory phases, they took on a creamy pallor and marched across the sea floor in large groups. They retained their white sheen until they settled on the offshore reefs and matured.

The decision had almost certainly been made then, when he opened the book and began to read, though he pretended otherwise. He would need to convince Alva yet. He considered the benefits and the drawbacks. Certainly, the lure of the place was strong: the medicinal salt air, the endless stock of fresh fish for dinner—and, of course, the money. But the islands were a godforsaken place in many ways, he had to admit. Isolated, harsh, inhabited mostly by men—foul-mouthed, hard-living, hard-drinking sort of men. Yet in them Onni recognised something comforting and familiar. In those three days on Little Rat, he had felt a stirring inside him. His roots searching down through coral tendrils, fastening. It had little to do with reason. To stay in Northampton seemed to Onni an impossibility. Even now, as he sat on the carrier boat chugging eastwards, he felt a prickle of something like guilt—the guilt of the deserter. He didn't want to leave Nalle out there on his own. On the island, in Nalle's shack, Onni felt the continuation of his brother inside him. No, it had nothing to do with reason. Onni was being swept along with the current of the Finns that had come before him. He'd started off at the mine because there was an opening. Now he would go fishing.

Coral

IT WAS A GOOD PLACE for getting pregnant, the women on the islands joked. By which they meant that once the boats were in and the fishing was done, there was little else to do. Yes, the islands had a way of coaxing you into the quiet belly of a tin hut on a lazy afternoon. There, rough working hands found smooth skin. They pushed aside the threadbare cotton of a summer dress, and a muffled gasp might escape the curtained window, to mingle with the lapping water all around.

It was a rather fertile place, thought Alva Saari, as she lay in the groggy aftermath of love-making, although at first glance it appeared as barren as a salt flat. The low-lying landmass looked as though it could go under at any moment—on a sudden rise in swell, at a turn of the weather. The ground they walked on was dry as bone, the skeletal remains of coral bodies deposited over thousands of years by the push and pull of the current. Only the hardy saltbush proffered a scant carpet here, and succulents shot through cracks in the veiny skin of the dried reef bed. But the sea was pulsing with life: groper darted beneath the keels of dinghies, oysters clung to the rocky shoreline in clusters, and blooming coral heads with creeping tendrils decorated the seabed in blinks of red, green and blue. At first glance they appeared as flora, but on closer inspection revealed themselves as fleshy creatures. Alva had seen the soft innards within the hard limestone casing when she had scooped up a piece of fresh, floating coral and broken it open in the palm of her hand.

Alva's small pregnant belly filled the space of the doorway. Her swollen midline appeared incongruous on her bony frame—she looked like a tall and spindly swamp bird that had swallowed too big a fish. Her quiet temperament meant that some people thought her shy, timid even, but Alva had left behind all her family and friends and travelled across two oceans and many seas to live in an unfamiliar place called Western Australia. These were not the actions of a timid person.

A few feet from the door of the hut, the island fell away. Alva looked out past the sheltered home reef towards Disappearing Island.

'No need to worry,' said her friend Helvi, who had come for coffee, bringing along her one-year-old son, Ismo. 'Onni's a careful fisherman. He doesn't go in the breakers.'

'It's those dead birds,' replied Alva. She had been unsettled that morning to find the island scattered with dead shearwaters.

Alva glanced across the kitchen and into the bedroom. On the timber shelf above the bed sat a wooden carving of a bird, the craftsmanship primitive but somehow perfect. It had a small head and a squat, plump body. *Sielulintu*, the Finns called it. The soul bird. Alva's aunt Iita had given the carving to her when she left Finland. Birds were significant, the old woman always said. Watch for their signs. Onni said those superstitions didn't serve anyone, that she shouldn't let them rule her movements, but Alva believed there was a kernel of wisdom at their base. She knew the natural world could tell you things. Back home, for instance, you could tell a storm was coming when the swallows fell silent.

'The swell's come up,' said Alva. Patches of white water had formed about the reefs where hours ago it had been calm.

On the floor, baby Ismo gurgled. He was learning to crawl and was testing himself, folding every so often under his own weight. When he neared the open doorway, Helvi stood and scooped him up, repositioning him at her feet.

Like Alva, Helvi had come from Finland, enticed by the sun and a young man with ideas of making good in this place of opportunity. Both women had spent a stint in the outback first, though at separate times, when their husbands had tried their hand at prospecting. They both preferred a fisherman's shack to a miner's humpy. Preferred the sea breeze to the stifling inland heat.

Alva had come to the islands with her husband after they inherited his brother's cray licence and tin shack. She'd agreed to the move almost immediately, despite the distance from the mainland and the ghosts of lost sailors, poor Nalle Saari included. And she had taken to it with ease, this island life. Tying a scarf around her short hair in defence against the never-ceasing wind, she gutted fish with precision on the outdoor basin. She noted with satisfaction the sparkle of approval in her husband's eye as he silently regarded her technique. Some days Alva went out on the boat too. She took on the deckhand's role—measuring the crays and tying off the hessian bags once full, with two ears at each corner so they might be easily transferred from the boat to a holding crate on the pontoon, and finally onto the carrier boat for transport to the mainland. She did not need directing. If the dolphins swam with the boat on the way out, Alva would quip: *Luck is with us today.* And then she and Onni would work quietly and comfortably together.

As the kettle sounded, Petra appeared at the door, her flock of kids trailing behind. She let herself in, leaving the children to play out the front. 'Not on the jetty!' she called. 'Matti, Saku, you two look out for Mika.'

Petra was one of the first women on the islands—the first since those poor ladies who had sailed on the *Batavia*. She came with her husband Esko, and those, she always said, were long, lonesome days. Now there was more going on. Friends to visit. Kids to feed and clothes to wash.

Petra sat herself down, her large backside leading the way, while Alva poured black coffee into three cups. She placed them on the table, along with a tin plate of arrowroot biscuits.

They sat in the kitchen, which also served as a dining room. In the beginning, this had been the entirety of the camp—Nalle hadn't needed any more room. As time passed, and the crays brought in a little money, slowly, slowly the rest of the hut had been built around this original room. Each camp on the island had a similar layout. They were built modestly but steadfast against the elements. The frame of the hut was two by four, cloaked and hatted in corrugated iron. Alva wanted to build a sauna next, out by the edge of the water.

The bucket and ladle will do, Onni said.

Well. She would work on him.

Petra surveyed Alva from her chair. 'Well, girl. Do you know what to expect when your time comes?'

'Not really—I'm terrified,' admitted Alva.

'And it's a terrible business,' Petra said. 'There's nothing to do but bear it. Sometimes you'll rip all the way to your bum.'

'*Herran jestas!*' said Helvi, glancing skywards. 'By God! No need for that talk.'

'I wish someone had told me!' Petra retorted.

Alva registered this quietly, staring at the swirling black liquid in her cup. Petra was a straight-talking woman who said what she meant and meant what she said. Some thought her severe, but Alva appreciated her honesty. She was as hardy as saltbush and as unyielding as the limestone earth underfoot.

'And then what?' she asked.

'Well, you won't be a young bride ever again after that,' said Petra, 'and it might take a bit more effort to keep him at home.'

Alva caught Helvi's appalled eye. 'Really, Petra, after all a woman suffers, it is he who has lost something?'

'It's the sad truth.'

'*Älä huoli kulta, se laps sieltä osaa*,' said Helvi, returning to the matter at hand. Don't worry, dear; the kid'll know which way to go.

'We have it easy,' said Petra. 'Our grandmothers gave birth on the steps of the sauna. Just the child-bringer there, chanting into their ears.' She began a quiet incantation: 'Open the gate, let the child come. Open the gate, let the child come.'

The women snickered together.

'I suppose there was some wisdom in it,' Petra conceded. 'It's all about rhythm, really. Rhythm and breathing.'

Alva thought of home. Thought of the sauna down the back of the house. That was where her mother was born and also where her body was put when she died. Alva remembered stealing glances at the body through the sauna door before they took it away. She hadn't quite understood that her mother was gone for good. No one talked about it.

Finally, Alva plucked up the courage to ask her father where she had gone.

Jumalelle. To God.

So she waited for her to come back, and when she didn't a sadness sat down in Alva and never really went away. Her father, who had returned from the Winter War with a shrapnel injury to his leg, did his best. They were a tight-knit family in a way, because they were poor and lived in such close quarters. Alva remembered her father as a stern, silent man in the next bed over. He slept in a single bed with her little brother, while across the room she and her older sister topped and tailed. Their great-aunt Iita, who had come to live with them after their mother died, slept on the wooden bench in the front room. They continued to sleep in that configuration until Alva and her siblings became adults and were married.

Alva looked out the window. That cold, dark country was a long way from here. Here, the sun always shone.

'They'll be back soon,' said Helvi, watching her.

'Esko will be on the bottle already,' said Petra.

One-eyed Esko they called him. It was said he'd lost his eye in a brawl back in Finland.

'Should have known from the beginning,' said Petra. 'That man already had a wife. He married the bottle long before he married me.'

It was true, Esko was a big drinker, and the drinking often led to other things. To fighting and gambling.

Petra and Esko had met at a summer dance.

'At the *tanssi*, a man smashed a bottle on his own head, and a woman fell off a chair. I saw him across the room and said to myself, *There he is*. And we only make one mistake in life.' Petra nodded. 'Finnish women are very loyal.'

Alva laughed and dipped her biscuit into her coffee. Let the soggy end dissolve on her tongue. Did all relationships deteriorate like that? she wondered. Would things fall apart for her and Onni, too? Would they despise aspects of the other? She hoped not. She hoped things would be different for them. And she was surprised by the hope she felt, because where she came from happiness was not something one was entitled to or expected to find. The minister at their small Lutheran church in Toholampi had often said that redemption is attained through suffering, and in moments of lightness Alva thought of him, of the downturned arc of his thin mouth. She carried her hope discreetly. It was a fragile white egg, something that could fall and break.

'What else do you wish you'd known about having a baby?' she asked.

Petra considered her.

'That you become like an animal, no different from the cows you've seen birthing back home. It's all fluid and stench and blood. Just the same. You'll grunt like those cows did. And when you take the baby back home, you are like a milking station. That's all you are for a while.'

Alva remembered a cold morning at Kepsala, the farm bordering her father's cottage, where she'd helped as a farmhand. The snow had started to melt, and the fields were bogged with water. The farmer's arm was plunged elbow-deep inside a cow as he attempted in vain to right her breech calf. She recalled the awful crimson colour mingling with the dirty yellow hay.

Alva grimaced, but Helvi laughed and shook her head. Again, Ismo had made his way to the open doorway. Helvi went and hoisted him onto her hip.

'Don't scare her,' she said to Petra.

'That's what it's like.'

Helvi planted a kiss on Ismo's pudgy cheek.

'But once it's over you forget all that,' she said, 'and then you have your own sweet baby.'

Petra rolled her eyes. 'Yes, you have your own baby, but then you have to see if it stays alive. That's when the real difficulty begins. Besides, babies are generally tedious, Alva. It's when they're older you get to enjoy them.'

On her way out, Petra stopped in the doorway and grasped Alva's hand.

'*Puhuuko veljestään?*' Does he talk about his brother?

'No,' said Alva. 'He doesn't seem to have the words for it.'

In the months after Nalle's disappearance, Onni had remained quiet, grieving privately for his brother. There were times when she found him sitting on the edge of the cot, looking out through the window at the endless water, his eyes full of guarded misery. She would sit beside him and pull his ox head towards her so that it rested on her breast. But he could not talk about what had happened. Onni was a house with all its doors and windows closed. Alva longed to be let in.

Petra nodded. It was no surprise to her. 'I know a joke that will cheer you up.'

Alva waited.

'There was once a Finn who loved his wife so much, he almost told her.'

When her friends had left, Alva began to make a fish soup. She'd caught the snapper herself the previous afternoon, when she and Onni had taken the dinghy out. She'd packed sandwiches and they'd skirted the perimeter of Big Rat. It was a rare windless day, and the water tapped lazily at the sides of the boat. They baited their hand lines and waited. She lost the first hook to a parrot fish. Tied a new one onto the line and tried again. The serenity was punctured by the frenzied flapping of the snapper when she wound it in. Wordlessly, Onni handed her the knife and she stabbed it through the head. So, this was her catch. Alva had gutted the fish on the outdoor basin, removing its slimy insides. Its wet guts had slipped free from her incision, intestines and shit tube all laid out on the bench before her.

Now, she divided the flesh into fillets. There was something that she could not quite put her finger on. Something connecting her and this snapper, the old cow at Kepsala and the blooming coral heads that made up the foundation of the home reef. She saw herself cleaved open on a hospital bed six months from now, and beneath the torn skin she saw it, the fleshy creature that lingered just below the surface.

She had just salted the broth—and tossed a little over her left shoulder for good measure—when Onni finally turned up. He looked strange to her, his t-shirt stiff on his back, his skin giving off a certain radiance. Alva scrutinised him, the shroud of his face, those hooded, almond-shaped eyes that seemed impossibly brighter than they'd been that morning. Those eyes that withheld things from her. But she was getting better at reading them.

'Don't go when the swell's up,' she said. 'You leave those pots for another day.'

Mutton bird

TOWARDS THE CLOSE OF HIS first season, Onni woke to find Little Rat covered in dead shearwaters, their dishevelled bodies in oily black heaps on the coral ground. Those shaggy mutton birds, as the Aussies called them. They flew thousands of miles every year, across open ocean, through torrents of rain and wind. They didn't always make it, and every so often they'd wash up on shorelines in their hundreds. A wreck. That was what they called it, when they washed up like that. A wreck of shearwaters. To travel so far, thought Onni, and all for nothing.

'A bad omen,' Alva said from the door of their hut.

Onni waved her words away. He considered himself a practical man for the most part, without time or patience for superstition. He did notice, however, as he motored out to check the previous day's pots, that the sea was in a restless mood. Out beyond the reefs, puffs of foam formed with the breaking swells, drawing brief warning signs on the water.

Upon arriving on the islands with Alva, Onni had vowed to learn his new trade systematically, carefully, unlike his brother. At first he had remained close to Little Rat, keeping an eye on the small ledge of coral that signified safety. He studied the reef, its troughs and contours, adding sections to the sea chart in his mind. He studied his prey. On a calm, moonless night, he went out in his dinghy and killed the lamp. Crayfish are most active under the cover of darkness, and Onni imagined them spidering along the reef below him, looking for food and new holes to settle into. He sat like that for a long while, feeling the pulse of water beating through the hull and into his own body. Soon he had read the crayfishing handbook in full, and could navigate his way by coral signposts.

Still, he felt Sulo's critical gaze on him at times, when Onni fumbled with a sheet-bend knot or when he motored back to the pontoon at mid-morning with his hessian bags half empty. But with each passing day, Onni's bags were a little heavier than the last.

During those first weeks, Onni had secretly continued the search for remains of his brother. He ventured to new grounds as much to look for crevices and nooks in which a body could have become lodged as to learn the layout of the reef. Weeks went by and turned into months and nothing was found of Nalle or his boat. It was harder to accept when he heard whispers about the skeleton on Beacon Island. A man they called Pop Marten had unearthed bones while digging a hole to bury rubbish. They could be seabird bones, or bits of coral, someone suggested. Others thought that the bones pointed to the true location of the lost ship. If they could find three-hundred-year-old bones, thought Onni, then surely they could locate something of his brother?

As Onni pulled his pots and re-baited them, his body bent in a U shape over the side of the cray boat, he was aware of Disappearing Island beckoning to him from across the water. The lively breakers rising up in fathom-deep water. Crayfish preferred movement in the water, Onni had noted over the course of the previous months, areas where the swell surged. He would not have admitted it to anyone, but each day he fished, Onni felt himself edging closer to that area. It acted like a strange magnet, that spot where Nalle had come into trouble, and where they all knew the crays were best.

Like a small battalion down there.

And so he had finally done it. Encouraged by a flat, guileless sea, Onni had motored right out to Disappearing. He circled the sandbank several times before setting his pots down, hoping nobody had seen him go that way. He hoped as much now, as he headed back there to haul them up.

Out on the line, Onni observed his orange and white floats bobbing happily on the surface of the water. He set to work on the first pot. It was unusually full, and the abundance buoyed him. Onni found himself imagining his return to Finland. Saw himself driving into town in a Mercedes-Benz. Stupid, really. He shook the image from his mind and continued along the line, each pot throwing up a similar bounty. Soon the abundance began to unsettle him. No doubt there would be some kickback, some counteraction, for such good fortune. He threw back a couple of undersized crays, including those on the cusp, aware of a strong desire to keep the balance. Even so, the hold was soon full of writhing crays, their heavy tails banging. And he was only halfway along the line.

He thought of his brother and his Sampo. *Nalle thought he'd found it out there on the reef,* Sulo had said. Afterwards, Onni had asked Alva what she thought the Sampo was.

'Since when are you interested in folktales?' she replied. Then she put down her sewing and looked at him. 'It's some sort of a machine you get everything from. Wellbeing, prosperity, the good life. It brought luck to Northland, where they locked it inside a rocky hill. But it was taken and then it was fought over and lost. So . . .' Alva shrugged, as though the meaning were clear.

A few wisps of grey cloud showed in the distance, but as far as Onni could tell the sea was calm enough and the wind brushed his bare arms without malice. Moving to the edge of the boat, Onni stared, transfixed, into the blinking blue water. It had the quality of air. Below him, he could see the cliffs and forests of the sea in perfect clarity.

What had it done with his brother?

'Nalle,' he said aloud.

'Nalle,' he repeated, louder still. '*Mihin jouduit?*' Where did you go?

The sun warmed his back and the sweat trickled down the sides of his face, and Onni felt an inclination to haul himself over the gunwale and dive into the sea.

As he went under, the sound of the terns and the stirring wind were muted momentarily. He came up, treading water, t-shirt slick on his back, taking in this new perspective. The cray boat was close by, confident on its anchor, bobbing up and down, up and down. Onni did the same, and the rhythm and the weightlessness felt good. The sand of Disappearing came in and out of view as he rose and dipped with the passing swells. He saw himself as an observer of evolutionary time. The island came and went before him.

Onni understood, then, the power of water. He knew how easily it could disappear a body, and even a whole island. It didn't seem so unbelievable now, that they couldn't find a trace of his brother. He knew it would take a long time to figure out how to read the ocean. And even then, you couldn't predict its movements, couldn't trust it entirely.

Across the water, he saw his boat, smaller now, and realised he'd been drifting. The secret pull of the current; he'd let it get the better of him. Onni saw Risto's torn groper in his mind's eye. Heard Sulo's hushed words: *Tiikeri hai.* The panic rose in his chest, and he knew he could not allow it to boil over. Kicking and paddling, he propelled himself forwards, but the boat wasn't getting any closer. He took a moment to regather himself; let the sea cover him over. He envisioned his own body, waterlogged, floating with the current. Joining the cycle of things, along with Nalle and others lost at sea. How easy it would be, to let himself sink down here in the liquid quiet. To give in to it. Either way, the world would go on spinning, as it had after Nalle died. Perhaps someone would remember him for a short while, and then his mark on the world would be rinsed away. Even if he did live to be an old man, he was only an arm's length behind his brother in the great wash of time.

A precious arm's length.

Alva came to mind next, the wreck of mutton birds and the gathering clouds.

Finally, Onni came up for air. He gulped it in, his lungs expanding. It was the first real breath he had taken in months, and the explosion of oxygen in his veins was white and glorious. Gauging the ebb and flow of the current, Onni orientated himself within the contours of the reef. He propelled himself into the current and let it carry him away from his boat at first, before he took a sidelong route back towards it.

Soon he was pulling himself with spent limbs onto the deck. He lay on his back, feet dangling over the transom, and squinted up at the afternoon sky, pearl-coloured and dazzling. When he looked across at the bags of writhing crays, he could not help but laugh.

Onni wiped the water from his face with a rag, peeled off his wet t-shirt and surveyed his position. The breakers on the south-west curve of the reef had doubled in size. The wind was picking up and those small wisps of grey cloud had merged, appearing now as a billowing wall marching towards the Abrolhos. He estimated their distance: they were perhaps an hour away.

He would let the remaining pots soak another day.

As the shard of the home island came into view, Onni knew he was looking at it.

The Sampo.

It wasn't the number of hessian bags on his deck but the whole sky, the coming storm, the little tin *kämppä* with Alva inside, sliding a knife skilfully through the belly of a snapper. It was that hard-to-catch fish called happiness. He could feel the smile inside him, and it took all his will to keep it in.

Birth

A YEAR FOR THE SAARIS was now lived in two parts: on-season and off-season. Their first season on Little Rat had been a moderate success, from an economic standpoint, and the couple looked ahead with a suspicious and careful optimism characteristic of their people. They had spent the tail end of the year back on the mainland, where they rented a weatherboard house in Bluff Point. Onni had set about preparing for the season to come—attending to the boat, doing repairs, mending broken craypots and the like. For this, they could prepare. For the baby, they weren't so sure. Without making a show of it, Alva did the things that her aunt Iita would have done in the circumstances. She left cupboard doors and drawers open, she let her hair hang freely, she untied the knot of rope that dangled from the verandah awning. And all of a sudden, Alva's time had come.

Her contractions came like a cloaked stranger in the night. Lying between the starched sheets of a single bed at the Geraldton District Hospital, Alva attempted to grasp the quick speech of the middle-aged nurse. She understood that Onni was asked to leave, and in a way she was glad. Better Onni didn't see her like that, her body split open, everything spilling out. With the cramping pains shooting through more frequently, Alva gathered that the moment was drawing near. As she lay in the bed, her heartbeat quickening, the walls of the small room began to bear down on her. She sucked in air. The stern sister narrowed her eyes and said words Alva had never heard before—a confusing drawl of indistinct vowels, no consonants to guide the way.

When the pain came proper, the nurse parted Alva's legs and placed her fingers inside of her. Alva's whimpers gave way to a terrified shriek. In her mind she was at Kepsala again, in the nip of the spring melt, watching as the farmer did the same to the birthing cow. The corporeal stench was heavy in the air, the smell of life and death that so often came hand in hand. Surely this was not right. This pain. It couldn't be. This was something else: this was the pain of death. She heard herself screaming, felt her fingers and toes tingle and cramp, and then the sudden, shocking blow of the nurse's open palm as she slapped Alva full on the face. Jolted from her hysteria, Alva pushed and heaved, as quietly as she could, and at last Hilda arrived in a squall of blood and fluid and heat.

Later, the baby Hilda was brought back for feeding time. It was an older nurse who returned her into Alva's arms and watched as the new mother attempted to introduce the baby to her nipple. The sister was a large woman, with matronly breasts and sure, purposeful movements. The kind of woman who made anyone feel safe. She reached over and gently corrected the angle at which the baby was suckling.

'Hurts a bit at first.'

The woman spoke very slowly, very deliberately, but not in a patronising way. Alva had noticed that people in Australia often used the same tone for her as they did for very young children or very old people.

'When it gets bad, wrap your breast in cabbage. It helps to soothe the pain.'

Alva was silent.

The nurse plopped down unapologetically in the chair by the bedside. She seemed extremely comfortable here in the ward, as if it was her domain. After some time, she reached over and squeezed Alva's hand. She nodded a few times, as though to convince them both. 'You'll be okay.' The nurse leaned back and looked out of the window, into the coming night.

Alva stole a glance at her baby. She could hardly take her eyes away. They'd cleaned all the muck from Hilda's skin, all the evidence of where she'd come from, the marks of her animal arrival.

'You know,' said the nurse, watching Alva watch the infant, 'you'll never have another worry-free day for the rest of your life.'

Alva went back over the words, trying to decipher them. She felt the nurse had said something profound. For Alva, trying to interpret the strange, drawling English of Australians was like being on one side of a thick stone wall while a conversation took place on the other side. Her ears were always pricked.

When Onni came to the hospital to see his new baby, he was in a borrowed suit a size too large. It hung from his frame as though still on the coathanger. Alva saw him enter the room looking all washed and scoured and sheepish, and wanted to cry when he took Hilda in his oversized, uncertain hands. The fishing season had commenced, but Onni had stayed back to wait for the birth.

'I sent a keg of beer to Little Rat to announce the news,' he said.

Soon Onni returned to the islands and Alva remained with Hilda in Geraldton. Each day the cray boat remained docked, Onni said, was money lost. The days were long and featureless. At first, Alva watched Hilda with a kind of astonished wonder. She noted the parts of the baby that were hers, and those that were Onni's. She was surprised at how quickly the memory of birth was fading, just as Helvi said it would. All she recollected was the blue-grey form of Hilda before the nurse gathered her up and coaxed the first breaths into her. The relief she felt at the sound of the baby's cry—yes, she was alive. Alva had not been prepared for that: the deathly, alien colour. When they put the swaddled parcel into her arms, her surroundings had melted away—the pain, the midwife and the sisters—and it was just the two of them in the room together. She was a mother. Her daughter nestled against her chest like a barnacle.

Now, Alva watched the meagre comings and goings through the lounge room window. She studied the trees, so strange and gnarled compared with the pines and birches of home. Harrison Street was dotted with peppermint trees, horsetail she-oak and coral gums. Only natives that drank little water thrived here. Alva's favourite was the Geraldton wax, with its spindly pink flowers.

Inside her home it was quiet, and comfortable enough—a repsite from the dry heat and the whirling dust. But it lacked the roaming freedom of the islands, the smack of salt air on your skin. She remembered lying in Nalle's old cot at night with Onni, listening to the ocean wind cry and, every so often, to the rain beating down on the tin roof like some ancient, booming opera. Something inside her had been opened up, unlocked, during those months on the islands, some wild and unkempt part of her, so that the eyes that now looked out of this suburban window were those of a caged bird.

Next-door's throng of kids played in their yard, sometimes spilling over to hers. She saw the eldest, a boy of six, pinching tomatoes from the Italian grower down the back and had to giggle. The sound of her own voice struck her as strange; she realised she hadn't spoken to anybody for more than a week.

She wanted so much for these first weeks with her baby to be a lovely, memorable time, and sometimes it was, but mostly she was lonely. She missed her friends, missed Helvi's carefree nature and Petra's austere humour. The seed of loneliness had been planted inside Alva on her very first day in Australia. She remembered arriving in Fremantle on the ship. How she had put on her most cherished garment—a floral chiffon dress—on the day they were to dock at the port. How they had stood on the top deck, she and Onni, with all the other new migrants, and she had become caught up in the excitement of it all, joining others to wave at those waiting below. Once they had disembarked, they found Nalle in the crowd and the two brothers shook hands, slapping each other on the back, laughing with glassy eyes. Alva was introduced, and then it was done, while all around her other newcomers were swamped by large families. They drank lemon squash on the foreshore and smiled into the distance, but underneath everything Alva felt the sowing of that small sorrow, knowing that, here in Australia, they were but a scant few. On the islands she had forgotten the feeling of loneliness, but here again she felt it.

Guilty in her idleness, Alva systematically cleaned each room in the house. Down on her haunches, she washed the bathroom floor with a scrubbing brush and a cake of Sunlight soap, flinching when she felt blood trickle from between her legs. Was it normal? Or had something broken inside her? It was a mess down there; she'd felt it with her fingers. There was a stone of worry in her gut, this feeling that she might be dying. That she might bleed to death, here in Bluff Point, and no one would know. No one would come for weeks—why should they? She imagined it pouring out from between her legs, all of the blood in her body, making a small river of her lounge room. And in the horrible fantasy, Hilda lay squirming in the rusty red puddle, and the sun went down and then rose again, and still no one came. Alva shook the image from her mind, telling herself in her grown-up's voice: *Of course it's normal.* Then Hilda woke, wailing, and Alva hurried to her, dripping sticky red spots across the clean lino floor.

Alva stood out the front in the watery sunshine, holding the four-week-old Hilda tight to her chest, a suitcase at her side. She heard Stewart start up the old Hillman next door, before backing it out and bringing it in sidelong at her front gate.

'Ready, love?'

She nodded and opened the passenger door. She had swallowed her pride when, in broken English, she'd asked Charlene for the favour.

'I want to go island, maybe you help me?'

Babies did go out to the islands, but four weeks was very young. Was she being brave, she wondered, or the opposite? A failure, because she wasn't coping here in Geraldton alone?

Her next-door neighbour's dyed blonde hair stood like a beehive on top of her head, brilliantly defiant of gravity's tug. Alva was in two minds about the hair—she thought it excessive, but also admirable, to go to all that trouble just to hang about the home. Most days, Charlene traipsed around the house, abetted throughout by a small amount of Bex powder, recommended by her doctor, which she dissolved into her cup of tea. That very week she'd suggested Alva give the stuff a try, sensing her struggle. 'It takes the edge off, dear,' she'd said.

So Charlene's husband Stewart was given the job of taking Alva out to the fishermen's wharf that morning. They spent most of the fifteen-minute drive from Bluff Point out to the boat harbour in silence. Alva watched the sparse residential lots wash by. She turned to check on Hilda, who slept in a cane bassinet in the back seat, her little head lolling to one side. They passed the railway line at Durlacher Street, and heard the sound of a freight train chugging along, bound for the harbour. It would be carrying lead from the Northampton mines, or perhaps grain from the wheat belt to the towering silos at the port.

'Nice day for a boat ride,' said Stewart.

She nodded, always agreeable in this foreign tongue. Stewart was not a seaman, and she looked out at the raving leaves of the eucalypts and started when she caught sight of three crows flying in a line overhead. She realised she had not given any thought to the weather, to the swell—she just wanted to get there—and a new anxiety bubbled inside her.

Thanking Stewart, she walked the length of the timber wharf to the fishermen's co-op, where three greasy men were loading the *Ida-Ray*. A short man wearing Stubbies and a worn singlet stopped his work and stood with his hands on his hips, eyes following Alva as she entered the shed. She noticed his broad arms, carpeted with bleached white hairs, and his nose, a beacon—a testament to his time ferrying back and forth between the islands and the mainland. The air was laced with the scent of fish. When she glanced past the wharf to the white-capped sea, it was big and dark and awful-looking.

'Alva Saari,' he said.

She nodded.

He spoke to her in that same slow way as other Australians, emphasising the consonants. But she heard kindness in his voice.

'Swell's up,' he said. 'You sure you want to take the little one over today?'

Alva nodded again, determined. 'I go anyway.'

Hilda squirmed in her arms.

The man looked Alva hard in the face, but she held his gaze. 'Well, come on, then.'

The southerly was blowing hard as the *Ida-Ray* left the port, headed for the bumpy horizon. The vessel smashed into the broad, heaving ridges of swell, one after another, lacking the rhythm that might rock a child to sleep. Across from where Alva sat, a rough sort of fellow shared a lump of cold meat with a kelpie.

'I'm the cook,' he said, his smile revealing yellowed teeth.

Above them, the sky swirled, the colour of smoked groper, and Hilda began to shriek.

A few hours into their journey, Alva reluctantly asked the deckie for a bucket. At the stern of the boat she balanced the baby in one arm and held the railing with the other, swaying on shaking limbs as she squatted. She recoiled at the sight of the acidic, bloodstained soup. Juggling Hilda and the bucket, her hair blowing across her face in the wind, she moved unsteadily to the side of the boat and threw the piss overboard, making sure it blew downwind. They returned to the cabin as Hilda resumed her protest. Her cries could be heard above the roaring surf, and Alva looked around at the gnarled faces of the men, their jaws clenched. Her heartbeat quickened when she imagined the vessel sinking. It would be every person for themselves, and she didn't even know how to swim. What sort of a place was this, she thought, to bring a little baby?

But halfway into the journey, they crossed that imaginary line. Alva let out a long breath. From here, she could throw it all to the wind: the quiet suburban house, the raggedy gum trees, her terrible loneliness and, worst of all, her inadequacy—her inability to cope, to go it alone. The fishermen described the islands as a parallel universe. And she felt it now, she really did. She was almost there.

In the blustery afternoon she saw it. The faint line that signalled land ahead. So thin and delicate it was, it might have been drawn on the sea's rippled surface with a pencil. She kept her gaze fixed on that sweet line, the white breakers revealing the surrounding reef. As they drew closer, she could differentiate the small arcs of land rising out of the sea, squat and low, in the distance. Leo Island, Alexander, Suomi, Vuti Vutti, Sandy Island, Roma, Big Rat, Little Rat.

As the boat reached the mooring, she saw the familiar activity of men on the water, heard the short, sharp calls between skipper and deckie. The fishermen would be waiting, Onni included, ready to come and collect their stores in turn. Then Alva Saari was seized with anxiety, her heart knocking in her chest. She would soon be face to face with him, her husband. What would he say? She had not sent word of her decision to come, because she couldn't accept his cautious response: that the seas might be too rough, that Hilda was too young, that it was dangerous to make the journey so soon after the birth.

The men on the carrier boat had sprung into action, passing crates and barrels from one man to another. She waited in the cabin until the flurry of movement subsided—best not to be in the way. After some time she recognised her husband's broken English as he talked with the carrier boat crew.

'Got something else in here for ya, Onni.' It was the short, burly man who'd said it.

She looked over the side of the boat and locked eyes with her husband. He raised his eyebrows.

'*Voi ei!*' Oh no.

He looked out to sea, where waves boiled white on the reefs, and looked back at Alva with questioning eyes.

She shrugged. 'I threw salt.'

Don't go when the swell's up, she had told him. But she was here now, and that was that.

Stepping off the *Ida-Ray* into the smaller skiff, Alva came face to face with her husband. She reacquainted herself with his scent: a mixture of tobacco, berley, fish blood and salt. When he took the baby Hilda into his arms he looked like a mountain. The smile was just a flicker, but she saw it there, in his blue, hooded eyes.

'Little precious,' he said, looking down at Hilda.

The small quiet comment, and the relief almost buckled her.

'Hey, Onni, give us a hand with this forty-four, will you?' It was another man from the carrier boat crew, calling as he prepared a water drum for hauling onto the island. 'There's work to be done yet, mate.'

Onni and Alva fell easily into domestic life on the islands. While Alva had been in Geraldton with Hilda that first month, Onni had built the sauna. A warmth spread out inside of her when he presented it.

'Makes sense out here,' he said, 'with fresh water being scarce.'

But Alva understood it was his gift to her, even if he would not admit it. From then on they used the sauna instead of the bucket bath, sweating out their day's work before briefly splashing their naked bodies with a ladle of fresh water. Oh, how it all shouted to Alva of home: the hot, dry air roaring up her nostrils whenever she took a breath; the sweat, gathering on her hairline and slippery on her thighs; and the dark, relaxing quiet. Afterwards, she would wash little baby Hilda in the bucket of water, adding a splash of hot from the stove, and then the clothes.

When Onni went out fishing, Alva cooked, watched over Hilda and decorated the tin hut. She'd collected a discarded float, a sun-bleached porous old thing, and fed fisherman's rope through the centre, knotting two lures and a gnarled fishhook to the end. When she was finished, she hung it from the rafters. Yes, the hut was slowly finding its character. Each day Alva would walk the rocky perimeter of Little Rat with Hilda wrapped tight and slung across her chest. She scanned the ground, looking for small treasures. A knob of dried coral to sit on the windowsill, a roe abalone shell in which to place the soap. A splinter of driftwood, its surface rubbed smooth by the water, on which she wrote *Little Rat Island, April 1960*, before putting it next to the coral fragment.

Now, Alva stood in the doorway of the camp, looking out at the skewed jetty and the scrappy islands beyond. She had a broom in her hand, and leaned her weight against its long handle. Hilda lay in a makeshift crib just inside the door, clenching and unclenching her tiny fists. The islands were a poor excuse for a home, thought Alva, as she took in the view of the archipelago. To think that people had looked at them and thought: yes, these should do just fine! She looked about and shook her head in wonder, her watery blue eyes giving away her overwhelming delight—for how glad she was to be here!

'We feel like strangers in that big, hot, dusty country,' Petra had said when Alva told her about the terror of birth and those quiet, solitary weeks spent in Geraldton. 'But these islands—these we can make our own.'

Alva smiled, feeling the sun crisp and warm on her bare arms. She was as happy as she would ever be.

Then, typically, her aunt Iita's old proverb intruded—*itku pitkästä ilosta*, cry after a long happiness. She swept her superstitions away, bringing the broom across the timber floor and boldly pushing the dust out the door.

Quietly Alva crooned a lullaby:

> *Tuu tuu tupakki rulla, mistä Hilda tiesi tulla.*
> Roll, roll, rolled cigarette,
> where did Hilda know to come from?

She sang the silly words as much to herself as to her daughter, a birdsong for this parallel universe, somewhere between land and water.

Alva waited for the sound of the boats motoring back to the home reef at mid-morning. Already the fishermen had pulled their craypots and tossed their catch into hessian bags before baiting the pots for the following day. She and Onni would have lunch, salted mackerel on black rye, and perhaps doze together in the hot blue noon, the tin camp cocooning this small family against all that lay beyond Little Rat.

Finch

STANDING IN FRONT OF THE small storehouse beside the summer sleep-out, Iita surveyed the woodpile, her mouth squeezed into a line. She allotted the logs into days and nights. They had a week's worth of wood; almost two, if they used it wisely. Winter had come down on them, heavy and laden. The snow glistened, weighing on the rooftops and the branches of the fir trees. It was always dawn or dusk. The sun rose only partway in the southern sky, behind a sheet of Arctic cloud. Its vague outline was like that of an old, ailing friend seen through an opaque window. Iita heard scuffling behind her as little Alva let herself outside. She joined her aunt in examining the woodpile. It was a sorry affair. Even Alva could tell. The girl traipsed across the puzzle of logs and bent over, struggling to lift one of the larger pieces into the cradle of her thin arms. Iita could see there was no stopping her. She would bear the load of the wood, and of the winter, as she had borne the death of her mother.

'*Minä teen*,' the girl said. '*Sää oot vanha. Voit kaatua.*' I'll do it, you're old. You might fall over.

Iita did not appreciate it. 'I'm old and you're young,' she said. 'It's really the same thing.'

Iita had grown better at managing the hearth fire, had learned that the logs would smoulder for hours, given the right amount of air. She'd been summoned to the cottage from Kepsala, the large neighbouring farm, one year ago. It was November 1939, after the children's mother had died and Arto had received the call-up. At the larger homestead, she was considered hardworking, reliable, her necessary departure regrettable. Lahja had been her youngest niece, and there was no one else, nobody like Iita without children of her own nor a husband. Arto was not gone long, but he returned with the bad leg, and Iita knew there were likely to be other wounds. Arto was a man of few words, and sometimes Iita wished to know him better. Talk is silver, she reminded herself in moments of yearning, and silence is gold.

Taking the small log now from the girl's trembling forearms, Iita cursed the long, bitter months ahead. If it were summer, she would wrap her hand with the pale violet flowers of the wood crane's-bill from the forest and ward off the spirits that hovered. Of course, if it were summer, there would be no need. Iita thought fondly about summer. How the forest would first be carpeted in flowers—bluebells, cat's-foot and buttercups. Then the berries would come: blueberries, lingonberries and, in the swamps, the precious cloudberries. Finally the mushrooms: ceps, chanterelles and countless others. How the mosquitoes would plague them, but the forest would provide.

Iita led the evening prayer. The littlest one, Pentti, was in the bed with his father, while the girls sat together in the other heavy wooden cot. The eldest, Aino, had begun work as a stablehand at Kepsala recently. She would soon be married to Timo, one of the farmhands, thought Iita, and there would be some relief in it. One less mouth to feed.

She began the recitation: 'We pray that You would forgive us all our sins where we have done wrong, and graciously keep us this night. For into Your hands we commend ourselves, our bodies and souls, and all things. Let Your holy angel be with us, that Satan may have no power over us.'

Coupled with the wood crane's-bill it might have been enough, but without it the unease remained.

The following morning, after Iita had coaxed the hearth fire back to life, she and Arto sat at the small round table and counted the money. Arto shifted the few marks from one side of the table to the other. The value of each coin was noted with a solemn stroke of the pencil on a piece of paper, until the tally indicated the truth of the matter. There was not enough.

'Twenty-six marks,' announced little Alva, who stood by her father.

The girl was proud of her counting.

'*Hyvin laskettu,*' said Iita—well counted—though there was no encouragement in her voice.

It was a devastating number. There is worse to come, she thought. If Arto was himself, he could go out into the forest and cut and collect the timber for the household, but that was not possible.

'Come,' she said to the little girl, 'let's bring up some potatoes and begin the soup.'

Potatoes sustained them. The family grew the root vegetable in the patch of earth at the back of the lot during the warmer months. Most years they produced a good yield of small oval potatoes with a creamy lustre, which they stored in the cellar under the floor through the winter. Iita moved the mat at the centre of the main room, lifted the heavy wooden latch and descended the short stairs. Alva followed, remaining close to her aunt in the narrow space and clutching at the fabric of the old woman's skirt. Iita thought she felt a slight quake within the girl.

'You can pick three potatoes,' she said, to ground the child within the dark void of the cellar.

When they stepped back into the dim light of the room, Alva moved away, as though she had not been afraid at all.

Beyond the cottage, Iita noticed Arto heading into the field. The large oilskin hung over his thin shoulders as he limped out across the snow with an axe in hand.

They set about preparing the soup. Iita chopped two swedes and a slender carrot, adding these to the pot with the potatoes and a small knob of butter that Aino had brought home with her from Kepsala.

'*Kuka on pelottavampi?*' asked Alva. '*Jumala, Jeesus vai metsän henget?*' Who is more frightening? God, Jesus or the forest spirits?

Little Alva stood on a stool pushing the vegetables around in the large pot. Her serious, angular eyes searched Iita's.

'If you have done wrong, you should be afraid of each of them.'

Looking outside now, at the faint ball of sun, low but centred against the frozen blue horizon, Iita estimated that it had just passed midday. There were perhaps two hours of daylight remaining.

'I'm not frightened,' claimed Pentti, who was playing on the floor with his hand-carved wooden blocks.

Just then a bird flew into the window. The impact of the finch's body against the glass was shocking, causing the children to jump. But Iita remained still.

'*Voihan sentään, nyt on jotain tapahtunut.*' Goodness me, now something has happened.

Pentti and Alva fussed over the injured finch all afternoon. They built a bed for the bird in a wooden box, cushioned with rags and thread and loose bits of yarn. Alva led Pentti around the house with a grave air about her. She drew the looped square of the *hannunvaakuna* on the front of the timber box with a piece of charcoal to ward off bad luck, just as Iita had done above the front door when she arrived at the cottage. Now the children stood above the doomed creature, Alva leading the homemade prayer:

Jeesus, siunaa tämä lintu.
Anteeks että olen syntinen.

Jumala, kaikkien valtias, anna linnun elää.

Amen.

Jesus bless the little bird.

We're sorry for all our sins.

God, ruler of all, let the bird live.

Amen.

Iita was glad to see that little Alva held on to her emotion. She must find the *sisu*, the grit, within herself, because life was full of suffering. But a foreboding now sat in Iita's stomach, in her throat, her limbs, as she waited for their misfortune to reveal itself in some solid shape or form.

Arto had resolutely refused the fetching of the municipal doctor, Arneberg, his mind on the remaining coins. He had correctly predicted that his good foot, which had been struck by the falling tree, would recover within a few days, but now the sound of his hacking cough pervaded the cottage. There was little to be done but keep the fire stoked. He had caught a chill as he lay on the forest floor, the cold fingers of frost reaching for his neckline. Iita had watched with resignation on seeing Anttila and his son emerge from the line of spruce pines dragging Arto behind them in the wooden sled. She wondered what they had done to invite this misfortune. Had she left a cupboard door open? There was a time and place for open cupboards and doors, for untying braids and knots. Had she passed little Alva those potatoes across the threshold of the cellar door? Had Arto angered the forest spirits as he attempted to fell a larger pine?

Or was it God?

The girl's query played on Iita's mind.

Though she knew the curse of vanity, she sometimes held the hand mirror to her face. It was an old woman who looked back at her. The thinning hair, loose chin and puckered mouth were visible in the small murky circle of glass even to her fading eyes. And she had wished for better. She had wished not to see the hag in the glass, for Arto not to have the limp, for Aino to be married.

Iita made a tea from a dried tangle of nettle and carefully held the cup to the man's quivering mouth. The intimacy was unsettling.

'*Lauletaanko, Iita täti?*' Can we sing a song tonight, Aunt Iita?

Alva was sitting in the rocking chair. She had pink cheeks and a running nose. Iita was wary of too much frivolity, especially under the circumstances, but she, too, enjoyed some entertainment.

When the stew was ready, the children slurped the watery broth, all of them prospecting for the few gristly pieces of sausage buried throughout. After the meal had been cleared and Arto had been helped to the rocker, the family settled again about the table. Iita's generous though raspy voice rose up in the dimly lit room. It reminded of the comforting bristles of an ancient broom. The youthful, high-pitched voices of the children and the lower timbre of Arto's cushioned hers, and together they sang the well-loved folk tune:

> *Tiedän paikan armahan,*
> *rauhallisen, ihanan.*
> *Jos on olo onnekas,*

elo tyyni, suojakas.
Sepä kotikulta on,
koti kallis, verraton.
Eipä paikkaa olekaan kodin vertaa ollenkaan.
Siell' on isä rakkahin, siellä äiti armahin.
Siellä siskot, veikkoset, riemurinnat, iloiset.

I know a loving place,
Peaceful, wonderful,
Where life is blessed,
Where life is calm and safe.
That place is my beloved home,
Precious, unrivalled in its riches
Without measure.
There is father most dear, mother most loved,
Sisters, brothers, my delightful companions.

As they sang, Iita felt a surge of happiness course through her. Afterwards, they said the evening prayer together. Before extinguishing the lantern, Iita placed the *sielulintu* by Arto's bed, just in case, heaven forbid, he required it. She then took herself to bed. Iita slept on the long wooden bench seat in the front room, over which she had laid a thin mattress. It was good for one's back to sleep on rigid surfaces; too much comfort made a person soft. But her bedding included the luxury of a bear hide skinned by her father, the remaining treasure from her own family home.

She woke throughout the night, her mind circling the dwindling woodpile, Arto's barking cough and the concussed finch. Before dawn she rose and pulled on her felt slippers. Iita looked at the smouldering hearth; the fire was almost out. She stoked it with a few miserable offerings then pulled her heavy woollen coat over her nightgown. There was the pitter-patter of a child's footsteps behind her. It was Alva, wide awake.

'I'm going for a walk in the forest,' Iita told the girl.

'*Saanko tulla?*' she pleaded, eyes raised to her aunt. Can I come?

Breathing the icy morning air, they walked out across the field and into the small pine forest that separated their home from the next property. The snow crunched underfoot as the black canopy enveloped them, but soon Iita's eyes adjusted. They came upon a spruce tree, about the thickness of a man's wrist. It would be at least fifty years old, and so it would do. Assessing the tree, Iita recalled the woody and sour taste of the *pettu leipä* during the famine years. The stringy flour they had produced from the thin cloths of bark. She would try to avoid the children having to eat the bark bread, but if it came to it, she would strip the cloth from the tree in May.

Iita took a long breath to focus her mind for the ritual. Removing her hand from the woollen glove, she let her fingers curl into a fist. She gave the trunk of the spruce a firm rap with her knuckles, then stepped back and spat over her left shoulder once, twice, three times. Beside her, the child watched closely.

As they walked back along the forest path, Iita explained: '*Vasemman hartian yli, siellä asuu paholainen.*' Over the left shoulder, the devil lives there.

A rustling nearby caused the pair to pause. Through the lifting darkness, Iita made out a reindeer and her calf. The child, too, had seen, and she held her breath, grasping a fleeting magic, before the animals disappeared silently into the forest.

They laboured on, filling their basket with slivers of birch bark. On the return march through the thick snow, Iita's unease began to shift. Behind her, Alva's stride was one of loyal determination, and it forged a renewed sense of purpose in the old woman. A tethering was taking place. She carried the burden of this family with a fierceness she had not known was inside of her. There was nothing she wouldn't do for the girl. She had to go and ask for help.

They took the *potkukelkka*, the kick sled. She brought Alva along with her, because who would turn away a small child? Iita had never had to beg before, and the shame of it was enormous. They had fallen to a yet lower rung.

The sun on the horizon appeared to embellish the morning with disproportionate hope. Little Alva sat on the chair and Iita pushed, listening to the sound of the metal runners cutting through the snow. It had fallen dry and powdery, as it does in the dead of winter. The girl had picked up a handful before mounting the sled and marvelled at the intricate ice crystals, offering it up for her aunt's pleasure. But Iita had refused to look. She wouldn't be able to see something so small anyway. The air was sharp and tingling as it entered her nostrils. They slid through the white landscape, which enclosed them in its mummifying silence.

Iita held in her mind the image of the children standing by the oak tree. That morning, once the house had begun to stir, Alva had coaxed little Pentti outside with her. She'd carried the injured bird in its wooden box into the yard and placed it ceremoniously at the foot of the oak. The girl had whispered brief instructions into her brother's ear, before they knocked on the trunk of the oak tree and then turned to spit on the ground to their immediate left. In this Pentti was a keen participant. The children spat with zeal, and Iita, watching from the window, felt her face forming the remembered fragments of a smile. Their repetition of the ritual gave it a childlike quality, but she did not mind. She hoped it would offer them solace. The burden of sin could seem insurmountable. The divine plan that bound ordinary people to this cycle. But Jesus endured. Her rituals, her prayers, they offered consolation in the face of uncertainty. *Sisu* in the face of adversity.

Now, Alva craned her head around to peer up at the old woman. Her nose was a frozen red button framed by her woollen hat and scarf.

'*Iita täti, mitä tapahtuu kun kuolee?*' Aunt Iita, what happens when you die?

The child, she thought, could sense the watchful presence of death. She recalled the girl's ardent prayer for the finch. Alva had been praying for her father as much as for the little bird, for her dead mother, for herself. Death loomed large for the girl, but so it did for all of them. That was what this life was like. She called to mind her own grandmother's warning: lice will get into your fur coat even without you putting them in there.

Iita remembered the days following her niece's death. She had arrived promptly to prepare Lahja's body, which had been laid out in the washroom by the cold sauna. Iita had come across Alva more than once dawdling at the back of the cottage, her curious eyes peeking down the garden path and through the dark entry of the outbuilding.

'*Jumala vaan sen tietää*,' she said now. Only God can know. But the girl was not appeased.

'*Tarkoitan, heti, heti kun kuolee.*' I mean, straight away, straight away when you die.

'When you die you take the shape of a migrating goose,' Iita told the girl. 'You will go north, but to get there you have to cross the black River Tuonela.'

Iita thought she heard Alva inhale. She did not tell the rest. That at the River Tuonela there is no sun or moon, and there are spears and swords and needles standing upright in the black water. That you can see the dead swimming in bloody clothes. That if you hear ringing in your ears during the crossing, it is the sound of your deceased relatives calling for you. She did not tell of the mountain; of the evil one. Iita had cut her niece's fingernails on the Saturday night following her death. She had cut each clipping in two, and slipped them into the neck hole of Lahja's dress. These would help her ascend Tuonela Mountain, which was said to be as smooth as an eggshell. Iita wondered who would cut her own nails when she passed on, who would put them in her smock for the journey ahead. Would it be the little girl in the *potkukelkka*?

They knocked on Antilla's door first, and the farmer nodded gravely at Iita's modest request. She did not ask for much. He offered Alva a piece of *pulla*, which the girl ate slowly and gratefully. Her eyes betrayed her surprise each time she bit into a fiery burst of cardamom. They too made *pulla* at home, but without the generosity of spice.

'*Onko meidän talo köyhä?*' asked Alva as they slid along the path, headed towards the next homestead. Is our house poor?

Our house. The word caught Iita off guard.

'*Tavallaan*,' answered Iita honestly, remembering how they had sung together in the cottage the previous night. In some ways.

'I had *pulla* like this before,' said the girl, 'at the funeral. Me and Pentti both ate three pieces each.'

'*Ahneus vie viljan pellosta.*' Greed will take the grain from the fields.

'Are you having a good time?' asked the child, unperturbed.

'*Ei nyt ihan*,' said Iita. Not exactly.

They skidded on, from one house to the next, Iita sighing out her shame before each exchange. *Forwards*, she said afterwards. Alva was yet too small to feel the indignity, though the child sensed something luckless about their journey. Iita had pushed the *potkukelkka* some ten miles before they returned home, finding the path through the fresh coating of snow, the wind biting like a wolf and the ice clumped on their damp mittens. Her hands throbbed with the cold and her old legs ached, but at the final small slope that led down to the property she did not disembark. Instead she let the *kelkka* gain speed, coasting to the door, Alva laughing with delight. Hearing their approach, Pentti waited for them on the covered porch.

'It's gone!' he said as they came through the door. 'The finch flew away!'

Iita stood at the stove and boiled the potatoes. She tried not to think about the pain in her legs. Instead, she wondered about the finch. Had the bird prevailed? Or had it taken itself away, to die on the forest floor?

The wood began to arrive.

It came by the cartload, delivered by one neighbour after another. The townsfolk offered far more than Iita had asked for. A different woman might have shed a tear. Iita did not. She nodded earnestly to the farmer, Antilla, to the butcher Virtanen, to the pastor, Mäkinen.

'Something has shifted,' she told little Alva, who smiled up at her. By the grace of God, the hearth fire would continue to burn. They had wood to last the winter, and Arto's cough had dried somewhat overnight. Looking at the child, Iita felt an unfamiliar swelling in her chest. Amid the deliveries of firewood, Iita had seen Alva skirting the edge of the pine forest. She had taken the bird's body in her hand, dug narrow hole into the deep snow, covered it and made the blessing over the grave. The girl had taken the blow, kept it from her brother, even from her aunt.

She had it, thought Iita. She had *sisu*.

Olive tree

IT WAS A TIME OF FIRSTS.

Alva had planted a line of fruit trees the year after they had bought the block, just a few doors down from their original rental on Harrison Street, and as February arrived, she noted with a burst of happiness that the first oranges had appeared on the branches. She had slowly built up the garden as Onni concentrated on the house, and each year, as her plants became more sure-footed in the sandy soil, so too did she. On the back page of her cookbook she wrote: *First oranges: 2 February 1965.* She wrote this below another entry: *First eggs: 20 January 1965.* Onni had built a chicken coop just after New Year, and on this morning Alva collected two perfectly formed speckled eggs. The chooks bristled and ruffled their feathers as she picked her way through their straw-lined dwelling. She carried the eggs in the bunches of her skirt, and was careful as she placed them into a basket on the kitchen bench, so delicate and breakable were they. These small offerings from the world filled her with hope. The first oranges, the first eggs, and it was Hilda's first day of school.

Hilda wore the uniform that Alva had sewn for her from the pattern. A white collared shirt with a green pinafore dress over the top. She was glad that they wore uniforms here; that her daughter wouldn't have to guess at what to wear. Everyone would be the same, and you wouldn't be able to tell who was rich and who was poor.

'Ready, darling?'

Hilda looked up at her from within the starched and stiff garment. She looked like a real Australian, and Alva felt a pang in her chest.

Out on the road it was already hot. Alva took a breath of the parched air and put one foot in front of the other, willing her daughter to do the same.

Hilda had bawled when she learned that Onni would be going to the islands on his own that season.

'Mun pitää mennä isin kans. Mulla on rapuja kolossa siellä.' I have to go with Daddy. I've got some crabs in a hole there.

'You have to go to school now,' Alva had told her gently.

'I hate school.'

'You don't know that,' Alva replied, smoothing Hilda's matted fringe and wiping the tears from her red cheeks.

But Hilda ran off into the backyard and crouched down behind the chicken coop.

After some time Alva went to her and pointed out the brown-and-white pullet, and told Hilda that it was hers. 'What should we call it?'

Hilda pointed grimly to the older chook and said, 'Can I have that one?'

She named it immediately—Iita Kana—and Alva was filled with mirth. She had named the chicken after Alva's old aunt, of whom Alva spoke often.

Alva was willing herself to accept that she and Hilda would be spending much more time in Geraldton from now on. With Hilda starting school, they would only be going to the islands during the holidays. Perhaps it would do them good in the long run, she ventured. Within herself, she felt unmoored, floating somewhere between Finland and Australia, somewhere between the islands and the mainland. She didn't want that for Hilda. Hilda needed a more solid foundation. It was such a transient life you lived out there, always unpacking and packing up again, closing up the camp until next season. In recent months, Alva had made an extra effort to make their Bluff Point house feel like their proper, permanent home. She had even organised for the Riihimäen glassware, gifted to her by Onni's family on their wedding day, to be shipped over.

On the mile-long walk to Bluff Point Primary, Hilda carried her brown clip-lock case with her arm at a serious right angle. With her other hand she held Alva's, joining the forced march with a look of resignation that made Alva want to turn and retreat, but instead she arranged her face to appear sturdy. Inside Hilda's brown case was a pencil box, which Onni had made before he left for the islands, and a lunchbox. Alva had prepared two Sao biscuits with butter and a polony-and-tomato-sauce sandwich. She'd also mixed up some green cordial for her daughter, funnelling it into a washed-out sauce bottle. These she thought matched Hilda's uniform. She knew they were the right things to send because she had seen what her neighbour Charlene packed into the lunchboxes for her children.

Despite the early hour, their bodies were daubed with sweat by the time they arrived at the school gate. Alva wiped away the moist line above her lip, observing the gathering of women and children. Mothers crouched before their sons and daughters, imparting some pearl of wisdom. Alva copied them. She bent down and gauged Hilda's sweaty face, which looked stricken.

'I wish I lived at Little Rat all the time,' Hilda said.

Alva sighed. 'We'll be back on the islands by Easter.'

Then Alva was aware of a presence beside her. Looking around, she recognised another of her neighbours—the woman from across the street. She had yet to make her acquaintance, even though they were no longer new to Harrison Street.

'Hello.' Her smile seemed painted on. 'Where are you from?'

'I too from Harrison Street. My name Alva.'

'Oh yes, I've seen you with your husband. But I mean where are you from?'

'I from Finland.' Alva sounded the words out just as she'd heard them pronounced on the record *Relaxed English*. She played it sometimes while she sewed or mended garments, but it was unbearably tedious.

'Oh.' The woman paused meaningfully. 'Finland.'

Alva nodded, let her eyes skip across the scene unfolding around them. A sea of white and green. All the children the same, as she had imagined, or almost. Over by the fence, an Aboriginal boy rocked on his heels, holding his mother's hand. Alva looked down at her own daughter, her difference camouflaged under her white hair. Until she spoke.

'*Äiti, Äiti.*' Hilda pulled on her skirt. '*Onko koulu loppunnut? Mennään kotia.*' Mum, Mum. Is school finished yet? Let's go home.

'Poor little love,' said the lady, eyeing Hilda. 'Does she know English?'

'Little bit. She here to learn.'

'Hmm. Maybe if you talk to her in English at home you'll both learn a bit faster.'

Alva looked into the woman's small brown eyes. They were not completely unkind.

'You wouldn't want her to be behind.'

Alva gave a slight nod of the head, but when her gesture was not followed by words, the woman cocked her head and pursed her lips.

'It's always difficult, the first day of school.' She looked from Alva to Hilda. 'You have a good day, honey.'

As she walked away, Alva lowered herself back down to Hilda's height.

'*Meidän rohkea tyttö, mene nyt.*' Our brave girl. Off you go.

Alva began the sweltering walk back to the house, feeling more alone than ever. She hoped Hilda would not break as she had done, just now. Outside she remained composed, but inside she was shaken. A yellow FJ Holden approached from behind, and Alva saw that it was her—the woman. She was sitting bolt upright in the driver's seat and, despite their encounter, Alva couldn't help but be a little impressed. She herself had toyed with the idea of learning to drive, but she had not yet worked up the courage to suggest it to Onni. Studying the bitumen, she felt a prickle of envy move through her. In that moment, she was the peasant girl she had always been. *I wish I lived at Little Rat all the time too*, she found herself thinking.

When she arrived home, she noticed that one of the small green-tinged oranges had fallen from the tree. Harvesting season was still months away, but she tore open the fruit anyway, just to see, and was unsettled to find the inside empty of flesh.

It turned out that Hilda's first day had been far worse for Alva than it was for the child, and this was a relief. The girl had drawn what she claimed to be a fish, which they now stuck on the fridge, and she had brought home a reader. They tackled the small hardback together on the couch that night. *Jane said, 'See it go. See it go up.'* Alva diligently struggled through the childish text, and Hilda followed.

But they had made a success of it. Perhaps Hilda wouldn't be behind after all.

Hilda and the little girl from across the street—that woman's daughter—gravitated towards one another. The woman introduced herself as Aileen and her daughter as Deidre, or Dee for short. Dee was a robust little thing, and Hilda enjoyed Dee telling her what to do. One afternoon Hilda showed Dee her chicken—Iita Kana—and they took turns carrying it around like a baby. 'I named her after someone who's dead,' Alva overheard Hilda say. 'She's my chicken.' Finally they let the poor creature down.

Alva was glad that Hilda had made a friend at school. She had the boys on the islands—somehow they were all boys—but it was nice for her to have another friend, a little girl to play with. She heard Dee and Hilda chattering away, so quickly and effortlessly, and felt the same ache in her chest that she had felt on Hilda's first day of school. Alva could hardly catch a word of their conversation, and she felt her daughter moving on, moving past her. She kicked at the immovable rock which was her own indelible Finnishness.

One afternoon, Hilda asked permission to go to Dee's house and, with a curt nod from Aileen, the two girls disappeared into the backyard. Alva busied herself with the washing, guiding the wet clothes through the wringer, turning the handle, and repeating the process after the rinse. All along her mind was with her daughter. The thought that she had gone there, across the road.

Later, Alva was surprised to see Hilda arrive home with Aileen in tow. With the washing drying on the line, she had been pulling apart some salted fish, and she felt somehow dishevelled.

'Off you go,' said Aileen, pushing Hilda through the door.

Once the girl was out of earshot, Aileen caught Alva's eye. It was the same look she had given her at the school gate, sympathetic and yet admonishing.

'Hilda didn't say please,' she said.

Alva's brow furrowed.

'It's polite in Australia to say please,' continued Aileen. 'A young lady needs to have manners.'

In Finnish they didn't have a word for 'please', only a phrase for 'may I'. Where she came from, too many niceties were to be avoided, lest one sound disingenuous. But Alva didn't say that.

'I tell her.'

It was a Wednesday, and the clouds were a whisper in the southern corner of the sky. While Hilda was at school, Alva planned to walk to Tall Tommi's place, which was halfway between Bluff Point and town. Tommi was heading out to the islands the following day. Alva dropped off supplies for Onni: Kraft cheese and fish roe in a tube, a bag of vegetables and a watermelon. A fresh watermelon. That would cause a stir on the islands. She added Hilda's wobbly drawing, some writing paper for Onni and a short note of her own. Her husband's last letter had told of two divers who had come to stay on Little Rat. They'd shown the fishermen some coins they'd found at the *Batavia* wreck site, the ship having been discovered the year before last—not in the Southern Group, as originally thought, but to the north, near Beacon Island.

On her walk home, Alva went over the words she had written in her own note:

Your girl started school.

The hens have laid.

I had to kill the sickly one. Not even good for a meal.

Hot wind in Geraldton.

Keep well.

She realised now that it was a curt letter, that she had prepared the package with an air of resentment. It wasn't fair that he was out there and she was here, walking this miserable road with her skirt bunching between her thighs. Ahead, the liquid mirage on the bitumen inched forwards with her own slow progress, while the humidity bore down from above.

The clouds had gathered across the sky now, so Alva picked up her pace. She was two blocks away from home when they gave way, and fat droplets of water began to spatter her forehead. At first it was a welcome relief, but soon she noticed her blouse beginning to soak through and stick to her body. It was then that the yellow Holden passed, going in the same direction—to Harrison Street—and Alva locked eyes with Aileen. There was another woman in the passenger seat, and the two heads, with their dry, bouncy hair, panned along with Alva as the car passed her, a half-drowned foal on the roadside. Alva was aware of her underwear beginning to show beneath her wet clothes. Aileen did not stop.

The Holden disappeared down Hosken Street, and Alva continued walking. Yes, she was a peasant girl. But she was not ill-mannered, she knew that about herself. *We may not have a word for please, but if I were the one driving that car I would have stopped to pick you up. That would have been the polite thing to do, Aileen.*

When she arrived, drenched, back at the house, Alva found a package on the doorstep. The Riihimäen glassware, sent to her from across the seas. Placing the box on the kitchen bench, she ran her fingertips over the blue-and-white postage stamp, the lettering that read *Suomi-Finland*. She missed it so much in that moment. A short while later, Alva pushed the unopened package into the back recess of the linen closet.

The following week, at around midday, she heard a woman's voice calling from the front step. Alva peered down the hall, and was taken aback to see Aileen standing there behind the screen door—a frightening apparition. She was holding a plate of something. Oh no, thought Alva. Oh no no no no no. But she remembered that she had asked Hilda to be brave at school, so she walked down the hall in her bare feet. It took a long time to get to the door.

The woman was holding a muddy brown cake. 'How are you, Alva?' she asked, her head once again cocked to the side. She pushed the cake into Alva's hands. 'Had the extra ingredients so I made two. It's a fruitcake.'

'Thank you.' Alva used her best Australian accent.

'It'll probably give you the runs,' announced Aileen. 'It's full of dates and such.'

Hilda nodded, confused.

'Thank you,' she said again. 'Would you like to come in?'

'No, no. Have to get back.'

Alva watched Aileen walk out through the front gate and across the street. She placed the cake on the kitchen bench.

Later, she told Petra about Aileen, about what she had said at the school gate, and about Hilda's lack of manners; the awkward drive-by; and then the thing with the cake. Diarrhoea, that's what the runs were, Petra told her. Alva had thought it meant something about being in a hurry. Going fast. Well, she was on the right track. Alva was baffled, though. Why would someone give you a cake that might give you diarrhoea?

'The woman felt bad,' said Petra. 'The cake is a peace offering.'

'I'm scared of her,' admitted Alva.

'And she is scared of you,' said Petra.

Could it be true? That the frightening woman was in fact frightened of Alva?

'What should I do?'

'You could take her something in return.'

It was a curious game they would play. Alva baked the wet sponge cake, a recipe she had learned from her older sister many years ago. She poured the sweet sherry and coffee mixture over the soft and porous sponge, then spread the tinned fruit and whipped cream across the middle layer. Was she going overboard? she wondered, as she carefully picked up the second layer and placed it on top of the creamy middle. The *täyte kakku* was something you made for special occasions. She drizzled a block of melted Cadbury chocolate over the top—an Australian addition she'd learned from Helvi.

She was not engrossed in the task like she might ordinarily have been. She was conflicted somehow. No, embarrassed. That was it. There was an uncanny sense of shame in the making. She kept hearing Aunt Iita's voice: *Mitä se meikäläinen siinä hienostelee?* What's a commoner doing getting so fancy? So much effort and yet she knew that Aileen wouldn't even like the sodden taste. But she had all those eggs to use, she reasoned.

She assessed her elaborate creation. Alva understood now that when Aileen had come by with the fruitcake, she had played down the offering. All that nonsense about the runs. So she cut the sponge in half, put a portion in her own fridge and wrapped the second half in paper for her neighbour. When she took it to Aileen's place, her nerves all churned up, she just about threw it at the woman.

'Here it is, please,' she heard herself say. 'It nothing special.'

And Aileen caught the cake with the most bewildered expression on her face.

'Thank you.'

'Have you seen the new family that moved into number thirty-four?' asked Aileen.

Alva had seen.

They were sitting on Alva's front verandah, having dropped the girls at school. The girls, now nearing the end of their first year, remained inseparable during the school term, until Hilda returned to the islands in holiday time and was restored to her rugged self. Each woman balanced on her lap a cup of coffee, boiled thick and bitter on the stove. Aileen had taken to it. 'Not too bad,' she'd said after several pots and half-finished cups. She didn't take it black as Alva did, though.

Aileen sighed. 'When I was a kid we lived down the way on Mullewa Road. There were just three houses on that street then—the Clarks', the Donnellys' and us. My brothers used to play cricket in the middle of the road. No dramas, you know.'

Alva conjured the area as it might have been. A straggle of houses on the edge of town. Rural even.

Mullewa. The word made you wonder. It sounded different from the other street names Alva knew: Edwin, O'Connor, Mitchell. Her mind took her back to the school gate. To the little boy and his mother.

Aileen took a sip of coffee, her cup meeting the saucer on the way down with a small ting.

'The Lings,' she announced.

Alva nodded, yes.

She had seen the Lings at the market the week before. Hilda had gone to speak to the daughter, having met her in school. Alva was startled by the girl's flawless Australian accent. She became aware of her mouth, set in a prim evocation of her neighbour's. Later, Petra had told her that another Chinese family, the Wongs, had been in Geraldton since almost the turn of the century, and there were the Chinese guano miners on the Abrolhos in the 1920s. No, they were not necessarily recent migrants.

'You know they're commies, the Chinese,' said Aileen. 'That's what I thought you were. But in the encyclopaedia it says you drove them out. The Russians, that is.'

It was a simple assessment of what had happened to her people, but Alva didn't argue. 'Was very bad time in Finland,' she said.

The women sat together on the verandah, and the silence between them was still uncomfortable, but more manageable than it had been. Was it friendship? Alva wondered. It was not the same thing she had with Helvi and Petra, but it was a version of it.

'I might have been exotic, you know,' Aileen said after a moment. 'My mother almost ran off with a wog, before she shacked up with my pa.'

Was she, Alva, exotic? She did not see herself like that. She was, like many Finns, pale and quiet and sombre. They were not an exotic people. Not like the fast-talking and big-gesturing Italian community that Aileen somehow longed to be part of. She understood that, in Aileen's view, she and Onni and the other European migrants who had flocked to the west coast over the past two decades, the Italians included, were not so different now. Not compared with the Chinese family that had recently moved to Bluff Point. There was a long, convoluted line of people waiting to be called Australian, and while Alva was nowhere near the front she was no longer at the back of the line either.

It was not long after this that Alva added an olive tree to the line of citrus. The seedling had come from Mr Vella, whose tomato garden finished at the strip of short timber palings dividing their two blocks. Alva had listened attentively to the instructions given in Italian English, adjusted for her ear with the knowing of one migrant addressing another. She dug the hole where he had said the sun would be best, filled it with water, let it drain, and then planted the tree firmly. With her knees in the soil and the foliage at her cheek, Alva inhaled the aromatic scent of the leaves and felt something like melancholy. It would take a long time to grow. Eight years even, Mr Vella had said, before the tree would be properly established, before it would bear a confident and worthy harvest. The slow-growing trees, he'd added, could take six to eight decades to produce stable yields. Planting it felt like a new beginning, but also a giving in, a giving away of something—of the sloping path down to the green, green field of her childhood, of the cows bellowing at Anttila's fence line, of the graveyard on top of the hill where Aunt Iita was buried. Alva joined her daughter now, on that forced march towards an Australian life that somehow, she hoped, would not elude her. She let herself imagine the sapling eighty years hence, shaped and twisted by the hot Geraldton wind, surviving, black with fruit.

Cuttlefish

HILDA CROUCHED ON THE SPONGY moss that grew on the flat, low rocks in the middle of the island. It was funny, that stuff. Squishy, while the ground elsewhere was hard and brittle. She pressed the moss down with the tips of her fingers and watched it spring back up.

There were so many surprises on the island, which at first glance seemed like a bare rock sticking out of the sea.

The boys were yelling in the distance.

They were always yelling and carrying on.

She gathered herself up and, leaving behind the secret carpet of olive-green moss, ventured back towards the busy side of the island, the side with all the huts and the jetties and the boats. She stopped when she reached the water where the boys were scattered. They were collecting crabs into metal buckets. She found Lauri waiting nervously, guarding a bucket containing several detained crabs.

'What are you going to do with those?' she asked him. Lauri was Ismo's little brother. He was the littlest one, and his and Ismo's parents came from Finland too, like hers. They were the kids of the migrant people.

'Can't tell,' he said.

He was cute in a babyish kind of way, that little Lauri. His mum had let his hair grow, and it curled about his neck in tufts of soft white down.

'I'm going to catch some too,' said Hilda.

'Okay, but you'll have to play your own game with yours,' answered Lauri. 'Mika said not to tell about ours.'

'Fine.' She didn't mind. Hilda was used to playing by herself.

Hilda found a metal bucket in the sauna at her camp and ran back towards the shallows. She climbed down into knee-deep water and shuffled her feet along the bottom, curling her toes around rocks and shells. Where the island rose up from the sea there was an overhang, as though the ocean was slowly eating the island away from the bottom up. From far off, it made the island look like it was floating. Underneath the overhang was a shallow cave, only accessible when the tide was low, and that was where the crabs were, scuttling around in the shade and hiding under the cover of darkness. To catch a crab you had to be quick. You had to lift up the bigger rocks, and, if you found a crab underneath, you had to snatch it up before it scuttled off—or before it challenged you with its angry nippers, as some of the bolder crabs did.

'Got you.' Hilda picked one up by the back and held it up to the light. Ten armoured legs struggled. 'You'll be my friend.'

Hilda popped the crab into the bucket, satisfied. One friend was enough.

She headed for the jetty and placed her bucket and crab down beside her. Belly to timber, Hilda positioned her eyes at the gap between the boards of the jetty and concentrated on the space below her. The water moved steadily past, urged on by an invisible current. It scared her sometimes, the thought of the undertow. It took her uncle Nalle—a long time ago now, before Hilda was even born. He was fishing out by Disappearing Island when he got caught in a storm.

The sun warmed the back of Hilda's bare legs, leaving salt crusty on her skin. Under the jetty, seaweed swayed and billowed. Rainbow fish revealed themselves from their hiding places in blue and green corals, while three little butterfly fish hovered above a red sponge. She saw lots of grey fish, too, the boring ones that were everywhere.

Hilda loved looking at all the things in the water. All the critters that hid in the rocks at the high-tide mark. Even on the island, she liked to weave her way through the saltbush and watch the little birds nesting. On the low rocky section at the centre of Little Rat, where there weren't any plants at all, Hilda liked to look for fossils. Sulo, the oldest and best fisherman on the island, had shown her a walnut-sized imprint of a fish there once, and it sent tingles all up and down her body. This old thing that belonged to the islands way before she did. But when she went back later to show Äiti, she couldn't find the spot.

Today the water was green and clear, with shafts of light shining through and dancing with the swirling current. It was a good day for spotting fish. On cloudy grey days, Hilda had noticed, it was almost impossible to see anything, because the sea worked like a mirror. She kept her gaze steady. You had to be patient, she knew that much, if you wanted to see something special.

The sun made Hilda sleepy, and she thought of closing her eyes, but then she spotted movement in the water. Pressing her forehead against the wood of the jetty, she watched as a cuttlefish swam underneath her. The thing had a long oval-shaped body with small wings along the sides, a cluster of trunk-like tentacles that sprung from its head, and two big black-and-yellow eyes. It glided in the dappled shade of the jetty and then something amazing happened: the cuttlefish started to change colour. The striped light thrown across the water by gaps in the jetty tessellated on its back. A mottled pattern of electric blue and green covered it, shot with shimmering white lines and a hint of peach through the tentacles. The fish became difficult to make out as it matched its colour to the mingling light. And then it was gone. Hilda stayed there, looking through the gap in the jetty for a few more minutes, but she wasn't really looking. She was trying to remember every detail of what she had seen, because she knew how quickly she would forget. She wished the cuttlefish hadn't left so soon; just like the fish fossil, it was now lost to her. Except in her memory, which changed and distorted things. But it was very special, what she had seen.

That afternoon, Hilda helped Äiti wring out the washed sheets. She was about to tell her about the cuttlefish when they heard yelling coming from the community hall. They hung a sheet on the piece of rope and went to see what all the fuss was about.

People were gathered at the front entrance, and Mika was being marched back to his camp by his dad. Lauri was standing to the side of the crowd, looking scared and excited.

'What happened?' asked Hilda.

Lauri let out a small gurgle and looked at Hilda wide-eyed. 'We let the crabs go in the hall!' He fizzed like a cup of lemonade.

Catches had been loaded into the holding crates on the pontoon and cray boats docked for the day. Which meant the fishermen—Isi, her dad, included—were in the hall drinking beer. They would be in shorts and tattered old t-shirts, and, best of all, they would be barefoot. You hardly ever wore shoes on the island. Thongs, maybe, but never shoes. Hilda thought of all the fishermen hopping around and saying bad words as crabs scurried under their feet. She laughed with Lauri, who looked like he might explode from the thrill of it.

'You boys, always mucking around,' she said.

The next day, Hilda was given the job of looking out for Lauri, since his older brother Ismo—who was also part of the crab game—wasn't allowed to come and play. Neither was Mika, who was the leader. She suspected that Ismo hadn't really wanted to be a part of it. He was a good boy. Hilda took Lauri to the centre of the island and showed him the squishy ground. They squatted down next to one another and pressed it down. Hilda looked sideways at Lauri, and he smiled, watching the textured moss puff back up as he took his hand away. He was good to have around. So easy to please.

'We could play wallabies,' suggested Lauri.

'That sounds like a game for little kids,' said Hilda.

They began to build a cubby in the saltbush nearby, but a nasty bird began to swoop and Lauri got scared. Waving their hands above their heads, they retreated back towards land's edge. They would play on the jetty instead. But first they went to the toilet together, at Lauri's request. It was a narrow shack that stuck out off the edge of the coral platform, with a wooden seat built over a hole, and below that the ocean. It was scary looking down into the hole with the whirling sea below. But they did anyway, tilting their heads together. When Lauri climbed on he looked like he could slip right through.

'Am I a little kid?' he asked.

'Yep. That's why I have to look after you. And that's why you're not allowed to go in the water by yourself. You can't swim yet.'

'No,' said Lauri, 'not yet.'

Hilda could tell that he was thinking about the water rushing beneath him.

Back outside, they made their way to Hilda's jetty.

Lauri held her hand and tugged it lightly when he said, 'Hilda, did you know my dad is the fastest swimmer, probably ever, and I'm going to be like him.'

They sat down cross-legged at the end of the jetty.

'There's an undertow,' said Hilda. 'You have to be careful of the undertow, or it'll carry you really far out and you might never get back.' She pointed towards the wide expanse of water that separated Little Rat from Vuti Vutti Island. 'That's what happened to my uncle. He drowned. Out There.'

Lauri stared at the water.

Out There was awful because of what happened to Nalle. Hilda loved the water that lapped at the edges of the island, she loved playing in the shallows where you could see through to the bottom and all its waiting treasures. But Out There was a dreadful place.

Then Hilda felt a shove from behind.

'Watch out for the undertow.'

It was Mika. He'd crept along the jetty without Lauri or Hilda having noticed.

'Hey!' said Hilda. 'You're in trouble! You should stop being so naughty, Mika, or God will drop a rock on your head.'

'Pfft. Mum's gone over to your camp for a cup of coffee. Said to come get you both. Your mum's made arrowroot porridge.'

They started back along the rickety jetty.

'Anyway, he got eaten by tiger sharks,' said Mika.

'Who?'

'Your uncle Nalle.'

'No he didn't, he drowned. The undertow took him away from his boat and he drowned. He couldn't swim. That's why you have to learn to swim before you go out on the water, Lauri.'

'How do *you* know?' countered Mika. 'They never found him, did they? If he drowned, he would have washed up somewhere.'

'He drowned,' said Hilda matter-of-factly. 'It's a peaceful way to go.' She'd heard her parents talking about it with Lauri and Ismo's mum Helvi. They sat talking quietly at the laminex kitchen table while Hilda lay like a rake, stiff with the fear of death, in her bed in the next room. Then Helvi had said those exact words. *A peaceful way to go.* Hilda liked peace and quiet.

Death was a terrible thing. But if you thought of it like this, as a long, muted sleep, then it was almost bearable.

It was true that they had never found her uncle Nalle. They had found other dead people out here, though. From the olden days. Over on the Wallabis.

After the snack, Mika's mum made him go back to their camp with her. He was grounded after all. And Hilda was triumphant; she liked having little Lauri to herself.

Together they returned to the jetty.

'Have you ever seen a cuttlefish?' Hilda asked.

'What's that?'

Hilda told Lauri about the funniest-looking fish in the world, with trunk-like tentacles coming out of its head like a sea elephant and skin as colourful as a kaleidoscope.

'A magic fish,' said Lauri.

They decided to lie down on the jetty just like Hilda had done the day before, and maybe the cuttlefish would come back to visit them.

The sun throbbed and they saw lots of regular fish, but no magic ones.

'I'm going for a swim,' said Hilda, groggy from the heat. 'You stay here and look for the cuttlefish.'

She climbed down the ladder into the water, its surface ruffled by a lazy breeze. Lowering herself down inch by inch, she felt the heat leave her skin until she was immersed completely. Hilda blew out her breath, allowing her body to sink down, down, to the rocky bottom, where she lay still and listened to the gluggy quiet. She thought about drowning. It sure was peaceful down here.

Hilda kicked up when she started to feel her chest tighten. She saw the sun shimmering above her and burst up through the lip of water, taking in a long, delicious breath. Lauri was standing on the jetty, looking down at her.

'What were you doing down there?'

'Just looking around. Listening.'

'What did you hear?'

'Nothing. Just the sound of water.'

'Did you see the undertow?'

'You can't see it, silly. That's why it's so dangerous. You feel it. Did the cuttlefish come?'

'No.' Lauri looked disappointed.

They decided to collect shells instead.

'Look for the colourful ones,' said Hilda. She knew that the sun bleached the shells white in no time. Everything was whitewashed out here—the walls of the huts, the discarded heaps of fishing nets and foam floats, the rocks, the shells and the very ground itself. That's why a colourful shell made such a good find. Even better if it was still in one piece.

They piled their shells on the jetty, and Hilda sorted through their haul while Lauri played at the far end. A dried starfish and a red abalone shell were the best finds so far. Then she noticed a bone in the pile. It was the jawbone of a fish, and it had little white teeth jutting out in two perfect columns, coming together at an apex. Little ones at the back, bigger ones towards the front.

'Wow!' she shouted to Lauri on the jetty. 'Where did you find this?' She held it up to the sun, mesmerised.

Then Hilda heard the splash.

And when she looked up from the jawbone in her hand, Lauri wasn't on the jetty anymore. She stood up and ran the length of the crooked timbers, and peered over the end. Lauri was already underwater, sinking down, his blue eyes looking up at her. His little arms attempted a few weak paddles, but it was useless. He sank down until Hilda could see him splayed out on the bottom through the streaked water. She wondered how long it took for the peaceful feeling to come. It was only for a moment that she stood there, watching, waiting, trying to make out the expression on his face.

He stopped struggling.

A bird shrieked nearby, cutting through Hilda's thoughts and bringing her back to the present. That's when the dread rose. It bubbled in her belly. She jumped from the jetty and frantically kicked down, found his rag-doll body and pulled him to the surface and into the shallows.

'Lauri!' she said, looking at his delicate, wet lashes, his eyes closed over as if he was sleeping. 'Lauri! Wake up!' But he didn't react. His plump little hands felt cold and his lips were purple.

Hilda could hardly take in air either. Her limbs felt paralysed, her head in a fog. She knew she had to yell but the sound wasn't coming. First it was only a squeak that escaped her mouth, but then it came in full: the sound of someone else's voice.

'Help!'

Äiti and Helvi came running. They got Lauri onto the jetty and
kneeled beside him. Helvi beat down on her son's chest and cried
out, '*Minun* Lauri, *minun pikku* Lauri.' My Lauri, my little Lauri.

It was Äiti who took Lauri's arms and started moving them
around. Helvi was still yelling, pleading.

'*Luoja, ei ei ei, anna elää!*' God, let him live!

Others had gathered at the jetty now, their expressions strained,
the colour gone from their faces. Was this really happening?

Äiti turned Lauri onto his side and water spewed from his
mouth. He was full of it. But even after he was empty, he didn't
wake up. She lowered her ear to his mouth and waited.

'*Hengitä, hengitä.*'

And it was like everyone could breathe again, not just little Lauri.

They carried him to camp and laid him down on his side, covering
him with a blanket. Hilda stood watching from a corner. Helvi
was crying and so was Äiti, although she was trying not to.
Hilda wanted to cry too, but she didn't think that would be
right after what she'd done. So she just stood there. And Lauri
didn't move.

They sat by Lauri and waited and talked about getting on a
boat. They talked in low, cautious tones. When Isi arrived back
from fishing he said there was bad weather coming and it would
be too dangerous to cross tonight.

Hilda hovered in the vicinity of the camp, stealing glances
at Lauri every so often. *Move*, she pleaded silently. *Please move,
little Lauri.*

Ismo sat with his mum and brother. He held Helvi's hand—the fiasco with the crabs long forgotten—but kept looking at Hilda. It was a sympathetic look, and it made her want to hit him.

Hot with bad feelings, she decided to jail herself in the dark sauna. By the door, she found her bucket and her crab, which she had left there yesterday morning and forgotten about. The crab wasn't moving either. She'd left it in the hot tin bucket in the sun for two days and now it was dead. Death was everywhere. And it could happen to your friends. And it wasn't because of the undertow. It was because of Hilda and her daydreams.

Later, as the sun was going down, Lauri came to with a cough and gasp and splutter. His nose ran and his eyes wouldn't stay open. He started shivering. Helvi swaddled him tight in a blanket and cuddled him while Äiti clucked nearby. Hilda thought again of a tiny, trembling chick, folded into the wings of the mother hen. The knot in her chest loosened a little.

But they didn't know what those few minutes without air had done. He mightn't be quite right after this. And if he was okay, would he be afraid of the water? He always loved the water, the grown-ups said.

The season ended and everyone went back to town. Hilda dreamed about drowning. She saw herself taking the dark plunge, vision distorting and sound falling away. She prayed for her crab. But by the time the next season came around and she found herself in the place of her crime, Lauri had learned to swim. He'd started doing lessons at the Geraldton harbour in the summer and he was the fastest kid in his group, he told Hilda. That season you couldn't get him out of the water. Even so, there was something different about Lauri. She strained to listen in on the hushed talk of the grown-ups, but nothing was clear.

Hilda lay on the jetty, belly to timber, the autumn sun warming the backs of her legs. She looked through the slats in the wood, watching the fish dart by in flits of black, yellow and grey. Then Lauri swam into her line of vision, gliding easily through the water. The muscles on his back contracted as he propelled himself on with a stroke of an arm and a small kick of a leg. The light ribboned through the gaps in the wooden jetty and mingled with the water on his back. His skin changed to match the swirling light show, an array of electric blues, greens and purples. Hilda could only just discern the outline of his body now, coasting expertly through the configuration of rusty sleepers that formed the foundation of the jetty. The water, thought Hilda, was in Lauri for good now. It was in his ears and veins and deep in his bones.

Cyanometer

THE CYANOMETER HAD COME FROM Latvian Igor. He had brought it with him to the islands along with his other worldly treasures, which were few but varied: a compass rumoured to have been used by Napoleon, a heavy iron rock from the Pilbara, an eighteenth-century pocket globe held within a spherical casing of fish skin. The sky that day was a deep cerulean blue, shaded at the edges with crosshatches of white cloud. Despite having raised her eyes to it, as she was known to do, and perceiving its particular splendour, Helvi Kalliokoski had been unaware that it would set in motion a slow but momentous change within her.

That morning Helvi had passed Igor on the path which ran along the eastern lip of Little Rat. She felt the furrows in the hard dry ground beneath her feet, and considered how each groove and crevice was unique, worn by chance exactly to its shape. She sensed the emerging furrows finding ground on her own still-young face. Until Lauri's accident she had not been the worrying type.

Igor's hulking frame moved towards her. He was an unsettling man, a bull seal, with an energy she didn't know what to do with. Igor stopped mid-stride, rather uncharacteristically, to ask how she was.

'*No, miten siellä teidän kämpällä?*' Well, how are things at your camp?

Of all the people to whom she might have voiced her troubles, she did not expect to choose Igor. But he listened attentively as she told him what she suspected he already knew, about Lauri, about his diminishing hearing.

'It started around this time last year,' she said. 'You know, after he fell in the water.'

Igor nodded.

'He had been playing on the jetty with Hilda.' Even as she said this, she knew it wasn't relevant.

He considered her. '*Lapset eksyvät omaan maailmaansa.*' Children get lost in their own worlds.

She held her stance under the comment, until he released her with a gesture of his hand.

'Come,' he said.

Helvi fell in behind Igor's heavy footfalls, following as he ducked through the doorway. This, she could see, was a camp built for one. Minimal but surprisingly tidy, it housed a single battered cot, one small table, one chair. Igor lumbered across the room to a timber shelf that had been tacked onto the wall by the cot. She noted with interest the array of fabled collectables. He picked up what looked to be a colour wheel, though it featured only one hue.

'*Laurille,*' he said, in his grammatically correct, though accented, Finnish. She imagined him learning the language from a book.

Helvi took the wheel in her hands and turned it over. It was an antique paper ring featuring squares in graduating shades of blue, with corresponding numbers extending from zero to fifty-two.

'A cyanometer,' said Igor. 'Invented by a Swiss mountaineer in the seventeen hundreds. It was used to measure the blueness of the sky.'

Helvi fingered the boxes of chalky ink. She loved colour, she thought now. Wasn't colour just a simple miracle of life?

'I once lost the use of my right hand for a while,' Igor said. 'Felling trees in Latvia. My younger brother had cut the wedge the wrong way. I had to learn to use my left hand. Nowadays I can hook a line with either hand blindfolded.'

Helvi looked again at the many-numbered wheel, and then through the window at the blue, blue sky. It invited her to see.

'Where did you come by it, Igor?'

'Austria—Vienna.'

'What were you doing there?'

'*Sitä ja tätä.*' This and that.

Helvi's gaze skipped along the shelf, hungrily inspecting each item in turn. The compass, the large rock, the globe.

'*Saisinko?*' May I?

An affirmative grunt.

She picked up the scaled pocket globe, unclipping the hinged casing to reveal the small earth cradled within like the yolk of an egg. It brought to mind the pagan creation story from home, how the world was created from the broken parts of an egg. The casing was marked with hand-carved map-like drawings.

'What are these markings?'

Igor pointed to the concave hemispheres in turn. 'This side shows the position of the stars in the northern sky, and this side shows them in the southern sky.' His large hand moved in a slow sweep around hers as she cupped the sphere. 'The earth is tilted on its axis, so here in the southern hemisphere we have a better view of the stars, if we care to look. A better view of where we are in all this.'

Returning the terrestrial globe to its celestial sheath, Helvi noticed that Australia was only partly charted, with the eastern half of the landmass dissolving into nothingness. Western Australia was marked *New Holland*.

Helvi wanted to thank Igor for the cyanometer, but, perhaps sensing this, he turned his back to her.

She left him and walked the path to her own camp, holding the image of Igor in her mind's eye. His towering yet wounded silhouette. He was a man who looked straight into people. In his presence, your public face had no standing. What made a man that way? wondered Helvi. Something very good, or something very bad.

Helvi placed the cyanometer on the top pantry shelf, hidden and beyond reach of the boys. She returned to it intermittently over the next few days, inspecting it closely and noting the different shades. A vague fear kept her from presenting it to her son, as if the offering would confirm something.

'But what's it for?' asked Lauri, when she finally found the courage to show him the instrument.

'You use it to measure the blueness of the sky.'

'But why?' he asked. For a moment he was her toddler again, her inquisitive, curious boy.

'*Räknätään yhdessä*,' she suggested. Let's figure it out together.

They took the instrument to the water's edge. She crouched beside him, holding her hand at the small of his back. With her other hand she held the cyanometer to the horizon. They tilted their heads together to gaze through the hollow centre, the wheel framing the scene before them like a painting. Turning the instrument slowly, Helvi compared what she saw to the shades on the wheel. Number twenty-two, they agreed. She recorded their measurement in a notebook, along with the date and time. In that moment Helvi was reminded of a former self: the schoolteacher. She had undergone the training in Helsinki before meeting Risto, because she liked the idea of having a profession. She would not live in the shadows, she had decided as a young girl. Risto had seemed attracted by it back then, she thought, that air of independence.

'We'll check the sky each morning,' she said.

Lauri was willing enough, as he scrambled to pull his swimming shorts up and over his knees. He couldn't get out the door quick enough.

She and Risto had argued about the swimming lessons. She thought it too soon, that perhaps Lauri would be afraid of the water, but in the end Risto's stubbornness prevailed. She had shown her dissatisfaction by refusing to be present at the harbour for that first session. Instead, she'd waited anxiously for them to return home, and then resolved to look busy as they came through the door. Lauri was all smiles, and she'd had to accept that Risto had been right.

Despite the accident, she found she didn't have to worry about Lauri being in or around the sea. He was a natural. Since arriving back on the islands, he had made the crossing to the pontoon, that rite of passage for the island children that separated the big kids from the small. The pontoon bobbed about in the darker water, some thirty feet from the edge of the island.

Helvi had noticed how the bigger boys let Lauri follow them in the days after his crossing. She crouched to his eye level and tucked a stray blond curl behind his ear. '*Äitin pikku kala*,' she said. Mum's little fish.

His face blossomed into a simple and happy smile.

'It's really far out.'

But as he said it Helvi caught a slight slur in his speech, the way the consonants had been muffled, smoothed over. She held her face steady as a wave of disappointment flowed through her.

Helvi spent the following morning with Petra and Alva. They sat in her kitchen overlooking the shimmering water, listening for the exultant sounds of the kids—Ismo, Lauri, Hilda, Mika, and the older two, Saku and Matti—as they shouted and hurled themselves from the pontoon. Helvi boiled coffee on one burner and a large pot of water on the other. There was a live crayfish sitting in a bucket on the bench, awaiting its fate.

'Bessy broke her ankle last night,' announced Petra. 'They were into the keg up at the community hall, and she went for a drunken walk and fell through a gap in the jetty.' There was a shadow of disapproval in her voice, but also something else. Satisfaction? Or relief? Relief that it wasn't Esko this time.

'Sometimes you just need to let your hair down.' Helvi was surprised to find herself defending Bessy Turner. She poured three jet-black cups of coffee and handed one to each woman.

'I was taught that drinking and smoking were the devil's work,' said Alva.

'*Kilteille Luterilaisille kaikki on syntiä*,' said Petra. If you're a good Lutheran, then everything is a sin.

Helvi had never known that kind of pressure, having never been a good Lutheran girl—not like Alva, who had been brought up on a confusing concoction of pagan superstition and Lutheran guilt.

'When I came over on the ship there was a group of Italian priests and nuns on board,' continued Alva. 'They spent the whole voyage drinking and smoking and playing cards on deck.' She laughed at this. Or perhaps at herself.

'Was it liberating?' asked Helvi.

'*Eihän siitä Jumalan pelosta koskaan pääse.*' You can't get away from the fear of God once it's put into you.

'Maybe God doesn't mind a bit of fun and frivolity,' offered Helvi.

She was glad she had not been introduced to Alva's God. In Helsinki, Helvi had been raised under a different influence. She had watched her father reluctantly trail the family to church on rare celebratory occasions, and afterwards she had listened as he dissected the sermon and derided the meekness of the congregation. 'Religion,' he had told her, 'is about class. Don't let them fool you.'

As far as she could see, God was not some spiteful, frightening authority. God was all around you. And if God had to be ascribed a gender, then She was most certainly female. That much was obvious. All that creation.

Standing by the stove, Helvi took in the scene from the window. Her gaze fell on Hilda, who was now lying face down on the jetty. Something in Helvi shifted, like a cloud moving across the sun. The other children played in the water, while Hilda lay stationary, peering between the timber boards. This somehow irritated Helvi.

'There's something wrong with that child.'

She turned to face Alva, who looked at her searchingly. Helvi could almost hear it, the barely perceptible fissures opening, forming ruts that would become an impassable gulf. But there was no going back.

'Hilda,' she elaborated. 'She's oblivious to the world around her.'

They appraised one another from the precipice.

The silence was broken by a loud gulp as Alva swallowed her coffee. Helvi could visualise the grainy liquid sliding down her gullet.

Alva's eyes searched the waterfront until they found her daughter. 'What do you mean?'

'*Täytyy pitää silmällä.*' You'll have to watch her.

Helvi sensed Alva recoiling into herself.

Meanwhile, the pot had come to a rolling boil, a hot column of steam rising to the ceiling. Helvi picked up the crayfish, which wriggled unconvincingly in her hand. Imagine putting up such a feeble fight! She tossed the animal into the scorching water and watched as the life seeped out of it. Certain situations called for brutality.

The air in the camp was taut, vibrating with discomfort, so that when Alva placed her empty cup on the table and made an excuse to leave, Helvi was relieved.

Petra remained seated.

'I'm almost certain,' Helvi confided. 'It began immediately afterwards.'

She pulled the blanched cray out of the water with a long set of tongs. Looking at the dead creature now just made her feel deflated. Something else had been killed alongside.

'I remember an old relative who was deaf,' said Helvi, her eyes distant now, searching in the blue wash of ocean for the half-forgotten memory. Sometimes it felt like home was becoming as vague as *New Holland*, fading into obscurity. 'My grandmother's brother, I think he was. Us kids used to imitate the way he spoke. Kuuro Kalle, Deaf Kalle, we called him.' Her voice strained on the final syllable.

They sat for some time sipping the dregs of the bitter black coffee.

'Do you know what the cure for ear trouble used to be?' said Petra. 'Someone would blow pipe smoke into the bad ear. My grandmother used to do it to me when I had an ear infection as a child.'

The story had its desired effect. Helvi smiled, if just a little.

Through the window, Lauri could be seen diving expertly into the water from the pontoon, his small body cascading like liquid to meet its equivalent below.

Petra squeezed Helvi's forearm. 'Water finds its way,' she assured her.

Towards the end of that week, Helvi found the cyanometer discarded between the cushions of the armchair. Lauri was in the dinghy with the bigger boys. Compelled by the canvas of a dappled light-blue sky, by the spectacle it presented, she recorded the measurements herself. And the day after that and the day after that. Sometimes Lauri stood with her, out of some sense of duty. He had the eye for it, but not the heart. In the end, his interest waned and Helvi more or less adopted the cyanometer, needing to begin her day with the ritual. She would step outside of a morning in her cropped chequered shorts, ignoring the eyes of the other fishermen's wives, who wore their impractical, knee-length dresses even on the islands. Now they had another reason to look. Helvi held the cyanometer to the shifting heavens until she arrived at the corresponding hue. No day was ever the same. She had a small book in which she copied the entries, and had begun drawing naive pictures and scribbling notes below the number. Soon, Helvi had memorised the wheel and could settle on the measurement without its aid. The number just came to her.

Risto appeared impatient.

'What's the point of it?' he asked, watching her one late afternoon as she slowly rotated the wheel. Number eight, she concluded; the faint and waning blue of evening.

'What's the point of it?' Helvi repeated, turning to regard her husband. His reaction was not unlike little Lauri's. And again she explained it to him. But she could only describe the process of finding the right shade, leaving Risto unmoved. Risto valued function, practicality, reason. She was reminded now of an evening during their early courtship when, feeling passionate after a nip of vodka, she had dared to recite a passage from one of her favourite poems, 'Iltamieliala', 'Evening Mood':

Avartuu.
Ilta niinkuin huokaus
vitkaan kiirii yli maan.
Tummuu puu,
riisuu värit oksiltaan.
On kuin jossain sois—ja sois—
Orpo laulu harhailee.

It's widening:
an evening like a sigh—
languidly spreading across the land.
The tree's unclothing
its branches of their colours, darkening.
As if something somewhere
were ringing and ringing—
a song straying like an orphan.

Helvi, standing tall before him in the muted summer dusk, had overflowed with sentiment as she recited the passage, but when she searched Risto's face for recognition, she found the words had fallen flat. He was embarrassed. He had clapped. No, they would not meet on that plain. But there had been consolation: on her first visit to Alva and Onni's home at Bluff Point she had sighted the thin volume of poems in the bookcase—*Glass Painting*, Aila Meriluoto's first collection. She had slyly pulled the book out while Alva was in the other room, and noted the owner's name, scrawled in longhand on the inside of the cover: *Alva Kotiniemi*. The discovery brought a lightness to her chest, an anticipation of what might come between herself and this quiet woman. It was not unlike the first stirrings of love she had felt for Risto.

'Who knows?' admitted Helvi now. 'But does everything need a use, Risto? Does art need a reason to be? Beauty a purpose?'

She had sufficiently confounded him. Weren't they talking about the blueness of the sky? About measurements and numbers? She slapped him on the backside with the cyanometer as they turned back towards camp.

'*Syömään!*' To eat!

Helvi had recorded fifteen shades of blue before it was time to leave. On the final day on the islands, she took out the children's watercolour tray and mixed water with the pale blue to put down a kind of likeness to the colour she had observed that morning. With the grey, she filled in her naive sketch of the boat.

Two hundred and forty-eight recordings of the colour blue, and at last they were on the islands once more. It was a reprieve, after the drab months in Geraldton. Dr Larkin had sent them to a specialist in Perth, who had asked whether either of their parents had suffered from hearing loss and they had both said no. On their return, Dr Larkin explained what the specialist had indicated: that the cause was unknown, but it was likely to be progressive as it had occurred after language acquisition.

'It can be difficult to pinpoint,' he'd offered. 'We still don't know a lot about hearing problems.'

Helvi had felt her shoulders loosen as the islands came into view. Somehow it all mattered a little less out here.

She had come prepared. She'd packed into her suitcase a set of watercolour paints with the intention of making her own cyanometer, having returned the antique dial to Igor before leaving the island the previous year. It hadn't felt right to keep it for herself; she suspected that Igor cherished it more than he let on. She began with cerulean blue—the base colour—and mixed it with white or black to create the graduating shades. In the encyclopaedia she had read that the word 'cerulean' came from the Latin *caerulum*, meaning heaven. Cerulean. She felt the word in her mouth. Tossed it around. It rolled off the tongue with a certain magnificence.

Risto burst into the camp midway through her making, giving her a view of herself from his perspective. Sitting at the table amid a mess of scrap paper and blue paint. It was child's play, she supposed. He raised his eyebrows.

One afternoon, as the children played outside, Helvi dared to paint the scene before her. She added daubs of white paint to blue, until she found the colour of the sky from her vantage point on Little Rat Island at that precise hour on 2 April 1968. In making the cyanometer, she had learned how to mix her colours. And through recording the measurements, she had learned about light, about the way it fell across the landscape and scattered in a hundred different ways. She had noticed that the sky was lighter towards the horizon and grew opaque at the centre.

The next week she painted the sky in its variegated hues. The cobalt sky of a clear day; the ashen sky of an overcast day; the conch-shell-pink yawn of the sky in the early morning. Soon she had completed a series, though she kept that to herself. In her mind she called it *Studies in Blue*.

Alva rarely visited during that season, and Helvi mostly stayed within the confines of her own camp and its immediate surrounds. Erecting her easel outdoors, she observed the slow movements of her island folk. She saw Alva from a distance several times, a scarf securing her short hair, standing somehow forlorn out the front of the *kivi kämppä*. She found herself brushing the vague and foggy form of a woman into the foreground of her painting. The woman stood by the rambling stone camp, blending almost ghost-like into the darkening sky behind her. There was satisfaction in having painted her, in having grasped hold of her in this way.

When Risto returned from the community hall that evening, he removed the lid from a pot on the stove and was shocked to find it empty. Helvi threw the final brushstrokes down furiously while the night settled in around them and Risto waited in the camp kitchen, baffled. She let him flounder until the sun had fully set.

'You liked the idea of a spirited woman, until your dinner wasn't on the table.'

Risto looked on helplessly. Was the fish he'd caught becoming too unwieldy? 'I didn't say a thing.'

'*Näinhan minä,*' Helvi said accusingly. No, but I saw the thought.

Risto, she knew, saw little value in these colours. They each worshipped such different things in life. For Risto, God could be found in the majesty of the boat's hull, in the horsepower of the outboard motor, in the cheque that came at the end of the month, in the house that he would one day build at Sunset Beach. For Helvi, God was in the small things, in the way the sun danced on the water of a morning, in the subtle shadows of the evening mood, in the rainbow hues that rippled across cuttlefish skin. There one moment, gone the next. Sometimes, she felt that Risto's eyes looked but did not see, his ears heard but did not listen. There was so much beauty, so much music in the world. Sometimes it deafened.

At 9 pm they ate rye bread with a few cold rags of groper on the side. Helvi dared any one of them to speak, but both the boys and Risto watched their plates as they chewed. When Helvi lay down, with her husband curled around her, her thoughts went to the shadowy figure in her work. The secret coil of accomplishment, of knowing there was something greater than herself in the blends of those blues, mauves, pinks and whites, warmed her into sleep.

Lauri was taking a keen interest in fishing that season, and joined Risto on the cray boat most mornings. Ismo went along at times too, though more out of a sense of obligation, Helvi thought, than any sincere interest. He preferred to wander the island with Hilda. They talked quietly and fished with their bamboo poles. Risto often reported back of an evening that Lauri was a great help on the boat and would eventually make a fine deckhand. Energetic, astute and, most of all, discerning. Discerning of small changes in the environment: of rising swells and shifting winds, of telling cloud patterns and the indicative movement of birds. When the boys worked together, Risto told her, Lauri was the eyes and Ismo the ears of the outfit. Have faith, he told her. She had never had faith before, she told him, and she didn't expect to find it now. 'You know what I mean,' he said, irritated. Sometimes she tried quite hard to irritate him.

Before the holidays came to a close, Risto suggested a picnic at Alexander Island, just the four of them. Perhaps he had observed her ruminating. They set out in the still morning, putting lightly across the channel. She watched as Lauri moved about the boat with ease, and was gladdened to see how the boys complemented each other. Ismo spoke to Lauri in gestures, she noticed, or positioned himself face on and sounded out the words with his lips. Helvi was struck by her own rigidity. Risto was right. She had refused to accept Lauri's diminishing hearing, continuing to speak to him as she always had, her voice growing louder with each passing day, and all the while Ismo was adapting, creating a new language between the brothers. Helvi had always thought of the men around her as stubborn, unyielding rocks, while she herself flowed like water. But now she saw herself as she was: a crouching, terrified boulder. She relished the subtle changes in the world around her while baulking at any small change in her own son.

Risto pulled the boat into the sheltered nook at Alexander, bringing them to a gentle, wavering halt. They were not far from shore, but the sea floor fell away below them. The deep hole was perfect for swimming—and for squidding, Ismo told her. Lauri was on his feet, uncoiling the anchor and readying it for the drop. As the rope unravelled into the water, Lauri followed it in, launching himself off the gunwale in a spectacular flip. She peered over the side of the boat and watched as he kicked down. His form blurred, until he was swallowed up completely by the great silence. What was down there she would never know. But she let go a little in that moment, allowing her grasp to loosen and the cable between them to unfurl like the chain that secured the anchor. Oh, how she grieved him—her normal little hearing boy.

He came up in a flash of glistening water and sunlit hair. Ismo and Risto followed him in, while Helvi dipped her toes into the crystal water. Afterwards, Risto brought the boat to shore and they ate sardine sandwiches on the sand.

The following spring, Helvi apprehensively entered one of her paintings into a group exhibition being held at the Geraldton Library. The label read: *Studies in Blue: 37.* She had asked the librarian if Igor's antique cyanometer, which he had again allowed her to borrow, could be included somehow, and she had been pleased to find it fixed to the wall alongside her painting, above the artist's name: *Helvi Kalliokoski.* The exhibition opening was simultaneously terrifying and thrilling. The fishermen appeared ill at ease in their good clothes, standing for a long moment in front of each painting. They didn't pretend to understand like other people did, and she decided she loved them for it. Helvi had hoped that Igor might come, that she might show him her progress, how his cyanometer had illuminated her world, added colour to it when she needed it most. Of course, he didn't come, though Alva did. She walked into the room wearing a smile of such genuine pride. It was then that Helvi realised she had been waiting for her. When Alva joined her in front of 37, Helvi waited for her friend to recognise herself, the ambiguous figure at the corner of the canvas. Although the outline of the woman was faint—a mere suggestion of a presence—there was no denying that it was Alva. Helvi hoped that the painting would explain something.

Earlier, she'd overheard some Australians talking about the picture.

'It's a ghost of one of the *Batavia* women, on Beacon,' a woman in a hat had ventured.

Helvi smiled inside.

Aave, that was the other title she had given to 37: *Ghost.* A different type of ghost, perhaps. Here, she thought, we walk among you, but sometimes you don't see us.

Alva located number thirty-seven on the cyanometer, and made the comparison between tones.

'It really is a wonderful contraption,' she said.

'Risto doesn't understand it. He only asks, what's the point?'

'There is no point,' said Alva earnestly. 'It's about noticing. It's like a pause.'

'Exactly.' They were navigating their way across the gulf. Helvi felt her heart opening, its ventricles inviting the flow of blood back into the parched chambers. 'As I painted, I was thinking about time. How each moment arrives and passes.'

If their souls were two birds flitting about on separate flight paths, then for an instant they came together, flying side by side. Helvi could have painted it. But just like the light moving across the landscape and scattering, falling across a rock or a face or an island, the moment lingered and then was gone.

Pink snapper

MORNINGS ON THE ISLANDS WERE marked by the shrill call of seabirds and motors chugging to life; by the sound of hawking and spitting, as crayfishermen purged their lungs of the previous night's tobacco; and by the soft sleeping breath of women and children, who would remain wrapped in woollen blankets inside tin huts for a few hours yet. But on this morning, Hilda Saari was up with the seabirds and the spluttering blokes. She was going out on the cray boat with Isi and the bearded deckhand named Woolly.

That morning, she had felt a large hand on her shoulder, gently shaking her out of a dream.

'Hilda, *tuletko?*' It was Isi's grave voice. Was she coming or not?

Hilda stumbled about the room, still groggy with sleep. She found her cotton trousers in a heap on the floor and pushed one leg through, but her foot got stuck down at the ankle where the material was knotted together with a sock. Isi hadn't waited; he was already down at the boat, its engine groaning in the cold. She understood the motor's struggle; it was hard getting going at this hour. Hilda rubbed her eyes and zipped her anorak all the way up to her chin.

She slipped quietly out of the camp, feeling the gravity of the early morning. This was the life of a fisherman. Hilda had asked several times if she could go with them on the cray boat. She would not be a nuisance, she promised herself. It was what she had wanted ever since Mrs Putnam had asked her what she would do in life, and her mind threw up the image of Hilda Saari, crayfisher. Or maybe it had been spawned earlier still, on her eighth birthday, when she had caught her first fish by herself. She used the hand line that Isi had made for her: a hunk of float with a length of green fishing line tied around it, with bits of octopus for bait. Äiti had given her some dry pieces of bread to scatter on the water to attract the fish, and she'd almost eaten it all herself before she finally felt a bite. Hilda carried the garfish proudly back to camp, and Äiti fried it up.

Now, Hilda fast-walked along the jetty in the pre-dawn dark and hopped soundlessly into the boat, breathing in the smell of dead fish and rotten bait. Taking her place at the stern, she gave Woolly the briefest of nods.

Onni steered the boat along the home reef and out through the channel. All three were silent as they watched the indistinct form of the island diminish behind them. It was too early to talk about anything other than practical matters. Isi and Woolly were communicating in grunts and nods. Fishermen's talk. Some fishermen, she had noticed, spoke like that all the time.

This was Woolly's second season working the boats. He was not young and not old but somewhere in between, and Hilda wasn't sure where to place him. Last season, she had sometimes found herself wishing she could switch her dad for Woolly. She thought that would be quite good, to have a young, handsome father. Then she would be overcome by guilt, and she would go to Isi, who was sitting at the kitchen table, and lean her body against his frame. Because although Isi was bald, she knew he was somehow good. She knew this because he sent her letters from the islands. Now that she was at school, she had to stay on the mainland with Äiti and could only come to the islands in the holidays. It was terrible. But Isi regularly sent a note back to Hilda with the carrier boat. The notes were short, just a few words, written on a torn square of paper: *A whale bone washed up on Vuti Vutti*, or, *Hello from the birds*. He often signed off with a wonky drawing of a fish.

This season, Hilda's feelings about Woolly had morphed into something more like a crush. He had worked as a shearer before, and that's why they called him Woolly. That, and the beard. Woolly was quiet by nature, though Äiti said she didn't think him shy, he just didn't talk for the sake of talking, like others did. His granny told him we have two ears and one mouth for a reason. So, when Woolly was in a talking mood, you listened. He'd told her the name of his home once, a word she'd never heard before.

'Show me where,' Hilda had urged one day, when they were in the community hall looking at a yellowed map of the mid-west.

Woolly had pointed to Geraldton.

'Woolly! That's Geraldton.' He was having her on.

'It wasn't always called that,' he replied softly.

Hilda looked again at the map, then back at Woolly.

'But this is the proper name,' she said that day. 'Look, it says right here.' She ran her finger over the official block lettering.

'Anyone can draw a map,' he'd replied.

So, on a blank piece of paper Hilda drew the outline of the island as it appeared in her mind. She had never seen it from above, but she had crouched in every nook, had walked its perimeter many times. She drew the jetties, like several arms, reaching into the water along one side, and then the adjacent camps, labelling each one. *Bob Dunn's camp, Esko and Petra's camp, Our camp, Kivi Kämppä (where Woolly sleeps), Tall Tommi's camp, Risto and Helvi's camp, Igor's camp.* She labelled *Home Reef,* just beyond the jetties, and this, for Hilda, was where the homeliness ended. Out beyond the reef, it was a different kind of place. There was the expansive dome above, and the fathomless world below, where ships sank and fishermen went missing. The island of Little Rat, on the other hand, Hilda knew like an extension of her own body. There was the old tumbledown shed that didn't belong to anyone anymore except the sea eagle who nested on its roof each spring with her babies. Hilda drew this and wrote *Eagle's nest.* There was the flat rocky section in the middle, where she wrote, *Fish fossil,* and added an arrow. Unfortunately, she was no longer sure of its exact location—like a faint birthmark on the dry and flaking skin of the island, she had traced it with her finger one day, and lost sight of it the next. *Little Rat,* wrote Hilda underneath her map, *is an island in the middle of the ocean. My father lives here during the fishing season, but my mother and I can only come in the holidays now, because I have to go to school. The islands are a lot better than town. It's good to sit at the end of the jetty and drop a line in. But you have to be patient if you want to catch a fish.*

Out on the water, the two men worked together to bring up the pots. Isi was on the winch, while Woolly guided each pot over the side of the boat and onto the deck. The winch was a new contraption, and it had made the work of crayfishing much easier this season. Now the fishermen could bring the pots up and send them back down without breaking their backs. But it was a frightening piece of machinery. A rack with teeth and a lever. Hilda had watched as the ratchet unspooled to send a baited pot back down. How the hungry teeth clamped.

Today, Hilda's role was to manoeuvre the crays from the pots into hessian bags. She handled the crayfish suspiciously, studying all their spindly bits, sticking out every which way. It was hard work. But that was fishing for you!

Then, suddenly, Hilda grew tired of it. Her stomach grumbled, her arms ached. She peered out over the side of the boat and noted the line of floats stretching on and on. She wished now to be back at camp with Äiti, warm and dry in her pyjamas, making hot tea and porridge. Perhaps Woolly sensed her waning enthusiasm, because he suggested they pause for a break.

'Already?' asked Onni. 'Bit early.'

Isi was being a real slave driver.

They pulled one more pot before sitting down.

The egg-and-pickle sandwich was more delicious than ever. Hilda gobbled it up, and then felt it sitting on her chest.

Woolly was playing with a bit of rope, his deft hands making easy loops.

'Can you teach me?' asked Hilda.

His eyes skipped over her father's face, as if to gauge his mood.

'Okay, young un.' He threw her the bit of rope. 'What do you know?'

She made an overhand knot, presenting it to Woolly with a smile.

'What else?'

She shrugged.

'Well, sorry, bub, but you'll need to know more than one knot if you're going to be a fisherwoman.'

Hilda smiled into her lap. Woolly was such a great guy.

'See, different situations call for different knots, right, Onni?'

'Oh yes. Woolly right on that one.' Isi gave a sombre nod, and Hilda felt a familiar sense of embarrassment on hearing his broken English. It was a kind of melancholy that spilled over, because Isi was better than those stunted words.

Woolly made loops in slow motion. He created a fixed noose at one end of the rope, then pulled it taut. 'The bowline.' He held it in his hands for Hilda to study. 'Your turn.'

She took the rope and attempted the knot from memory. By the second step, she had lost her way.

'Harder than it looks, isn't it?'

Hilda nodded.

'A good knot can tell you a lot about someone.'

Onni raised his eyebrows.

'What does your knot say 'bout you, Woolly?' Hilda asked.

'Well'—Woolly grinned—'it may look like I know what I'm doing, Hilda, but I'm just learning. I make them up as I go along. Your old man, on the other hand, he's a man who sticks to a few solid, reliable knots, doesn't stray into unfamiliar territory.'

Hilda thought about the knots her dad could do. They weren't fancy, but they were good knots.

This time, Woolly demonstrated the bowline in stages, moving his hands deliberately. 'The rabbit comes out of the hole—the rabbit being the working end of the rope—goes around the tree and back down the hole.'

He presented the finished product to her a second time.

'The good thing about the bowline is that it doesn't slip, but it's easy to undo.' Woolly turned the knot over, bent it downwards, and the whole thing came apart.

Hilda tried again, whispering the rhyme under her breath, and this time she got it right.

'Got a knack for it.' Woolly winked. A very quick wink; the kind that makes you wonder whether you imagined it.

The sun had risen fully now, and she felt its warm hand against her cheek. Small swells slapped the keel, the water glistening all around. Perhaps the open ocean wasn't such a frightening place after all. *Tämä se on elämää*, she thought, just as she'd heard her father say. It was true: this was the good life! And she almost said it out loud. Instead, she breathed in deeply and felt it privately— the goodness of the place. She felt it deep down in her bones. But then Onni got the engine going again, and it growled and farted below the waterline. He steered the boat towards the next pot in the line and turned on the winch.

'Let me, Isi.'

Later, she would remember reaching for the winch and wonder at that sudden stroke of confidence. Wonder what had got into her.

It happened so quickly. Like a fishtail on the gutting bench. She heard the crunch of meat and cartilage and bone, and then she saw the blood.

Isi swooped in. He was superhuman in that moment, seemingly in several places at once. He yanked the lever to kill the winch. There was a rag, and he was wrapping it around her hand, pressing down on the bundled finger with all his force. He was yelling to Woolly, who started up the motor.

Spurt spurt.

Petrol pulsed through it and the boat lurched forward. They turned one hundred and eighty degrees. Above her, the sky gushed by and then everything went blurry.

Her awareness returned as they docked at Big Rat. She was in Isi's arms, being carried along the jetty. With each footfall she heard the creak of the timber below them. Then the hard smack of his feet when they reached solid ground. Up ahead, she could see Woolly's bobbing frame.

They burst through the door of Nellie's camp. Woolly was already inside, talking, motioning. Hilda's dad laid her down on a mattress, and she clung to him with her good hand for a moment, before he shook her off. Looking sideways, she saw the rag, dark and soaked through, the colour of squished black berries. A little red tear fell onto the floor.

When she woke, she felt the throb first, like a heartbeat in her hand. It was only then that she remembered her blunder. She groaned. The sound of regret, not pain. Although there was that, too. Her hand was wrapped like a parcel, the finger—her ring finger—stupid and ungainly beneath the bandage. Onni sat in a chair at the foot of the bed.

'*Anteeks, Isä.*' Sorry, Dad.

It was the first time she'd called him that: Dad, not Daddy. He rose and walked over to her bedside, ran a hand through her white hair.

'*Minun pikku Hilda. No, on niinkuin on.*' My little Hilda. Well, it is what it is.

There was more to say. But the words struggled to escape the thin line of Isi's mouth, which preferred to speak of weather patterns, or boats or cray hauls. Disappointment was everywhere. It was in the sad droop of the blanket, half off the bed, and in the drab rag of curtain.

When Isi left, Hilda felt a sense of relief.

Nellie had been a nurse in the war, and out on the island she ended up looking after anyone who got sick or hurt themselves. She'd seen everything: endless blood and guts; grown men crying for their mothers. With the steadiest of hands, she dressed wounds and bandaged folks up, she splinted broken limbs and tried quietly to convince stubborn fishermen to return to the mainland for proper treatment. Hilda felt safe there, under Nellie's care.

'Showing off, weren't you?' she teased. 'For that young deck-hand. Weren't you, Miss Hilda?'

Hilda was shocked by the accuracy of Nellie's jibe.

After the Incident, Hilda was relegated back to camp with Äiti. In time, a brand-new layer of pink skin grew over the stump, but even so, it remained an ugly thing. She knew her mum was angry about what had happened when she said: 'No one will put a ring on that finger.'

When she wasn't helping her mother at their camp, Hilda wandered the island, as she had always done. She returned to the site of the fish fossil, hoping to locate it—feeling that, if she did, something would be restored. Here she met Sulo, and was overcome with embarrassment. She hid her hands behind her back.

With her permission, Sulo assessed the nub of her finger. It was a queer feeling, to lose a part of yourself. It still felt as though the finger was attached, but when she looked, there was just negative space. She felt reduced, incomplete. Hilda looked sideways, avoiding the old fisherman's gaze. She could hardly face him after what had happened.

'Good,' said Sulo.

Hilda let her eyes flicker over him. Sulo had been out on the islands for so long he had become part of the landscape. His skin was pockmarked and porous, just like coral, and his hair the same blanched shade. His eyes were a grey-blue mirror of the Indian Ocean.

'*Oppilasku pitää maksaa*,' he said, nodding gravely. Everyone has to pay the tuition fee. 'No, girl, nothing comes for free.'

She waited for him to offer something more concrete.

'We're all in fishing out here, aren't we?' he said.

She nodded.

'The crays are our lifeblood; they keep our bellies full and build roofs over our heads. But it's not an easy job, fishing. The bread is hard won out here. You've got to learn the ropes. And some lessons are harder won than others. Your uncle Nalle, he paid a large fee for the crayfish he caught. But by God, that man caught a lot of them.'

'Did you have to pay the fee?'

'I spent a long and terrifying night on the sea during a lightning storm. When I made it back to land, I thought I would never step foot on another boat.' Sulo laughed at himself. 'But everything fades. The important thing is the lesson learned. I misjudged the weather that day.'

After Sulo ambled off, Hilda gazed at the stump which was her tuition fee. She rotated her left hand, taking in the newborn quality of the skin. Everything fades, thought Hilda, even the blood-red horror of an amputation. She thought of little Lauri, who had unwittingly traded his hearing for the glistening body and pulsing gills of a fish. In her mind she saw a pendulum swinging back. An ear for a finger. Or something like that. But Hilda could only bear to think on it for a moment before pushing it to the dark recesses of her mind. This was where she had learned to hide the image of Lauri sinking down into the water, his little face staring up at hers. Instead, Hilda imagined the sea creatures that might have gorged on the end of her finger after it fell into the sea, and felt an odd connectedness. Her mind stirred with the great mystery that was life. She considered the fate of her uncle Nalle, who may have been eaten by tiger sharks after he got lost in a storm out by Disappearing Island. Hilda was struck by the liveliness of death; it would have been a grand and violent event. She could not hate the shark.

And there, just a few paces away, she caught sight of an outline in the rock. So faint, so ghostly—but it was there.

Things were always shifting on the islands. The wind switched from south to north, west to east, it whirled and flipped and changed its mind. The sun shone, and then the clouds gathered. The sea was flat, and then it was wild. So, too, people came and went, and now it was time for Woolly to go.

'When will you come back?' asked Hilda, addressing the jetty timbers.

When he didn't reply she raised her head. Woolly was standing with his arms folded, bracing against the wind, with a wistful look on his face. Hilda searched those good brown eyes for the truth of the matter. She knew he was going to see his family first, and then he was going north. To the very top, to work the pearl boats.

'Not sure, young un. You'll be the skipper of that boat before I get back out here, I'd say.'

So the vision reassembled. The future, grown Hilda, skipper of the cray boat *Riitta*—all boats needed a name, even if Isi didn't think so. But Woolly was not there in the vision, because he would be old by then, she knew, and he would have his own life. This pained her, and to escape it she looked out to sea.

The carrier boat was getting closer, and when it arrived, it would carry Woolly away. Hilda's heart galloped. As the vessel docked, hitting the jetty with a harsh and final bang, she knew she wouldn't be seeing the deckie again.

She drew the map from her pocket and pushed it into Woolly's hand. She had folded it over and over again, to a tiny square. Hilda thought of turning and running then, or she could snatch it back, a silly child's drawing. Woolly opened the map and studied it, a grin unfolding beneath his wiry beard.

'So that's what it looks like, hey? From down there at your level.' Was he making fun of her, at a time like this?

'I've heard Little Rat is the shape of a fishtail from above. Doesn't matter, but. This is *your* Little Rat.'

Hilda was hurt and puzzled, but she let Woolly pat her on the back before he jumped onto the carrier boat.

Later, when she had her first ride in the seaplane, Hilda looked down at the shape of Little Rat with dismay.

Indeed, you might call it a fishtail. And a small one at that.

But she could not erase her own image of the island from her mind. She thought of the place that Woolly called home, the place that she called Geraldton. There would always be more than one way to look at things, thought Hilda, as she rubbed, comfortingly, the stump of her severed finger.

Soon Hilda began to fish again, off the jetty with Ismo. They sat with their bare feet dangling over the edge, their lines floating to and fro with the current. Hilda held out her left hand for Ismo to see.

'The end of it fell in the sea, you know?'

She wagged the squat nub at her friend, who leaned backwards slightly.

'I fed the fish,' said Hilda, 'because the fish feed me. Nothing comes for free, Ismo.' She didn't tell him about the other part of the transaction.

Just then she felt a tug on the line. Hilda scrambled to her feet to haul it up, a pink snapper, the chalky colour of flesh.

Mackerel

ISMO STOOD IN FRONT OF the *Juhannus kokko*, warming his hands. Sparks rose, barely visible in the midday sun. He listened as the men who had gathered for the lighting of the bonfire offered their opinions on the shipwreck. The excavations had begun—they were taking the whole lot back to the museum in Perth, hull and all—and everyone was talking about the *Batavia* again.

'Those Dutch blokes went mad,' declared his dad, 'marooned out here for months, not knowing if help was coming.'

'This place would send anyone loony,' added Esko, 'if you stayed long enough.'

'Can't blame it on the islands,' said Onni. 'There's no excuse for rape and murder.'

'I'd agree with you, Onni,' said Sulo, 'but no one knows what they're capable of, in certain situations.'

The men looked down then, or away, and Esko chucked another broken bit of timber onto the fire.

Ismo had helped build the *kokko* after pulling the craypots that morning. A few minutes ago it had stood tall, a pyramid of old tea-tree craypots, leftover cuttings of two-by-four and other bits and pieces. Esko had doused it with petrol and thrown in a match, and it had erupted into life, flames licking and racing up the mountain of junk.

Winter had arrived as swift as a southerly change, and Ismo couldn't help but mourn the passing of another island season. Soon they'd be packing everything up and heading back to town. But it wasn't over yet, he reminded himself. Tonight was midsummer's eve. In Finland, people would be at their summer cabins, and there would be countless fires burning lakeside in the dusky midnight light. Each year, here on Little Rat, they had their own *Juhannus* celebration.

'You know what they did with the women? The ones they kept alive, I mean.' Latvian Igor had joined the conversation now. He was sitting on a lopsided rock a little way off. 'They made them women for common service,' he said.

He was a tall man with a face like a clenched fist. It was said that Igor spoke seven languages, though he was generally a man of few words. He'd worked on boats all over the world and had jumped ship, at one time or another, eventually ending up in Australia. Rumour had it he'd once worked for Al Capone, and he had the record for the biggest marlin ever caught on the islands.

'Common service?' Ismo whispered it to Mika.

'For rooting,' Mika said, as though it were obvious.

They'd been mates forever, him and Mika. Mika had taught him things, like where you might find a blue-ringed octopus (but they'd never found one) or how you could walk across the exposed reef between Little Rat and Big Rat on the low tide. Mika's dad Esko was one of the original five Finns, along with Ismo's own father, who had set up camp on Little Rat. At school, Mika liked to tell about the Five Finns and how they slept behind a windbreak during that first season. He would grow a few inches whenever he told it. Mika's mum Petra was one of the first women on the island, too, all on her own when the blokes were out fishing. She was a tough lady, and she had to be, to keep Esko in line.

Kyllä sillä akalla on sisua.

That's what Ismo's mum said. That Petra had *sisu*: like there was a quiet bear sleeping inside her.

'I've been reading about it,' continued Latvian Igor. 'Couple of people recorded what happened in their journals. And the Dutch wrote it down afterwards. This Jeronimus fella, he didn't believe in heaven or hell—which was unusual in them days.'

All eyes were on Igor now, surprised by this sudden volubility.

'Believed God was inside each of us. And whatever man did, he said it was God made him do it.'

He took a big slug from his king brown bottle—Igor brewed his own liquor—and Ismo watched as his Adam's apple bulged, his neck as thick as a jetty pylon.

Ismo felt important, standing in a circle with Latvian Igor and the other fishermen, talking like this. He was on the cusp of something; he was almost one of them. Ismo had been deckying for his dad during the school holidays. Soon he'd be sixteen; he could leave school and work the boats full-time.

'So that's how he made himself feel better about being the devil incarnate?' asked Uncle Onni.

It had all happened a long time ago.

Batavia.

The word lingered in Ismo's mind like a whisper.

The *Batavia* was a Dutch merchant ship sailing to Indonesia, carting gold and jewels and spices and all kinds of things to the new colony. Ismo's dad had told him all about it, when he'd asked. It wrecked over on the Wallabi Group. The islands were a trap for ships sailing at night, Risto had said, barely a fathom above sea level, so that the sailors didn't see them until they were standing on them. That was when the mutiny happened, and the killings and the rape. All led by that one man, Jeronimus Cornelisz. Apparently the Aussies over on the Wallabis said they could tell where the skeletons were because the soil was dark and greasy. And they saw things sometimes. Heading back to camp after a day on the cray boats, tired as anything and with the afternoon sun hammering their eyeballs, they reckoned you could make out a gallows on Beacon Island, a few bodies dangling in the wind. Ismo's mum reckoned it was just one of the fishermen's clotheslines they were seeing, a few wetsuits dangling, buoyed by the south-westerly. Ismo wasn't sure about ghosts. But if they did exist, the ones out on Wallabi would be an angry lot.

Everyone's eyes were on the fire, mesmerised by the flickering of flames. Igor removed a pouch of tobacco from his jacket pocket and started to roll a smoke one-handed.

'That bloke got his ideas from a Dutch painter. Torrentius. A great watercolourist, he was. Considered a heretic, though, by wider society.'

Heretic.

Ismo fought the urge to ask Mika to decipher this for him, too, but he needn't have worried. Igor lit his cigarette and took a drag, letting the white smoke curl up into his nostrils before he exhaled. He squinted through the haze at the other men.

'You know what "heretic" means?' Igor asked. 'The Latin root, I mean.'

The group looked at their feet. He was answered only by the crackling of the bonfire.

'Choice,' he said. 'Torrentius was a freethinker. And of course the Church didn't appreciate freethinkers.'

Others had started picking their way through the saltbush to the bonfire, rugged up in anoraks and beanies. Ismo's mum arrived with his little brother Lauri, along with Alva and Hilda.

'Enough of this talk,' said Onni.

Igor got up. 'Tide's on the way in,' he said. 'Might go drop a net.'

'*Onhan Juhannus, tässä otetaan votkaa,*' said Esko. It's midsummer, time for vodka.

But Igor wasn't interested in vodka. He lumbered off towards his jetty.

Ismo was sitting by the water with Hilda when Mika sidled up to them, eyes darting all over the place. He sat down and opened his jacket conspiratorially. There was a bottle stashed inside. A tall bottle of vodka.

'What are you doing with that?' asked Hilda.

'There's so much grog, they won't notice one bottle gone.'

Ismo looked over at the adults. The volume of their talk was rising. All these men who hardly said a word when you were on the boat with them, or even back at camp of a night. He heard Finnish swear words. *Vittu. Perkele. Paska.* He caught Alva elbowing Onni in the ribs.

'Let's take the dinghy and make our own *Juhannus kokko*,' said Mika. 'Over on Vuti Vutti.'

Ismo looked across the water towards Vuti Vutti Island. It wasn't that far. He looked to Hilda. She shrugged.

'I dunno,' he said.

'Come on, Ismo!'

'Your dinghy?' he asked.

The three of them trod along the brittle ground, pushing saltbush aside. They dodged seabird carcasses and sea lion poo on their way back to the eastern boundary of Little Rat, where the jetties ran out in kinked rows. The smell of drying fish heads and petrol laced the air and, in a way, Ismo was sorry to have left the warmth of the bonfire, the men and the buzz of *Juhannus* behind. He hoped Lauri hadn't seen them desert him—but he was too young for vodka. The outboard motor coughed into life and they pushed off, sitting in silence as Mika directed the boat through the channel. Over by the fire they'd started singing in Finnish. Raucous voices filled the air:

> *Tapa sinä kauhavan ruma vallesmanni,*
> *Niin minä nain sen komian lesken.*

> You kill that ugly sheriff from Kauhava,
> And I'll marry his handsome wife.

Out in the middle of the sound, the sun slipped behind a cloud and the wind picked up. Wisps of white hair escaped from the sides of Hilda's billowing hood, flitting about her pink cheeks. The dinghy shuddered along, the hull slamming into the messy lines of wind swell. Ismo felt Hilda's body next to his, moving up and down with the rhythm of the boat on the water.

The breeze stilled as they slid neatly into the sandy cove of Vuti Vutti. As soon as the boat was secured, Mika opened the vodka, screwing up his face as he forced himself to swallow the first mouthful. He passed it around. The antiseptic scent invaded Ismo's nostrils as the liquid washed down through his throat and chest, starting a little fire inside of him.

'Let's go find wood.'

They called this island Vuti Vutti. It was just a stupid Finnish translation of the Aussie name: Woody Woody. Woody Woody was one of the only islands in the Easter Group that had any trees on it, and this meant there was enough firewood lying around for them to build their own *Juhannus kokko*. They trudged around in the bushes, which shot up through patches of coarse sand. Ismo found some random things in the scrub. Petrol cans and old bits of rope, glass bottles weathered by the sand and sea. He gathered small branches and carried them to the site of their fire.

Once the *kokko* was lit it started to feel like *Juhannus* again. Ismo sat down next to Hilda and let his leg fall against hers. He waited to see if she would move, but she stayed put.

Silver gulls squawked and carried on nearby. Mika found an old loaf of bread in his dinghy, so they broke it apart and threw bits out to the milling birds. Ismo was starting to feel good, warmed by the fire and the vodka. They each had another swig, and it went down easier this time.

'Hey, I've got an idea.'

Mika soaked a piece of bread in vodka, tore it into strips and began tossing them onto the sand.

Ismo and Hilda followed suit. The flock was growing in size and becoming frenzied. Gulls toppled over one another in their race for food. They pecked at one another with greedy beaks. Ismo watched the scene unfolding, unsure if the vodka was having an effect, unsure if he wanted it to. But he decided to go along with Mika's game anyway. 'Drunks,' he said, 'got no manners.' Hilda started giggling. Ismo let his gaze linger on her a moment. He was a boy at the water's edge, watching a new current take hold. *Look at me.* Ismo willed her to meet his eye, and when she did, he felt his heart thump in his chest.

A few feet away, a quarrel had broken out between gulls, so Ismo threw a fresh scrap in another direction, to break it up. He was laughing along with Hilda when they noticed one bird pursuing another. It was behind it, then on top, while the other flapped and mewed.

'They're doing it,' said Mika, with a tinge of glee in his voice.

'Nah,' said Hilda.

No one said anything else, until Ismo got to his feet and ran through the flock of seabirds, dispersing them every which way.

'Get lost,' he yelled, with enthusiasm.

Ismo settled back down by the fire as the shrieking of gulls grew distant. He listened to the sound of his own slowing breaths. The three of them sat there for a while, not saying much, the smoke engulfing them one by one, as the breeze twisted and eddied, unsure of where it was headed.

'I need the dunny,' said Hilda. She stood, a little unsteady on her feet.

'Me too,' said Mika.

'You go that way,' called Hilda over her shoulder, pointing.

Mika wandered off one way and Hilda another, so Ismo stood up too and walked down to the shore. He looked across the expanse of water towards Little Rat, the clouds above like pink snapper fillets. Electricity pulsed through him. This place, the sweep of sky, the sea and the islands, made him dizzy with possibility. The *Juhannus kokko* back on Little Rat gave off a thin stream of smoke. Ismo imagined all the bonfires burning in Finland at that very moment, the endless summer day, and it seemed as if that old place, from his mother's stories and songs, could be just there. Just over the horizon.

When he turned back he noticed Hilda a little way off, squatting in the bushes. She hadn't picked a very good spot. Her shorts were pulled down past her knees and Ismo could see the whole side profile of her white bum cheek, her hip and upper thigh. There was a stirring in his pants. He looked up into the dunes, past the fire, and there was Mika. He was watching her too. It was like looking in a mirror. Ismo sensed a creeping sourness inside him, like milk starting to turn.

Back at the fire he washed it away with a good gulp of vodka. Hilda padded back along the sand, all red-faced and glassy-eyed.

'That Latvian Igor,' started Mika, 'he knows a lot about the *Batavia* wreck.'

'I've been in his camp with Dad,' Ismo told them. 'I saw the fish skin globe.'

'Reckon he really worked for Al Capone?' Hilda tucked her windblown hair in behind her ear.

'Look at him,' said Mika. 'He's huge. And that face. Must've had his nose smashed in a few times. Probably killed a man.'

'You don't know that.'

'You don't know that he didn't.'

'Give us a sip.' Hilda leaned over and grabbed the vodka. She swallowed loudly.

'Take it easy, Hilda,' said Ismo.

She let out a single hiccup.

'Hear what he said back there?' Mika's eyes were intense, animated. He searched Ismo's for recognition. 'Women for common service.'

Hilda was leaning back in the sand now, looking up at the swirling clouds.

Mika looked sideways at her, a wry smile on his face. 'You know, some girls like it rough.'

She propped herself up on her elbows and looked back at him, one eye a little out of focus.

'What would you know?'

'Plenty. I've been with girls.'

'Liar,' Ismo said.

'Just because you never have.'

'Piss off.' Ismo looked down. He grabbed a handful of sand and let it sift through his fingers. He'd have preferred to talk to Hilda, but she had closed her eyes now. Her head, resting in the sand, lolled to one side. He tapped her on the cheek, the skin soft and pillowy. She let out a low murmur.

'She's out of it.'

So they sat there, Ismo and Mika, not saying much. Ismo had lost his buzz. Mika shoved him with his elbow and motioned towards Hilda. Those loose shorts of hers had ridden up, exposing a strip of her underpants and the inside of her milky thigh.

'She wants it, eh.'

'What?'

'Jeez, you're a square.'

'No I'm not.'

'You've never even seen a fanny, have you?'

Ismo shrugged. 'Yeah.'

'Yeah, your mum's in the sauna.'

'Shut up.'

'Relax. Here's your chance.'

Mika rolled Hilda over and pulled down her shorts, then her undies. Her whole bare bum was exposed, round and flawless on the sand. She groaned, moved a heavy arm in the direction of her thigh.

'Look.'

Mika pushed one leg to the side, tilting his head to get a clear view. From where he sat, Ismo caught sight of two pink folds between her legs, a few messy wisps of hair protruding. It brought to mind the flesh of a fish, the good-eating, boneless part, white and fresh, hours after the catch.

'She won't even know,' he heard Mika say.

Ismo's heart was beating hard in his chest, and there was that pulse in his crotch, too. He felt excited and sick at the same time, and the vodka worked on him like an excuse.

Up above them, a gull shrieked.

Then there was the dim hum of a motor. The sound became clearer as the moments passed. And at last a dinghy could be seen, putting around the corner.

Latvian Igor.

Ismo remembered now. This was where he liked to drop his net, in the tidal channel at the northern lip of Vuti Vutti. Where, on the incoming tide, the water rushed between the island and a small sand spit, bringing with it schools of sardines, herring and bream.

Mika was up and stumbling. Tugging at Hilda's shorts.

'Shit!'

He managed to manoeuvre them up over her arse, and it was hard to know how much Igor had seen from that distance. In a synchronised motion they shifted away from Hilda. Then they sat and waited for the dreaded sound of the hull coasting up onto the sand.

Igor said nothing. As he strode up the beach the boys scattered. Hilda's body was heavy and drooping when Igor picked her up, but she curled around his shape. He carried her back to his boat. They were leaving, just like that. But before pushing out from the shallows he swooped into Mika's dinghy and grabbed the tank of petrol. Ismo swallowed hard. How much fuel did they have left in the motor? But Igor was already gone, his boat little more than a dot on the water between islands. They were headed back towards Little Rat, towards that line of smoke in the distance.

Ismo felt a wave of regret wash over him. He wanted to be back there too, back with his mum and dad, with Onni and Alva and all the rest. With Hilda. But instead he was here with Mika, and his stomach was as twisted as spliced rope.

The sun was slipping now, turning the sky a brilliant burnt orange.

'Goddamn it.' Mika had gone down to the dinghy and was checking the petrol levels. 'We're as good as empty. We're stuck here.'

Stuck. Marooned on Vuti Vutti.

Ismo sat on the opposite side of the fire to Mika. The embers were growing faint and feeble in the twilight. Mika glowered, breaking sticks in his hands, while Ismo concentrated on not vomiting.

He was thinking of the crew of the *Batavia*. Stranded like this, at the edge of the world, on islands of dead and sun-bleached coral.

After what seemed like ages, Ismo heard the familiar grumbling sound of a motor. It was well and truly dark by now, but across the water the *Juhannus kokko* burned on, both comforting and awful in the distance. Latvian Igor had come back for them, and he called from the shallows.

'*Pojat.*' Boys.

They were up in a flash, scuttling down to the water's edge, wading into knee-deep water and climbing into the boat. Ismo could make out Igor's massive form in the dark, sitting at the stern, hand on the tiller. Mika didn't say anything about his dinghy. They supposed it would be spending the night on Vuti Vutti.

Igor motored out into the middle of the sound and, shivering now, Ismo began counting the minutes till the journey would be over. All he wanted was to be back on Little Rat, but about halfway across Igor killed the motor.

'There's movement in the water tonight, boys.'

He baited his line, a gang of three hooks. In the torchlight, Ismo caught glimpses of his face. Eyes narrow, mouth like a scar, his skin fissured like the contours of a map. Igor knew this place. Knew the deep gutters and the sudden rises of the reef bed. Could steer the boat and drop his craypots blindfolded and still they'd come up full. The bone-coloured moon floated above them, and the black water was silky and serpentine. The only sound was of the sea, lapping playfully at the sides of the boat.

Igor dropped the line in, let it drift.

'There's nothing more glorious,' he said, 'than a really big fish. Except, of course, a beautiful woman.' Ismo felt the man's eyes settle on him. 'Breaks your heart to be the one to do it. It's a little bit of yourself that dies along with it.'

Less than a minute passed before he got a bite. The rod lurched forward, reel screaming as it unfurled. Igor adjusted his stance, gripping the handle as the tip arced away from him. He battled the fish: working it closer, losing ground, gaining some. The boat listing to one side. Finally, he managed to heave it up and over the gunwale, water pouring from its great body. A Spanish mackerel. It jerked and shuddered on the deck, scales glistening silver in the moonlight. And Ismo understood what he'd meant back there. It was strong, sinewy, the racehorse of the sea. To strike it down felt like a sin.

'She's a beauty.' Igor held the fish down with his knee, his long blade poised. 'But we're all in the business of killing out here, aren't we?' He made a slit just below the fanning, gasping gills. 'Have been ever since those Dutchmen ran aground here.'

Ismo looked across to Mika. His eyes were cast down, studying the deck.

'You want to believe you'd have been one of the good guys, don't you?' said Igor as he wiped blood and scales from the knife onto his threadbare trousers. 'If that Jeronimus bastard knew anything, it was how easily men could be corrupted.'

Mika looked away, out over the oily skin of ocean.

'Retribution finds a man in the end, though.' Igor looked out to the north. 'I've seen those gallows, shimmering like a mirage over on Beacon Island. Seen them more than once.'

The Spanish mackerel had bled out and its fluid nudged Ismo's toes. That was when it all came up. He wasn't sure if it was the fish or the grog or something else altogether, but he heaved his insides over the transom.

Igor didn't give his purging a second glance. He hauled the mackerel into a large holding tub and looked up, gauging the position of the boat. 'We've been drifting,' he said.

Suddenly Ismo was aware of the boil and spume of waves. They'd drifted right into the breakers. Igor wrenched the motor to life and directed the boat towards deeper water, racing a feathering peak.

'Hold on!'

They climbed the crest, up and up, until time stopped and they were weightless, suspended in space. Ismo could no longer discern the point where the sky ended and the sea began. Teetering on that fulcrum, the boat might've gone either way, and Ismo's mind pulled him back to Vuti Vutti. To that moment when he could have said something.

The dinghy pushed on, over the summit, and slammed down into the flats on the other side. Both he and Mika found themselves halfway off their seats, white-knuckled, staring up at Igor, a monument against the night sky.

The boat rocked in the aftermath of the set, water settled around them, and Ismo's insides, too, fell back into place.

Igor steered the boat towards Little Rat. At the jetty he directed the boys to secure the lines, and then, at last, he released them.

'*Menkää kotiin.*' Go home.

They hurried up the jetty, Mika a few paces ahead. When it was time to part ways, neither boy acknowledged the other.

Osprey

HILDA LEFT SCHOOL EARLY. Getting out of class was no trouble at all. At home, in the kitchen cupboard, there was a stack of blank notes that her mother had signed. She trusted Hilda, whose English was far better than her own, to fill out the note for the necessary occasion. *Hilda needs to go to the doctor at 3 o'clock*, she wrote.

She found Deidre at the public toilet in town, already transformed in her hot pants and halter-neck top. Hilda did the same, having crammed the change of clothes into her backpack that morning. The afternoon sun was warm on their newly exposed shoulders, and the wind blew, as it always did in spring, from the south-west. A giddiness rose in Hilda's belly as they neared the bottle-o. They slunk about the entrance, scoping the area for someone who had the right air about them. Someone's big brother, maybe. The hot pants would help.

Dee was Hilda's first proper Australian friend. She would go to the Sinclairs' place on a Wednesday night. They ate chops and veggies with a cup of red cordial, and had Neapolitan ice cream afterwards. She remembered when Dee had come to her house for dinner and found on her plate bread so black she thought Alva must have lost her senses in the kitchen. Later, when Hilda explained that it was rye bread and it came that way, Dee screwed up her face and said, 'I don't like it.' Hilda had agreed.

Having got what they needed, the girls walked from the bottle shop to West End. It sounded like a cosmopolitan suburb, but it wasn't. The far-flung neighbourhood was made up of weatherboard beach houses, their walls brushed with a layer of salt. A railway track snaked around the tip of the peninsula, leading down to the fishermen's wharves and the dockyards. The red-and-white-striped lighthouse sat at the edge of everything, blinking its warning signs into the coming dusk. The girls walked past an osprey's nest, built way up on the highest branch of a near-naked Norfolk pine. Hilda noticed the mother bird's majestic stance, could hear the little helpless chicks squawking. There had been a family of ospreys nesting out on Little Rat last year. She'd been lucky enough to spy a juvenile one day, preparing for its first flight. It had been spreading its wings and flapping for some time before it suddenly had lift-off. Hovering above the nest, it looked surprised at its own success, unsure of what to do next. It came back down. Rose again. Soon it would take aim at a nearby tin roof, flinging itself out and into the world. Hilda's heart had been in her throat as she watched.

Further up, in a dip in the dunes, they found a group of kids from school.

'What did youse get?'

'Summer wine.'

There was a pregnant girl there, her belly already swollen. Hilda was amazed when she saw the girl take a defiant swig of alcohol.

'Isn't it bad for the baby?' someone asked.

She looked hurt. 'It's my last chance,' she said.

Dee wanted to get pregnant soon. She said it would be fun. To have a little baby to dress up in pretty outfits. She said they could do it together, she and Hilda. Dee would call hers Elizabeth. She loved the royals. Hilda said she liked Victoria. They would walk down to the foreshore with their babies in prams and sunbake while all the other kids were in school. Only, whenever Hilda imagined it she felt a twinge in her chest. She'd always thought she'd fish for crays, like her dad. But the idea that she might become the skipper of her own boat was receding, slowly and gently like an outgoing tide. Maybe it was because he never mentioned it.

'Can't see us holding on to the lease in the long run,' she'd heard her father say in passing, while Risto talked non-stop about how his boys would one day take over his boat.

'Don't forget about the sea,' was all Isä had said the last time they'd gone out fishing together. He'd let her do everything that day. Start the motor, steer the boat, choose the spot, bait her hooks. They sat in comfortable silences, Hilda in Onni's big, baggy coat, her hair tangled. She felt like herself. There, on the sea, her many selves became one, so that Hilda wondered who that girl was, the one who got around in hot pants with Dee and talked about boys and babies and sex. He had packed sandwiches. They were bland parcels of mustard pickle and cucumber on black bread, no butter, because Onni didn't care about the taste of food all that much, only the nutrients and energy it gave you. Hilda's heart warmed when he passed her the sandwich, wrapped in wax paper. *Don't forget about the sea.* That was all he said.

The wine was warm and fruity and the colour of pee. It made them gag. It was intolerable. But someone had brought orange juice, and when they mixed the two together it wasn't so bad. Hilda felt the floating sensation coming on. She let a burp gurgle up from her belly and out of her mouth. Dee fell back into the sand then, giggling. They kept drinking as the sun slid down the sky, and a fire was built around them.

There was Ismo.

He sat cross-legged on the other side of the fire. He was a quiet, gentle boy. Always had been. Hilda loved him most because he could barely kill a fish. Imagine, a fisherman who couldn't kill a fish! On the islands they often sat at the end of the jetty together and dropped a line in. Ismo would blanch once he got the fish up on the timber slats, seemingly heartbroken by the look of its sad grey eyes and frowning mouth.

'Go on, Ismo,' she'd say, 'a quick one, straight through the head.'

He'd hold the knife above it, poised, and moments would pass.

'It's mean to leave it there, flapping in the air. It can't breathe up here, Ismo.'

'I know.'

'Give it here.'

So Hilda would do it, and Ismo would look away, and she couldn't tell if it was the dead fish or his own sissiness that made him look so sad.

They'd walk off, Hilda swinging the groper by its tail.

'It's okay, you can gut it if you want.'

Now, he and Hilda exchanged a wave. She gave him a warm smile, her eyes half closed. She was giving everyone warm smiles tonight.

Ismo plopped down next to her, so she offered him a drag on a smoke which had found its way to her fingers.

'Nah, gives me a head spin,' he said.

It gave Hilda a head spin too, and she didn't like it much. She'd have liked to stub it out now, but instead she took another half-hearted drag.

Her head was a hot-air balloon, weightless, and rising into the night sky.

She could see that Ismo's beer was still full. He was only pretending to drink it. *He's a fraud, and I am too.* Hilda was aware of her halter-neck top sitting against her flat chest, its garish orange colour, and all her back exposed. The stump of her finger was at its ugliest tonight. It gave her away. Sitting next to Ismo, who knew her in her trousers and anorak, she felt like an idiot. But Ismo's train of thought was not that. He let his hand fall just next to Hilda's, so that the outer edges of their palms touched. She knew he liked her. She remembered how he'd sat closer than necessary on the boat, going out to Vuti Vutti that day. But they'd known each other for so long. She didn't want to ruin it.

'You're like my brother, Ismo.'

She could tell she'd wounded him. Even in the dark, his frame shrank somehow. He kept his gaze straight ahead.

Poor Ismo.

I've always been the bad one, she thought. The one who can kill a fish, no problem. The one who can hurt another thing without it haunting me for days afterwards. The one who let Lauri fall into the water. Hilda carried her guilt around with her like an old suitcase. She shoved it in a corner or under a bed, but every now and again she noticed it poking out, and shuddered on remembering what was inside.

Ismo stood and walked off into the darkness.

Hilda sucked in a lungful of smoke. She took another gulp of wine, the grog coursing and fizzing in her veins.

She talked to the pregnant girl for a bit.

'Are you scared,' she asked, 'of when it comes out?'

The girl suddenly looked very serious and nodded.

It was much later when Mika found her. Hilda was sitting in a heap by the fire, her torso swaying as though buoyed by a slight breeze.

'Are you all right, Hilda?' He leaned back, studied her. 'You've had too much again.'

Mika pulled her up to standing. 'You going to puke?'

She half nodded. Maybe.

He linked his arm with hers, leading her away from the fire and the muted drawl of other kids, over the undulating sand to a gully in the dunes. They stumbled down the slope.

'Go on,' he said, 'throw up if you need to. There's no one around.'

Hilda stood, unsteady on her legs. Everything was spinning. She spat on the ground a few times, but no vomit came.

They collapsed in the scrub then, and after a while Mika turned and kissed her. He opened his mouth wide and filled hers with a fat, frenzied tongue.

When he tucked her underneath him and tugged down her pants, she wasn't sure how to react. He groped for her breasts and, she thought, withdrew disappointed. She felt like another boy underneath him, with nothing much to offer.

Then there was the hard knob of it, warm on her thigh. She felt the whisper of something electric down there, before the wine disguised it. A clouded voice in her head, too: don't do it. But then she didn't really care who was the first—as long as there was one, and soon. Dee was leaving her behind. She remembered what Dee had told her during one of their sleepovers: 'You should finger yourself. Otherwise you'll be too tight for it and they'll know you're frigid.' Hilda wondered about this as Mika fumbled on top of her, trying to find the spot. When he did, he pushed in hard and a small grunt escaped his mouth, sending a bolt of loneliness through her body. In the moments that followed she felt distances lengthen and contract. She felt very close to Mika—utterly and revoltingly entwined—and at the same time very far away. She saw herself, spread-eagled on the sand, so far below the blanket of stars. It was the sky that was magnificent, not them, not this. Beyond the dunes, the sea pounded the shoreline. Hilda wished she'd been laid out on the island. That might have made it all right.

And then it was too late.

'Are you okay?' Mika asked the dunes afterwards. Maybe he looked sheepish, standing there in the dark, his shoulders hunched. They both knew it wasn't good.

'Let's go back,' said Mika.

He was already walking off towards the fire as Hilda, bare bum to the night sky, searched for her knickers.

When she arrived back at the fire she saw that the crowd had dwindled. She went to stand next to Mika, only because she thought it polite, after a thing like that.

'It doesn't mean we're together,' he said, when he noticed her lingering there.

Hilda scanned for Dee. There was a groaning boy leaning over a puddle of vomit. In a little sandy gully, a boy and a girl knotted together. The pregnant girl was crying into her drink. No Dee.

Hilda started back to Dee's house alone. There was something about the way she walked, the way she held herself, that was different. She ambled, a little taller maybe, her back straight, her hips thrust out. Her steps were light and accurate on the bitumen.

But between her legs was something warm and animal, something far from elegant, that had grown her up all of a sudden.

Dee would be pleased. She'd crossed over. Now they'd be able to talk about it together, and Dee would know that she knew what it was all about.

As Hilda passed the lighthouse she heard footsteps behind her. Ismo.

'Hey,' he said, breathless.

'Hey.'

They walked side by side, listening to the sound of their shoes hitting the tar.

'Where did you go before?' Ismo asked.

'Nowhere.'

'You were with Mika,' he said. 'I saw you go off with him.'

A few moments passed, and finally Hilda shrugged her shoulders.

'You know he wanted to touch you on Vuti Vutti that day, when you were out of it. He probably would have done it with you if Latvian Igor didn't turn up.'

Ismo looked instantly regretful, as if he wanted to gather the words up and put them back in his mouth. If she were honest with herself, she would have to say she knew. If not what Mika had done, or wanted to do, then the kind of boy he was. But she had done it anyway.

'What did you say?' she asked now.

'What?' Ismo's voice broke as it hit a high note.

'What did you say,' she persisted, 'when he wanted to do that?'

Ismo was silent. Time ticked by, and still he did not reply. Hilda picked up her pace. She listened to hear if Ismo would quicken his step too, but he didn't. He stayed behind, and she did not turn around.

Some things had been lost tonight that could not be got back.

Up ahead, Hilda could make out the osprey's nest, quiet now. Did birds sleep? She hoped that the first dive for those fledglings would be a success. It was a sort of nostalgia she experienced, as she looked up at the dark mould of the twig and grass nest, for the little birds that were still on the other side of the plunge.

Marlin

IGOR HAD BEEN ON THE WATER long enough to know when bad weather was on the way. He battened down the hatches, so to speak, checking that the corrugated-iron roof of his hut was secure, that his cray boat was tied snug to the jetty. The smaller boat he left bobbing loosely by its side—anyone watching might have wondered at the small oversight, but no one was watching. He topped up the fuel in the outboard. Started it once, just to make sure. The motor let out the usual hiccup and growl upon ignition—a sound Igor had learned to ignore. It was too similar, that sound, to the sound of his past: the farm, the fields, the tractor. He scanned everything once more, thinking that perhaps the jetty might not survive this cyclone. Didn't give it too much thought. Igor made these checks not for his own comfort or safety, or because he valued his boat and his livelihood, but because he didn't like to make a mess. He'd made enough of a mess of things.

Lately, the Saari girl had been hanging around. He'd see her slight form lingering on the jetty as he motored back from a fishing expedition. She'd ask him practical questions: What had he caught? He'd grunt his replies, neither rudely nor politely. Squid, mullet, blackfish. He'd given up fishing for the big ones. The fight had gone out of him. Before, it had been the fight he sought, as much as the catch itself. The way they thrashed their great, whopping bodies around, overcome with the drive to stay alive. He wanted to see that will, that desire to live, in another creature. Needed it. Somehow it made him feel more alive. It was the marlin that had finished it. The record-breaking fish. He hadn't looked for another big one since then.

Where did he go? asked the girl.

Alexander Island, Disappearing. A little deep spot out there, by the north-east corner of Sandy Island.

And in that way they communicated. If he'd been out by Woody Woody, he wouldn't say. They didn't talk about what had happened out there the season before, even though he knew that the girl's visits had something to do with that. To mention it would have meant building some kind of bridge between him and the girl, and he didn't want that. He was an island: remote, inaccessible.

Two days ago, at her coaxing, they had practised tying knots. The seafarer's suite. She already knew the clove hitch and the bowline, had learned them years ago, she said, from one of Onni's deckies. Igor had demonstrated the triple sheet bend. She'd fumbled at first, blaming her missing finger.

'Stupid stump,' she said.

'We all have our amputations,' he offered, 'some more noticeable than others.'

She looked at him then, and he wondered what she could see.

Next, Igor demonstrated the blood knot: two discrete bits of rope tied around and around one another, over and over, until a sturdy bond was formed.

'Like family,' she said.

A malformed sound broke out of his mouth.

'My friend Dee hates her dad,' said the girl next, unperturbed.

Something rose in Igor. A purple cloud of envy. Even this he wanted, deep down in his marrow. The whole painful ordeal.

'Where's your family?' she asked.

'Don't have one.'

'Everyone has one,' she said. 'At least at the beginning.'

She was gazing out to sea, tugging distractedly at the blood knot with one hand. It would not unravel, but it could snap in an extreme weather event, or disintegrate over time, the salt slowly eroding its integrity. No knot was unbreakable.

Now, the king tide had begun to push in. The sea was a full bath, lapping at the sides of the island. It wanted to spill over. Consume them, on their brittle crag. Out of the corner of his eye, he saw her approach. He was in the pot shed, making the last arrangements. The wind, too, had arrived, and it whipped her white hair. She was wearing an oversized rain jacket—her father's—that fell to her bony knees.

'*Hei*, Igor.'

She looked down as she said it, still afraid of him, if only a little. She had been unable to dismiss the stories altogether, he guessed. Funny how stories can be born out of silence rather than talk. The bones of the stories were true: the ship jumps, the running from one port to the next. If he didn't stop, he had thought, he might outrun his own muddied shadow, his mind fixed on where to next—and then, having arrived, where to sleep and how to eat and how to get work. He had been a bodyguard in New York for a time, for some heavy Italian, and had visited Chicago, but he had never met this Al Capone. He let the stories wind and twist, go where they would—the wilder they got, the more people left him alone. Sometimes, when he motored back to the pontoon after a night spent in a storm on the open ocean, Sulo would greet him with a shake of his head.

'*Hullu ukko*,' he'd say. Crazy bastard. 'Are you not afraid of anything?'

But Sulo didn't understand. What was there to be afraid of, if the worst had already happened?

The girl held out her hand. 'Thought you might like this.'

Her wrist resembled that of a small child, protruding from the cavernous sleeve of the jacket. The tiny, white limb of a toddler came to mind. He remembered carrying Hilda, dead drunk, in his arms that day. How her body hung heavy in just the same way.

'It's from the *Batavia*,' she said, when he didn't react.

He moved his gaze from her wrist to her palm, an open oyster shell, and in it, an offering. Porcelain.

'Thought you might like it, since you're into history and that,' she said. 'I was thinking you could put it with your collection. With the compass and the globe.'

Needlessly, he rearranged the craypots. Stacked one on top of another. Coiled a bit of rope.

'Where'd you get it?' he asked.

'The Wallabi boys have got heaps of this stuff. We trade things sometimes.'

He'd heard there were remnants. That a few fishermen had located the wreck well before the divers came. The excavations were ongoing, and most of it would end up in the museum in Fremantle, but some pieces had been squirrelled away years earlier.

'What did you trade?'

'Pack of cigarettes.' She shrugged defiantly.

He could chide her, but she had a father. She swiped messy strands of hair from her eyes. It wouldn't take much to start caring.

'Put it over there,' he said, pointing. She let the shard roll from her palm onto the bench, and Igor caught a glimpse of the dirty white colouring, the flecks of deep blue.

A gift.

The first he had received in many years.

He'd tried to teach those boys a lesson that night. But who was he to talk about right and wrong? A small part of him had thought that helping the girl might wipe his slate clean. But he was still the same broken thing.

'I'm not a good man,' he said, the words tumbling out.

Hilda met his eye, and he could see how uncomfortable it was for her to hold his gaze. He knew how big he was—an oaf. A monster, really. He was the gaping marlin they'd heaved out of the water that time. He conjured its long and ugly snout. Its once giant yet agile body, now a mountain of useless muscle on the deck.

'You are,' she said.

He shook his head.

'There's a king tide,' Hilda said, returning to practical talk. 'Sulo reckons the sea's going to come up past all of these huts.' She made a wide sweeping motion. 'Everyone's going to shelter in the *kivi kämppä.*'

The words hung in the air between them: an invitation.

He could take her up on it. Join the families huddling in the stone camp, spend the night talking, reminiscing. Allow himself to be drawn in. They would accept him, he knew. They were accepting people. A patchwork community of the same species, wanderers of a sort. They would pass the time by playing cards, and the men would drink vodka and the babies would cry and the women would sing old songs in their own language.

A Latvian proverb came to him: *Solitary trees in the wind more easily fall.*

But some trees are rotten inside, he reasoned, no good. Some are better felled.

Igor remembered sheltering from a storm as a boy, back home in Latvia. The whole family had gathered in the farmhouse. The men, women and children, everyone sitting together around the hearth. He had felt a deep sense of safety inside that small cottage, the light from a single lamp fluttering with each crack of thunder, the hum of talk to pass the time—even his father had settled into it—and outside, the trees heaving. As though the world were a creature, drawing breath. The memory of that evening only made the sting worse. When he had seen his daughter for the first time, he had been slammed by such a tidal wave of love. He had been sure he'd make a better father than the distant man he remembered from his own childhood.

Now Igor nodded matter-of-factly, signalling the end of the conversation. So Hilda turned and went, and as she did, the first squall hit with a mighty boom. The sky opened up, and the rain came down in huge, broad sheets and he thought he heard her squeal in delight. He'd recently lost his appreciation for the physical world. It was one of the only things he'd found pleasure in afterwards. But this storm, rolling in from the north-west, did not give rise to that old thrilling sensation. He moved across the room and took the shard of porcelain into his hand, inspecting it closely.

Out beyond the reefs, the deep ocean swells galloped towards the south-east, gathering momentum. They feathered white at their crests, and Igor thought of an army on horseback. As he railed against it, hull smashing against the chop, the rain battered his eyeballs like small spears. He kept them open to the onslaught, staring down the huge mouth of ocean, which would soon swallow him up. Above the roar of weather and waves, he could still hear the growl of the tractor. It had been in his ears his whole life. At last, he let the image come. Her delicate seagull bones, crushed beneath the tractor's grotesque tyres.

He said her name out loud.

'Signe.'

He bellowed it into the storm.

Skipjack

MIKA NEVER IMAGINED HE'D BE anything but an islander. *Us islanders are different,* he often said, in a voice just like his old man's. *We're freer.* Because Esko had been an islander back in Finland, too. Finland was all islands. A jigsaw puzzle made up of a thousand lakes and small tracts of land. The family had lived on Saimaa. It was in their blood.

He stepped out of the house on Quarry Street. It was only 7 am but the sun already assaulted him. The dinghy was marooned on the front lawn, a forgotten craypot inside, frayed and fading in the elements. They hadn't been out on the water since the shit hit the fan. By now it was late November and the whites run had kicked off. The pale-shelled crays had set off on a great migration from their rocky coastline habitat to the deeper off-shore reefs. Usually, at this time of year, they would take the dinghy out and set a pot overnight. Just the two of them: him and the old man. The dinghy was called *Skipjack*. Mika had been allowed to give it a name, and it had seemed fitting, considering the way it skimmed across the surface of the water like those restless pelagic fish. But long strands of weeds now grew about the boat's perimeter. Nothing was in its rightful place. Mika kicked the hull as he passed.

He was stationed at a stainless-steel bench, one cog in a line of production workers—mostly women his mum's age. Several boiled crayfish stared at him through dead eyes. They were stupid creatures. Walked right into the traps the fishermen set for them. Mika avoided his own reflection in the stainless-steel workbench. The apron and the hairnet were laughable, but he wasn't laughing. The industry was at a crossroads, the manager said. New and exciting times lay ahead. Canned cray was on the way out. The consumer market was changing, with a rising hunger for crays in places like Japan, Singapore and China. A new co-op building was on the horizon, with tanks purpose built for live export. The man in the suit said there were opportunities for young blokes like him. Because he knew crays, because he'd grown up on the boats. Mika understood that he could become a man in a suit if he took an interest. Which he wouldn't. He didn't belong on this side of the ditch, holed up in the processing plant on the stinking waterfront, up to his elbows in crayfish carcasses. And he didn't belong in a suit either. He hated those types. Come next season, he'd be deckying, if nothing else.

This whole mess was his dad's fault—Mika knew that—but Esko was his best mate, and now he just felt sorry for the bloke. He understood it, in a way. In the off-season, betting was a way to pass the time. It charged him up too, made him feel alive. And there was always hope. No matter how many losses he had, there was always hope. It was like looking down your cray line of a morning, the anticipation before hauling them up. You just never knew how full those pots might be.

And that's all it took. Just one big win. While Esko hadn't got that big win, or not yet, there were always the smaller ones. The ones that kept you believing. Mika remembered nights after race day. If it had been a good day at the track, the mood in the house was light. Laughter, a few jokes, Neapolitan ice cream for dessert. Sometimes Petra would even get out the cloudberry liqueur, saved from Christmas, and pour a nip for Mika. Esko didn't drink that stuff. He drank Emu Export. The cans had become an extension of his own body: part of his silhouette. No matter the time of day, there was a can attached to his right hand, snug inside his Sun City stubby holder. After Petra had been warmed up by the cloudberry liqueur, Esko would grab her by the arse and she'd swat at him and Mika would turn his appalled eyes back to the telly. Those were the good nights, and yet they too could leave Mika feeling uneasy. If there had been bad luck, both he and Petra stayed out of the way. The day the debt collector came knocking, that was the worst day.

Then his mum left, if only for a measly week.

It wasn't fair that his older brothers had moved out and left him at home with his fucked-up parents. He felt like the odd one out, the leftover kid. They had got the best of it. The good years. The island years. They were both now working on the pearling boats up north, leaving Mika to bear the brunt of this mess alone.

Without Petra at home, Esko was a broken man, and Mika felt a vague fury bubbling up inside him.

You can't rely on them, said Esko out of his drunken stupor. *Women are all bitches.* Tall Tommi, Risto and Onni—back on the mainland for the off-season—had come around to console the old boy, and they nodded their agreement. But they all had wives and it didn't make much sense. It was only Onni who said something cryptic: '*Veikko, kaiku vastaa niin kuin sille huudetaan.*' Mate, an echo answers as it was called.

Mika wanted to smash those words out of the air, as they echoed in their own way. Stupid old Finnish sayings. Didn't Onni know that no one spoke like that anymore?

Something moved.

One of the buggers had survived the boiling phase. It happened sometimes, and Mika wasn't sure if they were actually still alive, or if it was just the nerve endings firing off a few final, stubborn rounds. The animal twitched as he pulled it from the pile. He looked into its wooden eye and did not recognise himself. Bending the leg backwards, slowly, slowly, he listened out for that satisfying crack. Then he waited for the sense of calm to settle over him. He had only been in a fight once, with Ismo, and it had started out as nothing. They'd been roughing each other up. Playing around. But then it got serious and he'd had to pull himself up, make himself stop. Sometimes he imagined what it would be like to let the rage take hold. He envisaged the first, glorious swing. All that pent-up frustration gathered like fish into a net and spewed out in one swift action. The old boy was famous for getting into brawls. That's how he lost his eye, all those years ago. One-eyed Esko, the best dart player on the island. That's what they called him. Now Mika scanned the shed. He hoped Maila hadn't seen. The old Estonian lady was always feeling sorry. Sorry for the crayfish, sorry for the prawns. Sorry for all the animals and all the people in the world. Mika threw the critter back on the pile, along with its severed limb. He would let it suffer there a while, before he cleaved it apart and picked the meat from within the claws, knuckles and tail.

After changing out of his ridiculous uniform, he skulked towards town. He had been glad to find out that the publican at the Geraldton Hotel turned a blind eye to young workers like him. What did it matter? He'd be eighteen soon enough. He passed the wheat silos and the fish shop. As he walked, Mika concentrated on all the things that made him angry. It was satisfying, to list the injustices in this way. But it also brought about a renewed wave of frustration, which rose in him, hot and red, until it reached the outer edges of his ears. He had a bellow inside him that had no way of escape. Ismo and Lauri and Hilda—they didn't know how good they had it. The islands were theirs. When he thought about Ismo lately he felt a fist in his chest; things weren't the same between them these days. And Hilda, well, she'd wanted it after all. How relieved he had been, to have put the first number on his tally. As long as he put it in then it counted.

Before turning east towards the pub Mika paused to take a look at the ocean. He knew that beyond the horizon were the islands. Hundreds of secret atolls like a mirage, just waiting for his return. To think, his dad, one of the original Five Finns who had slept behind a windbreak for a whole season, now had no remaining link to that place. Their lease sold to some other family, along with their camp, which Esko had built with his own two hands. It was nauseating.

Voices floated towards him from the town beach. It was Lauri and Ismo. They were doing peggies off the pontoon. Mika stopped for a moment and watched, mesmerised. He hadn't thought of swimming for so long. He hadn't thought of doing anything fun. Ismo noticed him just as Mika turned to go, and it was too late to avoid him. He was calling out and swimming towards the shore, sprinting across the coal-hot sand. Mika waved, arranging his face. As Ismo approached he slowed, and the awkwardness of their recent encounters returned to his body. In his rush to reach Mika he appeared to have forgotten it.

Ismo's hands sank into the pockets of his swimming shorts. 'What's happening?'

They stood a few feet apart. Round beads of water rolled off Ismo's bare chest.

'Just clocked off.'

'How's it going at the waterfront?'

'Pretty good. I'm probably getting a promotion.'

Ismo nodded, a polite smile on his face that did not belong to him. He wasn't impressed, not really. He was indifferent. Ismo didn't care about what happened on the waterfront and never would. He had no need, and Mika hated him for it.

'Did you hear about Latvian Igor?' asked Ismo.

Mika had felt relief on hearing that the Latvian had disappeared in the cyclone. But apparently he'd turned up again, once the weather had passed, wild-eyed and half drowned. Wordlessly returning to his camp.

'Yeah,' said Mika. 'Crazy bastard.'

'Yeah.'

Mika kicked at the concrete with his shoe.

'Coming swimming?' asked Ismo.

In truth, he wanted to hurtle down to the shoreline and lob himself into the delicious sea water. Take over the pontoon. Demonstrate his backflip. Way more impressive than a goddamn peggie.

'Nah. Meeting AJ for a knock-off at the Gero.'

Ismo's eyes ballooned for a short, sweet moment, and Mika savoured it.

'You allowed in there, are ya?'

'Yeah.' He shrugged. 'I'm a working man now.'

Mika lay on his stomach between crumpled sheets. He could smell himself—a sweet and sour scent rising from his pores, like overripe fruit. He'd put away several pints the night before. A dream still hung at the forefront of his mind. He didn't want to think of it, but the image kept returning. He'd been fucking Hilda from behind and Ismo had been there, shirtless, squatting on his haunches next to them. When Mika looked back, Hilda had turned into a Spanish mackerel, and he was fucking it through a hole in its white flesh. Ismo had smiled and said:

She's a beauty. Then he'd woken up and for a second he thought he'd pissed the bed.

Mika buried his shorts in the bottom of the dirty washing basket and put on a fresh pair. He crawled back into bed, and his mind turned to the night before. When they arrived at the Gero, he had been rattled to find the old man there, standing with Tall Tommi and a couple of Aussies. From the other side of the front bar, Mika had seen for the first time how pathetic Esko was. A sad old drunk, with hunched shoulders and a paunch sticking out. He was skinny but for the paunch—no tone—and looking at it had given Mika a feeling of vague queasiness. The missing eye, which as a boy Mika had taken pride in, was now somehow sickening. Esko had been standing at the edge of a group of men, laughing too loudly and for a moment too long. Then something erupted, and George from Port Denison punched the old man square in the face, just like that. Esko staggered and fell, his shirt up, exposing the shameful gut, a trickle of red falling in slow motion from his nose onto the beery floorboards. Mika felt AJ looking at him a bit sideways, heard someone push a coin into the jukebox. So he turned and said, 'What's this pop shit?' and took a swig of his beer, giving Dad time to stagger up and out of there.

Now Mika heard a knock at the bedroom door, followed by the squeaky turn of the handle. He knew she'd be hit with it, the foul scent of him. He didn't need to look at her stern round face to know she was frowning.

'*Ei enään laiskotella. Vaivalla se työpaikka hankittiin.*' Enough with that lazing about. Wasn't easy to get that job.

He grunted. Thought of the manager in his suit, shaking his head. *Just another dumb kid*, he'd say, *throwing away a sound opportunity.*

Petra pulled the blankets off him. He felt her astonished eyes pass over him: his strange body, part boy, part man. She stood above him, helpless, and Mika understood that he was the one in charge.

'*Ylös, poika.*' Up, boy.

She couldn't physically make him move. Not anymore.

'Why are you so angry all the time?' he shouted. 'What's wrong with you?'

He caught a change in her face—a tiny wince—something small breaking.

'Mika. Please.'

'*Painu ulos, akka!*' Get out, woman!

He had seen that look before, on a night when Esko, in a grog-fuelled frenzy, had locked her out of the house. And Mika had seen her through the window, standing there on her own dark driveway, bewildered. She looked pathetic, and because he couldn't stand the look of her anymore he had gone to watch telly. The look that Mika recognised: it was defeat, but he was not sorry.

He rolled over as the door clicked shut behind her.

Lying there in the musty sheets, the scene from the pub kept playing over in his mind. The frustration, tense in his limbs, made him reach for his cock. He would clear his mind in the only way he knew how. He tried to bring the body of a woman to mind, but all that came was the image of Ismo from his dream, his perfectly formed bicep. Smiling. Admiring. Mika longed for an eruption, but when he came, it was little more than a tremor, over before it had even begun. He watched the miserable cum dribble onto his stomach.

AJ said it was called hair of the dog. A couple of beers the day after would get rid of the sick feeling. So he was back down at the Gero. The red ball of sun was already falling into the sea. He felt like a useless shit, in bed all day. Tall Tommi was in his usual place. The fisherman was standing at the left corner of the bar, talking with two other blokes. They had their legs apart, feet planted flat on the floorboards. Mika felt the inadequacy of his handshake—his hand a small wet fish within Tommi's solid grasp.

'It's all gambling,' Tall Tommi was saying, and Mika felt a wave of discomfort wash over him. 'Prospecting, digging through the earth looking for gemstones, that's gambling. Crayfishing, too. It's about luck.'

Then one of the other men piped up: 'You're born with it or you're not.'

Was that how luck worked? wondered Mika. Could luck be inherited? Like eye colour or the way you walked?

Later that night Mika hit some fella. Some out-of-towner who was mouthing off. Well, not exactly. Mika just wanted to punch something, but it wasn't what he expected. His fist crumpled against the shocking hardness of bone, and the guy only teetered on his feet, didn't fall. Not like Esko had. And then Mika felt his own head flung backwards. The publican kicked him out, and he stumbled home cradling his right fist in his good hand, sucking on the salty sweet tang of blood, somehow appeased.

As soon as he came through the door Esko saw his swollen face. Had him by the front of his shirt, slamming him against the hallway wall. The hollow eye socket loomed just inches away, a puckered arsehole.

'*Mikä susta poika tulee?*' he growled. What you going to be, boy?

Mika held his gaze. I'm not scared of you, he thought but did not say.

'What you going to be, huh?' Esko repeated.

But there were tears in his good eye.

'You going to be an echo of your old man?' Esko's voice cracked as he said it, and right then Mika saw how much he hated himself. In his father's hold, hard up against the wall, Mika remembered Onni's saying: *An echo answers as it was called.* Esko let his grip loosen, shoved Mika to the side. Spent, they each went their own way.

There was a knock on his bedroom door early next morning. His dad's gruff voice: 'Going to set the craypot.'

Mika was grateful for the roar of the engine, which filled the wordless air between them. Esko backed out of the driveway, expertly swinging the boat trailer around at ninety degrees. Petra came outside in her foolish dressing-gown with a parcel in her hand.

'*Pitää pojan syödä.*' A boy's got to eat.

She handed him the sandwiches.

'*No, Äiti.*' Now, Mum.

He said this to the driveway, but she seemed satisfied.

The water lapped at the hull of *Skipjack* and for the first time in a long while Mika felt it, that lightness, the restlessness giving way as they capered freely along the sea's smooth surface. He imagined the salt water washing the stains of grass and dirt away from the bottom of the boat. Beyond the shelf, a proper cray boat fished for whites. After baiting the pot and lowering it down into the hole they'd spotted, they let the boat drift aimlessly for a while. He glanced furtively at his dad, who had his one eye closed, the hollow socket turned to the sun. Out here it didn't look so bad. It suited the sea. Mika's hand moved absent-mindedly to his cheekbone. He felt the swelling, and it hurt to touch. This morning, there had been a purple blemish spreading out across the side of his face, the same colour as the bruise creeping across the old man's jawline.

Sea lion

'A BLOKE FROM UP THE WALLABIS reckons he's seen a ghost.'

Sulo puffed air out of his mouth as they heaved the dinghy up and onto the jetty. Onni cringed as he heard the keel scrape against the timbers. A boat out of water always seemed to him somehow wrong.

'Ghosts live in your head,' said Onni, puffing now too, his hands on his knees. The dinghy was heavier than he remembered.

'*Totta on*,' agreed Sulo. That's the truth.

They reached under the gunwale now, one man at each end, and lifted the dinghy up fully. Walking backwards up the jetty, Sulo said, 'Doesn't mean they're not real.'

'You're no believer,' Onni stated, eyeing the old fisherman.

They turned the boat over behind the camp.

'Better weigh those down with something,' said Sulo, pointing to a pile of corrugated-iron sheets.

The cray season was coming to a close, and each of them was preparing their camp for the long off-season ahead. It would be eight months before they were back. During that time, the islands would almost become a true ghost town—a floating village of vacant huts, save for one or two—and the birds and sea lions would claim back what was theirs.

Onni gathered two lengths of four-by-fours and stacked them on top of the pile of corri sheets.

Sulo stood and watched him, his hands low on his hips. 'Living on top of those bones would do it. It'd start to play on your mind, I mean.'

Onni looked down at the alabaster skeleton of coral that formed the island. 'We're all living on top of bones.'

'Well, ghost or no ghost, this godless old fisherman is glad his camp is not on Beacon Island.'

Onni bent to collect a tangle of stray floats from the ground nearby. He liked to think it wouldn't worry him. A few old bits of bone. So what? We would all end up in the ground eventually. And after that you were just matter—atoms and molecules.

'Right then. I'm off to do my own camp.'

Onni watched Sulo pick his way back through the sparse tufts of grass and saltbush.

The scent of eucalyptus invaded his nostrils as he approached the sauna. Alva had just finished scrubbing the benches with the *juuri harja*. He poked his head in the door as she was closing the latch to the sauna stove.

'Will you be storing anything else in here?' she asked.

'Just these floats.' He held them out for her to take, but her hands remained at her sides. After a moment he understood: Alva avoided passing objects across a threshold. It led to conflict or strife, according to her aunt Iita. Onni made a show of stepping into the sauna and handing the floats to Alva. Unruffled, she added them to the knotted pile. Onni had noticed that she often became more obsessive at times like these. Times of movement or change. She and Hilda would be taking a charter flight back to the mainland tomorrow, and Onni would bring the cray boat across in the coming days. Hilda was often hard to find towards season's end. She spent whole days on the water in that small dinghy of hers—filling herself up with it, Onni thought, before the mainland slowly drained it from you in the off-season.

Onni continued the preparations. He gathered all of his cray-pots except two, which he might make use of in the off-season—he put these in the boat—and stacked the others in the small lean-to off the side of the sauna. He then secured the stack with a heavy rope. Cyclone season had passed, but you could never be sure what to expect out here.

Inside the camp, Alva was packing. She folded the last of the island clothes into the trunk and then stood up. 'Make sure you strip the bed before you leave.'

'Will do.'

He watched her walk over to the timber shelf above the bed and turn the *sielulintu*, the little hand-carved bird, just so. It now faced due north.

'And don't leave the cupboard door hanging open,' she said.

'Hm?'

'Be sure to close the cupboard door.'

Alva wore a grave expression. Who was this woman who was his wife? wondered Onni.

He couldn't help but say: 'It'll make no difference, Alva.'

'Just because you've got the name doesn't mean you've got it.'

And by that she meant luck, the word *onni* meaning good fortune, or happiness.

'What will happen will happen. It won't have anything to do with my name or a door left open.'

With her stony eyes fixed on him, she moved to the cupboard and pressed it closed with a small thud.

'Just remember, Onni, bad luck doesn't call out as it arrives.'

They skirted around one another in the kitchen. Alva sorted the remaining food, leaving only that which would keep until next season: the powdered milk, the instant coffee, the cans of spaghetti in tomato sauce. Onni scraped the last bit of fish roe paste out of the tube onto a dry biscuit. Watching his wife's sullen back as she stood facing the kitchen window, Onni was inclined to reach out for her. He ventured to touch her shoulder, but she brushed him aside as she would a fly.

Later that evening, while dinner was being prepared, he edged closer to her and reached his hands around her widening waist. In this way he told her he would do it, he would close the cupboard door.

'It was the Johnsons' boy who reckoned he saw it.'

Sulo was still going on about that goddamn ghost over on the Wallabis. They were sitting on two folding chairs facing east, with the wind on their faces. The island was emptying by the day. Alva and Hilda had left that morning, along with some of the other wives and kids. Sulo passed Onni a black coffee.

'Johnson's deckie found a coin and pawned it back in Geraldton.'

News on the islands came in dribs and drabs. Yesterday a cray boat from up north had brought some new information.

'It was after that the boy claimed he saw the woman down the cove. Apparently kept turning her head one way then the other. Like she was lost.'

'Those ghosts never seem to have a clue where they are,' said Onni.

'It's the ones who've suffered that seem to hang around. Have you ever heard of anyone being haunted by a happy ghost?'

The two men watched Moukari, the ugly old sea lion, as he ambled up onto the island a few feet away. He barked at them. They knew Moukari by the scar on his ear. The creature had a head like a mallet, and that's why they called him that. Sea lions could live for over two decades, and this one had to be fairly ancient. He'd been hanging around for years. The two men felt an affinity for old Moukari. They had all been visitors to the island for such a long time now.

'*Hei*, Moukari,' said Onni.

'*Hei*, Moukari,' said Sulo.

They sat in silence for some time. Onni was thinking about how Moukari had led a harsh and perilous existence but had survived with only a scar on his ear. He would die an old sea lion, and this pleased Onni.

'There are no happy ghosts because ghosts live in our heads,' said Onni, returning to their conversation. 'It's only the bad deaths that haunt us.'

He pushed the memory of his brother's death aside, put it next to him but out of sight.

'Could be,' said Sulo. He paused, eyes fixed on Moukari, his rumpled skin tough as an old boot. 'Brings to mind my father.'

Onni waited for Sulo to go on.

'Dad was a man of reason. But he had the curse of the sceptic.'

'How's that?'

'He left the Church—that was hard for Mum—said those fairytales didn't serve anyone.'

'Sounds like a rational thinker.'

'He was. But he saw ghosts.'

The last rays of afternoon light caught Sulo's white beard. Onni saw that familiar look in his eyes: he was far away. In another time and place. Back home in Karjala.

'Haunted by something, was he?'

Sulo cleared his throat. 'He was a timber getter.' He spoke facing the water. 'When he was felling in the forest he'd sometimes catch sight of a boy soldier from the corner of his eye. It happened for years. He would dismiss it as a trick of the light or the shadows of the fir trees. It wasn't until he was on his deathbed that he admitted it. He was certain that he'd seen Tervasen Oski, the son of the drunken lot farmer who was shot in the forest.'

After the civil war, some of the young soldiers who had fought on the side of the reds were slaughtered. They were killed by the whites, by their own people. *War*, Onni had been told, *does not determine who is right, only who is remaining.*

'Your dad went mad,' said Onni.

Sulo straightened up in his chair. 'Have you ever sat with a dying man, Onni? There is a moment of lucidity just before death.'

Onni had witnessed death in sudden blows. A bomb in the forest. A rail accident. A lost boat. He had never sat with a dying man.

'I have heard of that,' he said.

'Those boys,' said Sulo, 'they'd followed their brothers into war before they'd even learned to do up their britches. They hardly knew the difference between a red and a white.'

Sulo didn't know it yet, but Onni was one of those boys. A different time, perhaps, and a different war, but his were the same misguided motives of boys through all time. It was on these afternoons that Onni felt like he might have been something other than a labourer, something other than a man who worked with his hands, because Sulo would move into history or philosophy, and he would take Onni with him.

'I was a messenger boy on the front in 1942,' he said now. 'I was fourteen.'

He had lied about his age, but all it took was one look at his war photograph and you knew.

'Shit myself,' he continued, 'during an air raid.'

Sulo nodded. 'Grown men have found themselves in that situation, too.'

The rolling sea was blue and endless. Humanity seemed an absurd thing. Imagine that, a boy sent to war.

Afterwards, Onni had confided in his brother about the bomb, told him how it had blown up that boy Juha who was only a few feet away, sheltering behind a rock. It would have obliterated Onni, too, had he not found himself snagged by the branch of a spruce, unable to make it to the boulder in time. Thinking about it now, the memory was sickening. The nearness to death—it made you shudder. But it was something else, too; something like a prize. Like fortune had smiled on you for no reason at all. And here you were, alive. *Luck*, his brother had said in a low voice. *Who knows why it visits some of us and not others?*

'Check the sky at dusk,' said Sulo, as he rose to his feet.

Onni nodded.

'See you on the other side.'

Sulo would be making the crossing back to the mainland a few days after Onni. Walking back to camp, Onni could hear Sulo's voice carrying after him on the wind. He was chanting one of his *Kalevala* verses: '*Onko selvät ilman rannat*,' he sang, '*onko selvät vai sekavat*.' Well examine the horizon, whether clear or filled with trouble.

That night Onni dreamed of Nalle. It was unusual—his brother had only come to him once before, almost two decades ago. They'd spent the day searching for him in Sulo's cray boat, and late in the night Onni thought he felt his presence down at the lean-to by the jetty. So why now? In the dream he had seen Nalle's empty boat. Just drifting. The licence number on the side of the hull: LFBG302. Or was it *his* boat? Onni sat up in bed, shaken by a sense of panic.

He lay back against his pillow, wishing that Alva were still there in the bed next to him. Her soft, puffing breaths might have calmed him. Onni let himself remember. He could see the two of them, two siblings, in his mind's eye. They were boys in uniform, just kids. He recalled Nalle's twinkling disposition. The way he'd grab Onni by the neck, take him in a hold and wrestle him to the ground. There was no memory of pain, none whatsoever. And afterwards, when they were standing up again, straightening out their clothes, Nalle would tousle Onni's hair and then punch him in the arm. Before his brother had taken the train back to Äänislinna, he had shown him the marching pattern over and over until Onni got it right. He'd sounded like a father when he said: *Niin poika, nyt on rytmiä.* Okay, boy, now you've got rhythm. But the marching hadn't mattered in the end.

As Onni started the motor and untied the boat from the jetty, he heard the bark of a sea lion. In the lifting darkness, he could make out Moukari mooching up to the front porch. Honking as he went, he slumped against the door, his flipper sideways. He was like a fat family dog who had come to take up his post. Onni felt a brush of something like envy for the old boy. He had the long quiet months ahead of him.

For Onni it was time to go. He steered the boat out through the network of reefs and islands. As he came upon the open sea he looked back at the diminishing Abrolhos, several vague lumps in the hour before dawn. Unknowingly, his eye searched for something else, perhaps for the dolphins that sometimes followed in the boat's wake. He dismissed the brief discomfort he felt on not seeing them there, which was followed by a small prickle of annoyance. At Alva. When sea water came rushing across the deck from the starboard quarter, Onni was taken by surprise. A rogue wave? It lifted the cray boat by the stern and set it gliding, briefly and majestically, with the running swell.

The morning had begun to unfold in its slow way, and Onni inhaled it in one long breath. Now, with the sun risen, he could assess the day. The flocks of gulls, which had surrounded the boat on departure, had disappeared. Just a lone mutton bird remained with him, gliding low across the roughened surface of the sea. The wind was bracing in its chill, but he wouldn't have called it strong. Maybe twenty knots, and increasing. The ocean was dark blue, with whitecaps here and there. He was bouncing along nicely. But when he looked to the south-west, Onni saw the fabric of a mackerel sky. He considered this. A change could be on the way, or perhaps not. Nothing was ever certain. If there was a low-pressure system coming, the scaled sky suggested its distance. Six to twelve hours away.

Onni spread canned tuna on a piece of bread. He had to make a decision. He said the rhyme in his head, the one he'd learned from the Aussies: *Mares' tails and mackerel scales make lofty ships take in their sails.* He remembered that Mario, who lived on Roma, the tiny island to the south of Little Rat, had told him that in Italy they likened those same cloud formations to little sheep rather than the scales of a fish. But the meaning was the same.

He had not yet travelled three hours, which meant he could be back in the safety of the archipelago in time, if there was a front lurking. Now he thought of Nalle. How he hadn't taken in his sails that day. He'd pushed forward. For what?

Why did death come to some and not others? He considered Latvian Igor, who had taken himself into the eye of the storm—looking for it, Onni thought—but had returned. It had been a miraculous sight, to see the speck of his boat growing clearer, just as they'd been gearing up for the search.

Onni's thoughts meandered as he checked and rechecked the darkening sky, the wind now whipping up the water in earnest.

According to his compass, he'd been swept north a little way. To be fair, though, he was only marginally off-course. Then again, if he missed Kalbarri, there'd be no reprieve for hundreds of miles. Another half-hour passed before he turned the boat.

By now the sea had become tipsy, flopping this way and that beneath a gun-barrel-grey horizon. A brief period of warm calm gave him pause. Perhaps he had overreacted? But when he saw the black thunderhead swimming towards him, Onni's mind connected the signals: the rogue wave, the absence of birds, the cloud formations, the wind building from the south-west. His stomach dropped along with the needle on the barometer.

He shoved the loose paraphernalia—his tin coffee cup, ropes and floats, the extra life jacket—into the hatches before securing them, his hands stiff and uncooperative. The rain coming down in splinters. Onni stood foolishly then, at the helm of his boat, a man awaiting his adversary's arrival. He had one eye on the sea and the other on the temperature gauge, aware that he was redlining the engine, and had been for some time. Ahead, the deep ocean swells were lined up like cavalry, the top sections erupting in rogue slops of white water. It was the broken sections of the waves that would bring him unstuck, Onni knew. But he was feeble in his cumbersome cray boat, which was not built for this. The swells were now spilling over his port bow, the water careering across the deck and up his shins before draining out of the scuppers. His worst mistake today became apparent: he had waited too long before deciding to turn the boat. Now he rode directly into the onslaught. Some nonsensical feeling of fate began to grip him, as though everything, his whole life, had been leading him to this moment. Then the first liquid mountain rose up before him and Onni felt an awful lightness take hold. The boat lurched over the summit, dropped out of the ceiling and came slamming down on the other side. Onni lost his footing, ramming his shoulder into the side panel of the wheelhouse. It was the valley between waves that scared him the most. Down there in the crooked elbow of the sea, where it was eerily still. Then the sudden rush of wind as the boat heaved skywards again. The world now shattered at intervals under an electric shimmer. It was the most beautiful and terrifying sight Onni had ever seen.

A moment of reprieve arrived, but he knew the sea was only gathering its strength for the next assault. And sure enough, before long a set of waves appeared in messy rows of dark water. Hoisted once again above the sea, the boat teetered indecisively. The ocean was toying with him; it did not care for him, his puny soul. Onni saw himself as if from above: a tiny dot on this forgotten curve of earth, thrashing hopelessly against the elements. He was such a long way from home. On landing, a fresh shock of sea water swamped the deck, and the boat was set back on its haunches, before being slewed sideways. If there was another wave in the set, it was over. How could it be, Onni asked, two brothers lost to this place?

He was crouched in the cockpit like a petrified crayfish. Time moved around him, but he could not join it, his body immobilised in the false safety of the wheelhouse. When he finally raised his eyes, he saw the next wave was smaller. The boat, still angled dangerously sidelong, rocked on its keel. Regaining the use of his body, Onni corrected the cray boat and pushed on. He could have called out to death, who sailed alongside him now.

But he could see the Easter Group at last.

As the boat railed against the smaller swells making their way into the sheltered network of reefs, Onni felt the tension in his muscles give a little. A metallic taste in his throat.

He killed the motor and tied his boat to the jetty. Watching his hands making the loops, Onni saw the faint tremble and looked away. He knew that he was a different man from the one who had untied that same rope only hours earlier. He was aware of some shapeless fear following him. It was something like dread.

At the entrance to the camp, Onni shucked off his raincoat and hurried through the door. He was truly drenched. Wet to the bone. He dried himself off and fished some fresh clothes from the trunk by the bed. As he pulled the pants up around his waist and the jumper over his head, he had the impression that these items belonged to someone else. He looked into the small mirror hitched onto the wall, and a jolt ran through him. He could see within it his own reflection, which was frightening, but it was something else that had alarmed him. It was the cupboard door, hanging wide open.

Three moments came to him. He saw himself as a boy in uniform running through the forest, the deafening sound of the bomb ricocheting in his ears. Then he saw himself jumping into the water out by Disappearing Island, where his brother had been lost. It was his first season on the islands. He had not noticed the current, had not yet learned how to see it. He had been a stupid young man, out of his depth, but he had survived then, too. And now this: the abandoned crossing. It had felt like the ocean was out to get him. How much luck could one man have? Onni remembered how, back in the mines, they used to talk about instinct. How when you got that claustrophobic feeling, it was time to get out. An old saying from home came to mind: *Ken kuuseen kurkottaa se katajaan kapsahtaa*. Who reaches for the spruce plummets onto the juniper.

He would not follow his brother, not this time.

The movement was automatic, determined. He pushed the cupboard door shut, and was somewhat pacified when he heard the conclusive thud of wood against wood. He might have laughed if he wasn't in such a state. He had acquired the curse of the sceptic.

Puukko

ONNI WALKED WITH HIS BROTHER through the forest towards the site of the summer dance, where a temporary outdoor stage and dance floor had been constructed in recent weeks. A drone of mosquitoes accompanied them as they made their way along the well-marked path. Chickweed and yarrow waved between the thin, straight trunks of fir trees, and lichen unfurled like a mottled green carpet across the rocky floor of the forest. Onni and Nalle had attended a town meeting earlier that day, where Martti, a veteran of the Workers' Party, had been campaigning for the reopening of the old dairy. There had been a feeling of promise in the air, as if something might just come of it. But as the men had wandered home, scuffing their boots, they caught sight of the dilapidated dairy in the distance. A forlorn cow, chewing cud, had watched them shuffle by, a doubtful expression in its knowing eye.

No matter.

This evening they could leave all that behind. They would go to the dance, sip vodka and make jokes. Perhaps they would talk to girls. Walking beside him, Onni sensed Nalle's energy, his excitement. For too long now, there had been nothing to do. A day at the railroad, a few with the timber cutters. In the decade since the war ended, the careful sense of optimism with which Finland's youth looked ahead had been whittled away by the reality of a nation in recession. You'd line up at a building site of a morning and men would be picked to work, but there were never enough places. The word on everybody's tongue was *inflaatio*. What were they to do when a mark was worth this much one day and a fraction of that amount the next? In recent months Nalle had turned his gaze outwards. As Onni did his chores around the homestead, Nalle was looking further afield, waiting for something to happen.

'Brother,' said Nalle now, his arm slung lazily over Onni's shoulder, 'what will happen to us next?' He was feeling nostalgic. As though whatever it was that lay in store for them had already come to pass. Onni had seen the creased notice among Nalle's things. *There's a man's job for you*, it read, *in Australia*. And he'd seen another pasted up in the window of the general store in town: *Come to the sunny side*.

Australia.

Onni had heard of other men going, some to Canada, others to the United States of America. Some had returned home, many had not. Onni didn't want to think that Nalle had made up his mind, but something about his wistful look suggested he had. After all, there was little keeping him here, neither work nor wife. Nalle couldn't seem to settle on a woman, to their mother's dismay.

They neared the clearing by the lake, and Onni saw the raised timber platform. There were packs of young men milling about and several women talking in small groups. Nalle was drawn to a gathering of men standing at the edge of the pine glade. Onni followed him.

'It's so hot,' someone was saying, 'if you put a tin plate in the sun for a while, you can fry an egg directly on it.'

The group erupted. Onni glimpsed a rough sort of fellow, a little older than Nalle perhaps, in a cattleman's hat. He'd seen one just like it in a picture show.

'You never have to put long pants on,' he continued.

The men nodded and grunted with satisfaction.

'Not a tree as far as the eye can see.'

Again, the crowd was agreeable.

'You can eat as much meat as you want. Steaks that cover the whole plate.'

It was unbelievable.

'Where is this place?' asked Nalle.

'Mount Isa,' said the man. 'Queensland.' Then, continuing his spiel, 'You have days off when you can go into the field and look for a place to make your own claim.' There was a glint in his eye, and hunger in everybody else's. 'You just start digging.'

'What else?' someone asked.

'I saw an emu running through the street. As dumb as a chicken but as tall as a man. You put your hand up and make a beak and he thinks you're one of them.'

Everyone erupted again.

The group separated when the piano accordion started up. Bottles of vodka and *pontikka* were passed between friends and enemies. Young men tried to catch the eyes of young women.

The first brave couple skipped the polka across the timber dance floor. And so the event was underway.

Onni stood at the edge of the platform with his hands dangling by his sides. He looked around. The Kotiniemi girls were there, across the way. They were quiet girls from Toholampi, a tiny village twenty kilometres to the east. Around him, the confident boys were going and picking girls from the perimeter of the dance floor. Onni thought about going to ask the younger of the Kotiniemi girls for a dance, but what would they talk about? And he wasn't much of a dancer. Thinking through the steps sent Onni to talk to Kari, a friend from the railways, instead. He'd wait till the vodka grew his confidence.

The accordion player floated them through the evening, which took on the usual pastel hues of midsummer.

Then the voices of men grew gruff, until the posturing became discernible. Onni greeted the boisterous scuffling sounds with a comfortable familiarity.

'It's your brother,' said Kari calmly.

Sure enough, it was Nalle clutching another man's shirt-front—Timo, the blacksmith's son. Onni saw the glint of the knife blade in Nalle's hand, his treasured *puukko*, acquired in a trade with a traveller from the north. The two men stood a good arm's length apart, the squat knife held back at a safe distance. Nalle was all mouth.

'Take it back,' he was saying. '*Ei tämä mies puukkoa säästä.*' This man is not afraid to use a knife.

'Well, neither is this one. This one is the dangerous man!' Timo was thumping himself on the chest.

'*Vien saunan taakse,*' warned Nalle. I'll take you behind the sauna.

184

The crowd did what was expected of them: the men were cleaved apart and each of them talked down. It all had the air of a well-practised ceremony. The piano accordion started up again, and now couples moved onto the dance floor with ease, because the awkwardness of the evening had been shattered by the excitement of the fight.

Later, Onni found Nalle sprawled at the base of a hay bale with the blacksmith's son. They were sharing slugs of vodka and admiring one another's knives. A well-forged knife, his brother had told him once, is the measure of a man.

Standing at the edge of things, Onni wondered about men, about what kind of a man he was or would become.

Before leaving, he spied Nalle making grabs at a girl at the outskirts of the glade. She laughed, encouraging him. Onni walked home on his own, and all around him the forest was showing off. The wildflowers pushed their heads above the scrub, and the blackberries and juniper glinted like glass shards among the dark green of pine needles.

One month later, Onni stood on the platform, his ears full of the thrum of the approaching train. It arrived too quickly. Their father shook hands solemnly with his eldest son, his throat wrestling with possible words, which did not eventuate. Their mother rested a cold cheek on Nalle's warmer, livelier one, and then it was done. He turned to Onni.

'No need to be so glum, little brother.' Nalle's lopsided smile was difficult to resist.

He pulled out the *puukko*, snug in its casing of reindeer hide.

'You look after this for me.' Nalle had never let him use the knife, not even for spoon carving.

'*Enhän minä.*' No, I won't take it.

'*Ota.*' Take it.

'*En minä.*' I won't.

'I'll set it all up for us,' he said, pushing it firmly into Onni's palm. 'Then you come over. Give it back to me when you get there.'

The train whistle pierced the air, and Nalle was slapping him on the back. He was pulling him in by the neck for a brief, violent embrace. He was jumping up and into the carriage with his duffle bag and then he was gone.

Loping home alongside the railway line, Onni stared down the iron sleepers that vanished into the distance. The tracks were like a protracted arrow, pointing to a place called Australia, where the sun was so hot it would fry an egg on a tin plate. Onni had been trailing his brother all his short life, into the fields, into forests, into war. Nalle had looked proud and honourable in his uniform and Onni wanted some of that too. He didn't feel so honourable, nor manly, standing in the pine forest after the air raid, ears ringing, trousers soiled. He remembered what the lieutenant said afterwards: that he belonged at home with his mother.

Nalle sent word of his arrival in Queensland. He told of hot air and blinding sun, of the red dirt that had become a fixture in the grooves of his browning skin, of steaks that covered your whole plate (it was true). It was difficult to conjure while in Finland the melancholy hues of autumn gave way to the bleak, monolithic white of winter. With the waning season, Onni felt the first phase of his life drawing in. As he swept the dung from the horses' stables, he was only partly present. He was looking further afield, as Nalle once did, waiting for something to happen.

An entire year passed before they received more news from Australia. Enclosed in the envelope was a cheque for his mother, a handsome figure, earned in the mines of Mount Isa. But Nalle had left Queensland after finishing his contract at the mine, the letter told them. He was now headed to the western side of the country, where there was also money to be made.

I have heard of a group of islands where the waters are teeming with crayfish, Nalle wrote. *Like the little freshwater crustaceans we used to find in the lake by the summer house. But these ones are four times bigger and red in colour. The Americans like to eat them. I am going to buy a boat.*

Onni found it hard to believe. Nalle, a fisherman. He thought of his brother flapping ludicrously in the shallow lake at the summer house. Onni could see the mixture of fear and hope in his mother's eyes as she sat knitting a pair of woollen socks. The click of the needles accelerated in the quiet kitchen.

'With God's help he'll get by.'

But she lost her usual, easy rhythm, dropping a stitch.

'*No, voi nyt.*' Well, goodness me.

Onni sat quietly at the kitchen table with a sense of things coming apart, unfurling.

This, Onni thought, could be his last summer dance. Word would come from his brother soon, he was sure of it. He arrived with Kari, wearing his Saturday clothes, with his brother's *puukko* tucked into his belt. As he lay in bed the previous night, Onni had run his fingers along the inscriptions carved in the sheath. He could not decipher the lettering, nor the symbols. Pulling the knife from it, he had admired the smooth pale hilt. It had been forged, certainly, by a master smith. Onni had sharpened the blade with care, imagining what might happen if he pulled it out at the dance. He could make a fine show of it, as Nalle had done. His brother had left the dance last summer with a new air of conviction. As though he had arrived someplace.

Nearing the clearing now, Onni greeted several acquaintances. Men he had met while felling trees, or at the mill, or at the railways. He spoke with Timo, Nalle's opponent from the previous dance, about the situation in Helsinki—there were whispers of a coming strike—but this no longer concerned Onni much. He saw Benjami, who had married Onni's cousin Ulla in the spring.

'How's the old ram getting on, then,' Onni asked, 'now that he's found himself a ewe?'

They laughed in their best men's voices, Onni pretending that he knew what it was all about.

He assessed the scene before him. Searched for some form of tinder, for something that might ignite. The problem was, he felt no ill will towards anyone.

When someone generously gifted him the remaining third of a bottle of vodka, he took small sips, emptying the last of it into the grass while his companion relieved himself. To the west, the evening sun hovered low, casting a soft pink glow across the dance.

And finally, something did happen.

He caught the gaze of the younger Kotiniemi girl. The slight turn of her closed lips, what might have been a smile. She was wearing a simple cotton dress, with her hair down, and flat shoes. There was something about her that drew him in. Some purity to do with her lack of adornment. An honesty to the way she carried herself. He might go over there and talk to her. Ask her for a dance. Perhaps when the tango finished. He sensed that the two of them were not the tango type.

'*On mökkiläinen.*' She's a cottager.

Kari's voice rose above the music. He had followed Onni's gaze.

'She works on a farm in Toholampi. I did a day's work there in the spring. Anttila said she's been working for him since she was a girl. The mother is dead, the father's a cripple. There's an old aunt there who must be about a hundred.'

Onni nodded. He noticed her broad, worker's arms.

'They're dirt poor,' said Kari, just to make sure Onni had understood.

Watching the girl, Onni let his mind race ahead, imagining the two of them married, packing their things. Her single, shabby suitcase. Because she was a cottager and had few possessions to take with her to the other side of the world.

It was ridiculous really. And yet.

The music slowed and couples dispersed. Between tunes, the accordion player cracked his knuckles. The familiar sound of the polka rose up into the night.

And Onni, feeling the outline of the *puukko* against his groin, summoned the courage to make the long trek across the floor. The flat grind of the knife was not made for fighting, he reasoned, not really. It was the natural choice for carving, slicing, whittling, to clean hunters' and fishers' catches.

It was a tool for home, for the day-to-day business of life.

Driftwood

HILDA WALKED AROUND THE ISLAND, as if in a dream. She wanted to remember every detail of the place. Every rut and rise in the coral ground, every succulent, every shell. Each leaning jetty, each ramshackle hut. At the western cove of Little Rat, she lowered herself onto the coarse sand cross-legged and watched a sea lion frolicking in the shallows. It waved at her with its flipper. *I won't go*, she said to the sea lion. *Or I'll come back in a year. You'll see.* A pile of driftwood had collected on the sand and Hilda picked up a small shard, fingering its smooth, alabaster surface. Where had it come from, she wondered, and where would it end up? She kept her back hunched towards the east.

Sauntering back across the island, she headed to the jetty where she knew her father was waiting for her.

'Hilda, *mennään*.'

The motor of the cray boat rumbled. They were going for their final fish, she and Onni. When Hilda got to the end of the jetty she noticed another figure in the boat. Ismo. He was obscured behind the pots and clutter on the starboard side.

She almost said: *What's he doing here?* Instead, she conveyed it with her scowl.

If Onni noticed, he didn't make it known.

Hilda stepped off the jetty and into the boat. There was a surliness to her movements now as she lowered herself down at port-side.

The boat punched through the swells, and she and Ismo stared out over the sea in opposing directions. Her dad was at the stern with his hand on the wheel, looking slightly baffled. Surely he had noticed that they didn't hang around together like they used to. Surely he knew that much.

After killing the motor at the deep hole near Alexander Island and throwing the anchor overboard, all three baited their rods.

'So you're driving across?' Ismo attempted.

The sea lapped, until Onni came to his rescue: 'We'll cross the Nullarbor then follow the coast around the bottom end.'

'Reckon you'll come back for a visit?'

'Long way,' said Onni.

Hilda thought now about that immense desert between Western Australia and New South Wales. She'd never seen it, but she could imagine it. The Nullarbor Plain, that's what all the talk had been about recently. Flat, treeless, unending. Like the sea, but red. She had bumped into Ismo's dad out the front of the community hall the other day. 'Ismo has been looking at the map of Australia,' Risto had told her, 'running his finger from west to east. Such a long way, huh?'

She'd had to escape then, sprinting off towards the far end of the island.

Now, Hilda made the first catch: a baldchin groper. She went about it methodically. Slid the hook from its mouth, slapped its blue body against the timber bench, took her knife, cut it just below the white chin. Tossing it into the bucket, she baited her rod again. The water glinted in the sunlight and Hilda took a long breath, reminding herself that this was it, she had to savour it. She couldn't let Ismo's presence ruin it. Glancing sideways at her dad, she saw the desperation in his eyes. Her surliness was robbing him of the farewell fish he had planned. But this was their decision. She was still furious that they'd made it without her. *Dad can't do it anymore*, her mum had said, as she stood with her hand on Onni's shoulder. They had formed an alliance against her. *His back is giving him too much trouble. He can't do another season.* His back? Right then Hilda hated Onni and his back, for being too weak.

Ismo's rod jerked forwards. It was a coral trout that eventually came up, huffing and puffing on the end of his line. Gripping it around its spotted midsection, he pulled the hook out of its lip and automatically passed it over to Hilda. It had always been this way. It was their system. She made the kill, with Ismo averting his eyes, and later, back on the island, he gutted it. But not this time.

Hilda handed him the knife. 'You do it.'

Ismo's blue eyes looked at her pleadingly. She hadn't planned it, but now she was determined.

'You act like you're so gentle and good,' she whispered in rapid-fire English, knowing Onni wouldn't be able to make it out, 'but you're just as bad as anyone.'

'Get it done,' ordered Onni from the other end of the boat.

Watching Ismo kill his first fish was awful. As the blade entered, Hilda felt it move in her own flesh. She watched his innocence run down his fingers in red, stinking rivulets. And so it was done. She wondered if he felt the same emptiness she had that night beneath the lighthouse. He baited his rod with eyes fixed on the water.

The first gust of wind whipping in from the south brought a mixture of relief and disappointment. Her dad called it, and they packed up their things, securing their rods for the journey back to Little Rat.

Onni motioned to Hilda. 'You take the wheel.'

She sensed that there was something beneath this offer. Some demonstration of solidarity. But it was the crumbs he was throwing her now. She was just steering; she wasn't the skipper.

Hilda knew the reef around Alexander. And she showed him now, moving the boat with the map of the reef below her. She had one hand on the wheel when Onni pulled the Instamatic out of his jacket pocket. His fingers looked too large as he pressed down on the trigger.

'*Hildan viimeinen päivä Pikku Rotalla,*' he said, smiling sadly, so that she had to look away. Hilda's last day on Little Rat.

It felt as though none of them wanted to go, not even Onni. And yet they continued to make movements towards leaving.

Earlier that morning, Hilda had watched her mother pack up the camp kitchen, wrapping the cups and plates in newspaper with the most desolate look on her face. Taking the anoraks from their hooks, Alva had folded each one mounfully, placing them into a bag as though placing flowers on a grave.

We don't have to go, Hilda wanted to yell. *Let's stay.* But she remained silent. As they went about Little Rat, moving in slow motion, performing the small rituals and tasks of season's end, it felt as though they were hurtling along at a great speed. So Hilda held the wheel with two hands. The boat had been set on its path and you couldn't turn around now. But she would come back, she promised, in a year or two, when she was old enough to make her own decisions.

Back on the island, Onni left Hilda and Ismo at the outdoor basin. They each pulled a body, one orange, one blue, from the bucket and began scraping away scales.

'You know it wasn't like that,' said Ismo now, 'the way you think it was.'

The words were being prised out, like a fishbone caught in the gullet.

'So how was it, then?'

'I wouldn't have. If it had come down to it.'

Hilda let the words sit there in front of them on the gutting bench, mingling with scales and fish guts.

'Why am I the bad one?' continued Ismo. 'You went with him, that night.'

So that Hilda was aware of the thrusting swells all around, and the hard backbone of the groper under her fingers.

'He's not my friend,' she said. 'He never was.'

Looking out to sea, Hilda could make out the islands that made up the Easter Group: Big Rat, Leo Island, Alexander Island, Woody Woody, Roma and their island, Little Rat. They were one network, and yet ultimately separate. Almost in sync, she and Ismo threw the viscera into the sea and the fillets into the bucket between them. The contrast between the two species was plain to see. Hilda knew then that things would never be as they were. The system had broken—they would no longer fish together, acting out their respective roles. Eventually you had to go it alone.

That afternoon, Hilda did a loop past Latvian Igor's camp. She hesitated by his new lean-to, which he had rebuilt after the cyclone smashed it down, along with the jetty. Her visits had become less frequent this season, not for any particular reason. Only that it didn't seem so important now, for either of them. He had recently told Helvi, who had told Alva, who had told her, that he had once had a daughter but she had died very young. It was too sad to think about.

Hilda found him under the shade of the open structure, securing his pots for the coming off-season. He had a tin cup of coffee on the bench next to him.

'We're leaving tomorrow,' Hilda said to his large back.

Igor turned and surveyed her. 'They say that new beginnings are often disguised as painful endings.'

At times, over the course of recent months, Hilda had let her mind run, and she would even find little scraps of hope for the future, like the flickering tongues of distant lightning. Who knew what waited for her in the east? Another sea, above which the sun rose of a morning rather than set. Things would be back to front, or different, at least. Maybe she would be happy.

'I'm glad you came back.'

She had been wanting to tell him this but it had always seemed too hard. Too forward.

He might have nodded; it was hard to tell.

'*Hei*, Hilda.'

'*Hei*, Igor.'

As the sun was beginning to set, Hilda looked around their camp for some memento to take with her. They would be leaving on the boat, at first light, and she had to be ready. There was an aged, sun-bleached float that she considered. An eroded coin from the *Batavia* that she'd acquired from one of the boys from the Wallabis. But neither seemed fitting. She could see her mother doing the same: picking things up, putting them back. Hilda picked up her tackle box and walked over to Ismo's camp.

He was sitting on his own jetty, looking out to the horizon.

'You should have this,' she said, offering him the box of fishing tackle, but more.

'Won't you need it over east?'

'You're the one that's going to be the fisherman.'

They sat together at the end of the jetty, as they had so often done, bare feet dangling over the edge.

'You know,' said Hilda, 'you did it good today. The way you cut it. It would've died straight away.'

As the light diminished, Hilda felt a pang for their receding childhood. She remembered the taste of Sunshine powdered milk and arrowroot biscuits, of cold smoked mackerel and pickled herring straight from the jar. She remembered the feel of a crab's hard carapace in her fingertips, its little squirming legs fighting for release; the phantom imprint of a fish fossil, reminding her of her smallness.

In the end Hilda took nothing with her. What could you possibly take, when you couldn't take the island itself? She sensed her mother experiencing the same struggle. But as Alva stood with her suitcase in the camp kitchen for the very last time, Hilda noticed the small piece of driftwood in her mother's closed palm. It had sat on the windowsill in their camp forever, alongside the little knob of dried coral. In Alva's scrawled handwriting was written: *Pikku Rotta, April 1960.* Hilda was just a tiny baby then, not two months old, on her first trip out to the islands. There were a handful of them: the kids who weren't quite born there, but almost. She thought of rounding out the inscription: *Pikku Rotta, April 1960 – June 1975.*

Onni and Alva made their way to the jetty lugging the remnants of their island dream.

And furtively, in the pre-dawn dark, as they called her name from the cray boat, Hilda crouched and ran her hand across the rough coral skin of Little Rat.

PART 2

EAST

Birch

THE YEARS OF WIND AND coral were over, and Alva Saari attempted settlement for a second time. Word had spread of a building boom, a continuous supply of construction work in the nation's capital. Many Finns had relocated there in recent years, setting themselves up in the dusty, half-built northern suburbs, which were really just paddocks of brown grass, a leftover yellow box or ironbark tree punctuating the landscape here and there. Alva had refused to live that far away from the sea, and so they had compromised and bought a modest weatherboard house in a small, quiet beach town called Sunpatch, two hours from Canberra. Onni travelled to the capital for work during the week, staying with Jouko, an old acquaintance from his mining days. Sunpatch was nestled behind a craggy headland that leaned out to the south. There were mountains set back from the sea and long, deserted beaches. It could be a good place. Sunpatch: the name gave her hope. She'd even unpacked the Riihimäen glassware. Though Alva was aware of a hollow feeling inside her since leaving the islands.

And there was the problem of Hilda.

Alva found the letter in the hand-built mailbox when she returned from her cleaning shift at the Clarkes'. That morning, Onni had left before sunrise to make his way over the mountain for work, and Hilda had dressed in her school uniform and set off in the direction of the bus stop. Alva struggled through the contents of the letter, a hot wave of anger moving through her as she deciphered its meaning. Hilda had not attended classes for several weeks.

'There's no point,' Hilda said, when Alva confronted her in the afternoon. Her daughter's tartan skirt was hitched up unevenly, rolled at the waist, her skinny thighs suggestive.

Alva called Onni in Canberra.

'*Tyttö palaa suoraa päätä kouluun kun näkee mitä se työ oikeen on,*' Onni announced down the phone line. A girl will go straight back to school once she sees how hard working really is.

But the image that appeared in Alva's mind was that of Hilda on the boat back out west, working as hard as anybody. And there was a silence down the line that implied Onni was thinking the same. Alva had watched her girl floundering since arriving in the east. She was unmoored, looking for something to anchor herself to. They all were. But there was more to it. She was pulling away. That invisible cord between mother and daughter was growing taut. The Christmas just past, Hilda had sat sullenly in her armchair, half-heartedly mouthing the words to the songs.

And then she had refused to join them on New Year's Eve for the *uudenvuoden tina*, the melting of the lead. Instead, she'd gone to a beach party. Onni said there was no point doing it, just the two of them, but Alva insisted, out of a sort of stubbornness. She secretly hoped that Hilda would rush back at the last minute, not wanting to miss out. Alva watched the melding of the elements, the molten liquid making smooth silver shapes on the ladle. Even as it was plunged into the ice water, before she'd seen its final shape, she was overcome by a familiar feeling. And of course it came out brittle, a thin, fragile archway of tin connecting the two more solid lumps, and Hilda did not come. Alva held her New Year's fortune in the palm of her hand, reminding herself that it was all about perspective. She attempted the sort of optimistic thought appropriate to such an occasion: I will talk more to Hilda. I will let her be herself.

Following Onni's instruction, Alva put the girl to work. They would go to the Clarkes' first, then to the big house on Ainsley where there was never an item out of place. Alva was a good, thorough cleaner, and after she found work at the first house, the others had come to her. For the first time she was earning money, negotiating her own fees, and although she knew it was a lowly occupation, it felt good all the same. She looked her employers in the eye. And she was getting better at the small talk.

Today, Hilda was to scrub the bath and shower recesses while Alva vacuumed. Surely she would begin to see. To understand that she had a chance to be something else, something better than a cleaning lady, if she just went back to school.

Halfway through the shift, Alva found Hilda sitting on the bathroom floor, her face drained of colour. This is it, she thought, a cautious triumph moving through her.

'I won't have you sitting down and wasting time,' she said, more proudly than necessary. 'We have the second house to do yet.'

Hilda moved in slow motion across the sickly white tiles, and there was something recognisable in her glassy eyes. Some vague, bodily memory that nudged at Alva.

'Please go back to school.' Alva hadn't meant it to sound like a plea.

'Mum, there's no point.'

There it was again. No point?

'Of course there is. You won't have to do this.' Alva gestured with a sweep of her hand. 'You can do better.'

Hilda looked into her eyes. Her nausea was palpable.

'*Äiti. Ei vauvaa voi kouluun viedä.*' Mum. You can't take a baby to school.

They drove home in silence. Alva could not get the picture out of her head. Her own child, all gangly legs and jutting knees, growing something inside that narrow pelvis of hers. Her child looking up at her from the bathroom floor with those eyes; the eyes of a girl who knew things, knew what went on between bedsheets, all the sticky, sordid details. But worse still was the pity with which she'd looked at her. Her stupid migrant mum, who knew nothing. Had she been unwell in some other way, Alva could have held her hair aside and rubbed her back as she threw up. But she couldn't do it. Instead, she'd fought an urge to hit her daughter, and in order not to, she left her alone, head in the Clarkes' porcelain toilet bowl. Somehow that made it worse: being at the Clarkes'. This sort of thing wouldn't happen in their family.

Alva turned into the driveway and brought the car to a stop. She pulled on the handbrake and sat motionless, staring through the windscreen at the tin shed.

'*Miksi?*' she asked. Why?

Alva turned to look at Hilda.

'*Miksi ei?*' her daughter replied at last. Why not?

Inside the house, Alva dropped the car keys on the kitchen table and marched straight back out. She burst through the screen door and made her way up the road to the beach. At the north side of the Cove, Alva crouched in the dunes and conjured Hilda in Western Australia. Hilda in the off-season, feeding the chooks in their backyard at Bluff Point. Hilda in the boatshed, helping Onni with the upkeep of the cray boat. She used to ask so many questions of him. Hilda on the islands, in her blue anorak, her hair across her face. She had her fishing reel in one hand and a bucket in the other, weighed down with fish. She always caught something.

But they had left all that behind.

So, why not?

A bobbing head caught her attention, someone taking a walk along the beach. Alva sank lower in the dunes, certain she saw the head of the walker turn, just for a moment, to glance in her direction. She was a ridiculous sand crab, frozen in place, thinking itself camouflaged.

When the walker had passed, disappearing down the track at the base of the headland, Alva let herself indulge again. Had it all been in vain, all of their hard work? What was the point of it all, of crossing seas, of leaving family behind? Hilda would drop out of school, work some monotonous, unskilled job, as she herself was doing. Alva imagined an entire lifetime. A drab domestic struggle through the years. No, no, no, no, this was not what she had envisaged for her daughter.

She was having a tantrum. But slowly the sea breeze hushed her, and the perpetual rhythm of the swell surging up the shoreline pacified.

Later that night, as Alva lay in bed, turning the secret over in her mind, she wondered what sin she was guilty of, what sin had caused this. She had wanted too much, of course. She had thought they might make a success of it. Alva remembered how, years ago, Onni had asked her what she thought the Sampo was. She had played the puritan, as though she did not dream of material wealth, of success. She said the evening prayer privately, as she had always done before going to sleep. She asked for forgiveness.

Hilda's body began to change, and soon Alva could hardly look at her. She glimpsed it through a crack in the bedroom door when Hilda was dressing after a shower. Her swollen white midline, imitating the perfect oval curve of a chicken's egg. It was demanding to be seen. And her breasts fuller, her thighs fleshier.

How could it be, Alva wondered, that this child would soon endure that crude act? She remembered Hilda's birth. The utter terror she'd felt, and the nurse's brutal slap to quieten her. But now, as Alva looked back on the scene from a distance, she understood that it was perhaps the only possible course of action. She had been wild with fear. Onni wanted to try for another child at one point, but Alva could not go through with it again.

'You'll need to tell Dad soon,' she said that night.

Hilda was on the couch with her feet curled underneath her, her little girl's nightie pulled taut over her expanding stomach. It was all wrong.

'You know people will start to notice it now.'

Alva let her wide, frightened eyes fall on the offending body part.

Hilda glared. 'So let them notice. I'm not embarrassed, Mum.'

'No, *niin se sitten on*,' was all Onni said when the moment finally came. Well, that's how it is then.

The defeat in his voice wounded. Alva would have preferred the angry words that she knew were there. She wanted them to be in it together. This tide of fury on which she was being carried.

The father, they learned, was a boy from a small inland town who had come to stay at the caravan park in the summer. Alva imagined it. A hurried minute when the rest of the family had gone out. A cramped fold-out bed in an airless caravan.

His family were in the automotive business. Smash repairs. There was a granny flat, Hilda said, where they could live with the baby. Alva stared at this stranger child who was hers.

'You'll move away from the sea?'

Hilda just shrugged.

Alva calmed her nerves by tending to the garden. She lugged a large watering can across the yard and sloshed the contents onto the base of the ever-thirsty birch. She had planted it, along with the Geraldton wax, soon after their arrival in the east. Onni had grumbled, 'You should choose plants that belong here.' *Or none at all* was what he really meant. Onni preferred a practical yard of well-shorn grass and concrete rectangles. But the birch reminded Alva of Finland and the Geraldton wax of the west.

A second letter arrived, this time from Western Australia, from her friend Helvi. Helvi the artist. The letter told of the cray boom. Of an insatiable hunger for the red-shelled creatures. How could anyone have predicted it? That just months after they'd sold their lease its value would have soared? The letter told of Petra and Esko, who had followed their sons north to start anew. And of Helvi's boys, who were becoming fine fishermen. The reason for writing, though, was young Lauri, to explain what they knew of his condition. The letter was an offering, and it should have brought relief, but reading Helvi's scrawled hand, Alva only felt a sort of grief, as sharp and painful as a needle, for their friendship, for the islands, for a life that was still on track. What did it matter now? It was too late. The protruding belly mocked her, and Alva put the letter in a shoebox under the bed.

She found herself shying away from small talk. When Alva took her pay packet from Mrs Kennedy, she looked at the clean, carpeted floor, which she had vacuumed methodically, and went away. She could not bear the questions. Simple, innocent questions, like, *How's Hilda going?*

They had met the boy a handful of times. He spoke in a drawled accent, and although the words were stretched out, it was still difficult for Alva to understand.

The kid had a rumbling EH Holden that was his pride and joy, and when he came to visit, he and Hilda would go for drives.

'Where to?' demanded Alva.

'Nowhere. Just for a drive.'

Nowhere. Hilda's words were full of the hopelessness of the life that she would have.

'Who drives around for the sake of driving?' Alva asked Onni.

'They do in Australia,' he told her.

One night, Alva met Hilda unexpectedly at the kitchen sink. It was after midnight, and they converged in the dim glow of moonlight flooding in through the north-facing window. Hilda was soft in the pale light, her body flowing. Something niggled at Alva, threatening to break open her staunch indignation: a recognition of form. Of the processes of life. Of beauty. She felt the ebb of the tide give a little. Was aware of her own, now thick-set body beside this young, blossoming one. She had become rigid with age.

'I can't sleep,' said Hilda.

'You won't sleep now for years. Not after what you've gone and done.' It escaped from her mouth as a snide hiss, and the thread of beauty fell away. Outside the moon remained visible, creamy yellow and perfectly full.

It came time for Hilda's final check-up before the event. In the car, Alva circled the block several times.

'There's one,' Hilda said, pointing to a park on Main Street.

'Too tight.' Alva drove on as Hilda eyed the space, easily big enough.

'There.' Hilda pointed out another car space, but Alva drove on.

Finally she pulled into a spot in the back car park, off River Street. From there, you could enter the surgery from the rear. Alva collected her handbag from the back seat and waited. Out of the corner of her eye, she watched the rounded belly, like an open umbrella, thrusting its way out of the passenger door. It was a small elephant that walked beside her.

'*Kylläpä minä olen kauhea häpeä sinulle,*' said Hilda, and there was fire in her eyes. Well, aren't I a great shame to you.

The air caught in Alva's throat, but she kept on walking. As she pushed open the surgery doors, she recognised her own reflection in the glass. She pretended it hadn't been a harsh woman that stared back, but a mother.

Alva sat in the clean, antiseptic smell of the waiting room with her hands knotted together. A memory came to her. Herself as a young woman, walking along an empty Geraldton street in the pouring rain, and her neighbour Aileen, before they had become friends, driving by with another woman in the car. She recalled the look of embarrassment on Aileen's face. The way she had pretended not to know her.

Alva was seated beside an older lady with a creased face that reminded her of her aunt Iita's. The lady had seen Hilda waddle into her appointment, and she sat as though wanting to say something. Alva avoided her eye.

'You forget all about it when the baby comes,' the woman said eventually. 'And it grows them up real quick. You'll see. She'll be less of a worry to you after than before.'

The door to the consultation room swung open and Hilda appeared alongside the midwife. Hilda said something, and the woman laughed. Then, before turning to go, the midwife placed a friendly hand on Hilda's stomach, just for a moment. Alva thought: But I have not touched it. She noticed that Hilda held her body proudly during the exchange.

That afternoon, Alva went about the house opening things up. She opened cupboards and drawers, flung windows open, let the curtains loose from their ties. Every piece of twine, of looped string, of knotted rope, she untied and let hang freely. She did what Aunt Iita would have done to prepare for such an occasion. For the movement of a soul across a threshold. She put the *sielulintu* by Hilda's bed, making sure it faced due north. And for the first time, Alva let herself imagine the baby that would be born into their family. This, the opening up of things, was her first act of solidarity, and it was easy after that. With each cupboard door, each window, Alva felt herself opening a little too, her pent-up shame and anger drifting out. Out and away.

Unlatching the large window in the lounge, Alva found herself looking out on the birch. It had sprung up in two prongs, as they often do. A novice might perceive them as two separate saplings, but a true gardener would know they were but one tree, born from the same root. Alva noticed now that the smaller branch, shadowed by the larger, had grown to the left, searching out the light.

In the evening, she cooked a liver casserole for Hilda. It was time to begin preparing her system for the blood loss. Of course she knew Hilda would hate it, and perhaps this was partly the reason for making it.

'You'll think you'll die,' she told her daughter, again recalling her own experience. 'But you won't. What you'll die from is the exhaustion afterwards. You become like a cow,' she told her. 'A milking station. That's all you are for a while.'

And so things were more or less peaceful between them.

New Year's tin

THE HEAT WAS AN ASSAULT.

The dry, crackling kind of heat, that settles down on wheat-coloured land. Nothing moved, neither the people nor the animals—the old wolfhound, and the couple of docile cows they had milling around in the yellow paddock. Hilda sat with the baby under the whirring fan in their granny flat. Randle had skipped across to Ma and Pa's for tea. He preferred to eat there because the food was better. Ma was quietly triumphant. And that way, he wouldn't have to help with Riitta. Rida, he called her.

Riitta was feeding, or not quite.

Earlier, the baby had shrieked for two hours, until Hilda had stopped trying. She sat in the armchair given to them by Pa, looking straight ahead. The bawling became indistinct, a far-off sound that had nothing to do with her. She just sat, and didn't feel a thing. Thought about leaving, going down to the dam to look at the water. But even that seemed too much.

Then Ma, Randle's mother, had come charging in.

'It's too much,' she'd said. 'It's too much.' She'd taken Riitta into her matronly arms and, cocooned in all that warmth and pudginess, the baby had let up.

Now, as she held little Riitta in her own arms, attempting to cradle her as Ma had, Hilda willed her to latch on, to suck, but felt her instinctively drawing away. Did she know? Creatures like this, they had an instinct. She thought about the gentle wolfhound, Betsie, who looked into her soul with knowing eyes. They had an instinct about the goodness of a person.

Ma didn't hold it against her. Once the baby had settled she bustled right out of there.

'You'll get the hang of it, dearie.'

But all Hilda could think about was little Lauri.

'There is something wrong with me,' she said.

Lil, Randle's sister, was at the door. She was fifteen, two years younger than Hilda. She liked to come for a cuppa after dinner.

'I can't wait till I can leave school and have a baby. I'll call her Dianne.'

Hilda remembered how she and Dee used to talk like that.

'You should finish school,' she said.

'What for? You didn't.'

'Maybe I'll go back.'

'What, when you're old? That would be weird.'

Here, no one questioned her choice. Here, life was lived, and no one asked why or how. Life was not a set of choices but something that happened to you. It was a relief, in a way, after living for nine months under the weight of her mother's disappointment. She remembered Randle's reaction when she told him. The way he puffed up and out. Randle didn't think about the little baby that would be born. He was proud because his boys were swimmers. To celebrate, the family went to the Soldiers' Club one Friday night. Hilda had never been out to dinner. On Ma's recommendation she had a prawn cocktail followed by chicken Maryland.

'Can I hold her?' asked Lil.

Hilda passed the baby over.

'New Year's is going to be a hoot.' Lil was giddy with it. With life, and all it had in store for her. 'You just wait till you see the bonfire.'

'In June every year, we make a big bonfire for the Finnish midsummer's eve celebration,' Hilda told her.

'What's midsummer's eve?'

'It's the longest day of the year. In Finland, it doesn't get dark at all.'

'Wow.'

Hilda could see the *Juhannus kokko* on Little Rat. The smoke billowing into the chalk-blue sky, everyone standing around in their winter jackets.

'Did you like our Chrissie?' asked Lil.

'Sure, it was great.'

Hilda had spent Christmas with Randle's family. She had wanted to get a real Christmas tree, something resembling a spruce. Even a raggedy casuarina sapling would have done. But Ma said she didn't want the leaves dropping all over the carpet. So Hilda helped them decorate the plastic tree. They did the presents on Christmas morning, and she'd been given a vacuum cleaner.

'It has all the latest features,' said Ma.

Hilda had made *pulla* for the occasion, her mum's recipe. It was a long process, especially with the baby waking so often. First she'd had to hunt down the fresh yeast and the cardamom, which she'd finally found at the deli in Cooma. After the dough had tripled in size, she'd punched it down like she'd seen her mother do, and kneaded it a second time. She rolled it into long lengths, and at last it was time to plait the dough: this was the part she'd enjoyed as a kid. But on Christmas Day the plate of *pulla* had gone untouched.

She'd waited for something to happen, some ceremony to mark the day. Instead the blokes just went out to the shed with their stubbies in hand, and the women tidied up. As she was clearing the table, Hilda found one of her scrolls discarded among the dishes, a single bite taken out of it. How ridiculous, to feel hurt over a thing like that.

Later, when she was alone in the granny flat with Riitta, she sang her the Finnish Christmas song that she knew best:

> *Joulu puu on rakennettu,*
> *Joulu on jo ovella,*
> *Namusia ripustettu*
> *Ompi kuusen oksilla.*

> The Christmas tree has been built,
> Christmas Eve is at the door,
> The sweets have been hung
> Upon the branches of the spruce.

Imagine if Alva could have seen her then. But she wouldn't have given her the satisfaction.

On the last day of 1977, at about midday, Hilda joined the family out in the paddock. The men and the kids were running around like busy ants, lugging all sorts of bits and pieces from the sheds to the site of the bonfire.

Lil joined her under a lone eucalypt.

'Randle and the boys from next door went to Deep Creek Dam,' she said. 'There's going to be a party. Mum said I can't go.' Lil's chin jutted out with the injustice of it.

Hilda remembered when she and Randle had gone for a drive out to Deep Creek. She'd packed her bathers, but there was hardly any water. Just a murky brown puddle at the bottom of a ditch. Randle was excited about his new wheels. The car was cobbled together from the spare parts of wrecked Holdens. He'd revved it a few times, smiling sideways at Hilda.

'It's got to have grunt,' he'd yelled over the roar of the engine.

They didn't even get out to have a walk around. Instead, Randle did a couple of burnouts.

'I don't know if we should with the baby,' yelled Hilda, over the top of the grunting engine.

'She loves it!' yelled Randle.

'Are they coming back for the bonfire?' asked Hilda now.

'Dunno.'

They both tugged their dresses down at the armpits, where the fabric had become wet with sweat.

Hilda tried to figure out whether she cared or not.

Uncles and aunts from Cooma arrived, and cousin Tina, the snobby one, who worked as a public servant in Canberra. Hilda had been shown the photo of her wedding, Ma pointing admiringly to the dress, its leg-of-mutton sleeves. Others came from the surrounding area: the drunken bloke from one of the nearby farms, and the lady who worked at the roadhouse, along with her throng of kids. Randle's Holden didn't make an appearance.

Aunt Ness found her. She waggled her head in front of the pram, coo-cooing at little Riitta.

'How are you lot getting along then?' she asked.

'Good, thanks, Aunt Ness.'

'And Randle?'

'Gone to Deep Creek Dam with the boys.'

Hilda felt Aunt Ness's eyes studying her.

'Are you keeping him how he'd like to be kept?'

Hilda smiled, but Aunt Ness was serious.

Luckily, Lil saved her. 'I just love New Year's. Don't youse?'

'On New Year's Eve,' said Hilda, 'we do this thing called *uudenvuoden tina*. New Year's tin. Dad melts lead and tin on a ladle over a flame and then it gets dunked in a bucket of cold water, so it cools into a shape, predicting your year ahead.'

'What's it look like?' asked Lil.

'They just look like these bubbly lumps of lead.'

'How do you know what it means?'

'You hold it up in candlelight and see what kind of a shadow it casts on the wall. If it looks like a ship, then maybe you're going travelling. If it looks like a horse, then maybe a new boat.'

'A boat?' Lil was furrowing her brow.

'Or a car,' said Hilda. 'But if it's all fragile and breaking up, then it might mean bad luck.'

Aunt Ness and Lil just looked at her. A fly buzzed around Lil's nostrils.

'Now that's a bit different,' said Aunt Ness finally.

The sun was just beginning to set when Uncle Bernie threw a match on the bonfire. Everyone squealed, especially Lil. A carload of boys pulled up, making a big dusty show of it. When Hilda saw that Randle was not among them, she felt her body give a little. To her surprise, it was a sigh of relief that ran through her.

She didn't have to stay.

Hilda threw a few things into a carry bag. A summer dress and her bathers. Her skin almost tingled with the thought of it. Of salt water.

Ma saw her packing the car. 'What's happening, love?'

'Sorry, Ma,' she said. 'I've got to go see Mum and Dad.'

I've got to do the *uudenvuoden tina*, she thought. She wasn't sure why, but suddenly it seemed vitally important.

'You do what you got to do,' said Ma, and planted a kiss on her cheek.

It was an hour-and-a-half drive back to the coast. Before pulling into the driveway, Hilda did a loop up to the headland. The black mass of water heaved in the moonlight, and as she opened the window, the sea breeze hit her face. Hilda turned to the baby in the back seat. Riitta had just woken. She looked at Hilda with lake-water eyes. They were Onni's eyes.

'We're going to be all right,' Hilda told her. She didn't know if it was the truth, but she had to be hopeful, for the kid's sake. You have to look into your New Year's tin and see something good. Something worthwhile. She thought of Latvian Igor then. About how he had left, but he had come back.

Hilda found her dad in the kitchen. A glimmer of happiness moved across the surprise on his face.

'*Voi ei. Hilda on tullut kotiin,*' he said. Hilda has come home.

She smiled, swallowing the lump in her throat. Took in the quiet house. On her way inside, she'd noticed that the shed was all closed up.

'Aren't you doing *uudenvuoden tina*?'

'We didn't think we'd bother, just the two of us.'

Perhaps Onni discerned the desperation in her eyes.

'*Helposti se järjestyy.*' It won't take long to set up.

Stingray

ONNI DROVE DOWN THE CLYDE MOUNTAIN on Friday afternoon. He wound his way around the steep corners, and exhaled as he took in the first welcome glimpse of the ocean. The construction of the new Parliament House had kept him making this journey for longer than he had planned. Every Friday, at around this time, he felt the salt air slap him on his now rather rough and slackening cheek, and was glad.

He'd been troubled all week by a photograph that had arrived from Western Australia. Risto hadn't meant it as a barb, but that's how it had felt: like something sharp and gnarled lodging itself inside him. In the photograph, Risto stood, barrel-chested and solid on his feet, in front of his new jet boat. The vessel was dry-docked, so that the magnificent hull thrust forwards. *There,* said Onni, as he laid another brick, steam escaping his mouth in the brittle and frosted morning. *There are the dollars that I have missed.* Somehow it had brought everything into his line of sight: here he was, trowel in hand, and he was no longer in his prime. His body ached. There were the young guns on their crew—the sons of other Finns—who went hard, as he once did. And at the end of the day, when he got into his groaning Land Cruiser, also past its best, he knew he had not made it as Risto had. But maybe there was still time.

On weekends, it was his granddaughter who filled his mind. Saturdays were theirs. She would follow him down to the shed mid-morning and watch as he hammered some nail or restrung the fishing rods. Sometimes he gave her a lump of wood and a few old nails of her own that she would hammer in. When she was finished, she sat on the sawhorse and asked him questions. And he found he didn't mind answering.

Later, if the tide was in, Onni would take Riitta fishing at the long, open beach to the south. This afternoon he was down in the shed getting prepared, and the girl, as usual, trailed him. Onni had the tackle box open on the bench, checking and refilling their stock of hooks and sinkers and line. Riitta loved the old birchwood knife that once upon a time had belonged to his brother. Nalle had never wanted it back. As a young man, Onni had kept it perfectly oiled and sharpened, presenting it to his brother on his arrival in Australia. Nalle had waved him away: *It's your knife, little brother.* It was merely a pretext for getting him there.

Riitta slipped the knife from the box and carefully pulled it from the reindeer-hide casing. It was a routine of theirs.

'When did he die?' she asked, as if she didn't know.

'Two years after arriving in Western Australia.'

'How?'

'You know how.'

'I wouldn't want to drown,' said the girl.

She gazed at the old knife blade admiringly, turning it over in her smooth hand.

'When you die, will you leave this knife to me?'

'*Tietysti*,' he said. Of course. 'Who else?'

'You won't die soon, will you, Ukki?'

'Not just yet,' he said.

'Good, because we still have lots to do. I haven't shown you the shark egg I found.'

Onni considered how different his own death would be from his brother's. He compared Nalle's sudden and spectacular end to the slow demise of ageing. His joints were starting to give him trouble, and his back had never recovered from all those years bending over the sides of cray boats. He wasn't sure which type of death was more terrifying, but he could no longer ignore it: the fact of his own mortality. He had passed over the summit of life without even noticing, and now he was on the other side. The inevitable, downhill slope.

Onni chucked the rods and the picnic gear into the back of the Land Cruiser, along with Riitta. She always rode back there. There were no proper seats, just a wooden bench that he had put in himself. She liked to be thrown around by the ruts and grooves in the long, sandy road that led to their fishing spot, so he looked for them, listening out for her gleeful squeal.

Onni pushed two pieces of PVC pipe into the sand, about thirty feet apart. On an upside-down bucket, he cut a large pilchard into sections and threaded one piece onto each hook. His granddaughter squirmed beside him. Next time, he would make her do it. Riitta battled her rod, attempting to cast it on her own. After two tries she surrendered it to Onni with her bottom lip jutting out. He cast the line into the high tide trough, and placed the rod into the PVC pipe holder. Riitta sat cross-legged in the sand and soon forgot her frustration. Onni moved to his own spot, and they each settled into it, gazing absent-mindedly at the tips of their rods.

The wind blew and their lines moved with the current. Onni's mind drifted back to the photograph. Why had he given it up? People often asked him this, and he always told them it was because of his back. That, and the downturn in the industry, which, as it turned out, was a blip in its otherwise endless upward trajectory. It wasn't as if he hadn't been aware of it until now. He had watched it from afar for years, quietly noting the rising price of crays. And then Risto had told him, in a roundabout way, when they'd come to visit them in the east—him and Helvi. But the photograph somehow confirmed it.

As he baited and cast his rod, the memory of the islands lingered, like a lover lost. He started to wish he'd never seen them, those damn islands. His thoughts circled that particular moment in time, the moment he had decided to leave, and as he refocused on the wide blue Pacific before him, he felt a kind of anger. When it proffered up a stingray, thrashing at the end of little Riitta's line, he was determined.

He got hold of the tail with his pliers, and covered it with a rag. This way he could grasp the barb securely. He flipped the creature over onto its back, meeting its strange, triangular smile.

'Remove the hook,' Onni said, holding the pliers out to Riitta.

She gaped at him, frozen in ankle-deep water.

'No, Ukki, I'm scared.'

He could hear the beginning of tears at the back of her throat.

'You can't let it get the better of you.' The words came out more forcefully than he had intended.

'No, Ukki.'

'Now, Riitta.'

So the girl had to take the pliers. She reached with trembling hands for the stingray's mouth. Once she had a firm grasp of the metal, she began to pull, but it wouldn't budge.

'Wrench it,' he told her.

When it finally came free, he carried the ray by the tail into the shallows and flung it out. It shot off through the waves and disappeared into the sea. Onni pretended he didn't hear Riitta's waning sobs.

They walked back along the beach, Riitta trailing behind. Up ahead, Onni saw the Koori beach haul fishermen, with their four-wheel drives parked up along the ridge of sand. The sun was beginning to set.

He slowed as he neared the group. The men had their eyes on the water, scanning for shoals, perhaps.

'Going for a fish?' asked Riitta, when she caught up.

One bloke nodded. 'Any tips, little one?'

'We went up there but it wasn't much good,' replied Riitta, pointing to the section of beach where they had been set up. She turned back towards the group. 'Where are your fishing rods?'

'We use a net,' the man said. 'We'll put it in the water up that way.' He gestured, raising his chin to the north. 'In the corner where it's not so rough. Been doing it this way for a long time.'

'My grandpa's a fisherman too,' she told them. 'He had a boat in Western Australia.'

'Is that right?' The man looked to Onni.

'Used to be in crayfishing,' he said. 'Abrolhos Islands.'

'Ah, the Abrolhos Group.' The fisherman nodded. 'I hear those cray licences are worth a pretty penny these days.' He searched Onni's face for confirmation. 'Anyway,' said the fisherman after a moment, as if sensing some wound opening, 'mullet's just starting to run.'

The sun had disappeared behind the dunes now, and the low light softened the faces of the men who stood leaning against the bonnets of their trucks.

'No luck today?' the man asked.

Onni showed his empty bucket. 'My timing wrong,' he said, and it was the story of his life.

Riitta had made off up the beach track now, so they nodded goodbye, one fisherman to another. Or was it?

Onni followed his granddaughter, padding his way towards the quiet car park, where a windsock swayed in the light offshore breeze. Riitta had climbed solemnly into the front passenger seat.

Onni took his time packing the gear away in the shed. Inside, Alva was almost certainly waiting to accost him. As he shuffled across the lawn in the near-darkness, Onni stopped to take in the scene before him—his life, at fifty-five. It was a small but sturdy house, which held within its walls his steady and adequate wife. His one daughter, his one granddaughter.

Somehow, it wasn't enough.

When he finally pulled open the screen door, Riitta was sitting at the kitchen table with a plate of sausages and mashed potato. She seemed okay.

'Well, how did you go?' asked Alva.

'No luck,' he said. 'A stingray came up on Riitta's line, and that was all.'

She nodded. The moment almost ticked by, but then he heard Riitta's small, proud voice. 'I took the hook out.'

Alva paused, and Onni felt her gaze drilling down into him.

'A stingray?' asked Alva.

Riitta nodded to her dinner.

'What on earth were you thinking?' hissed Alva later, once Riitta was tucked into bed. The girl's mother was out—working her usual weekend night shift at the hospital.

'She's fine.'

'It could've gone badly.'

'It didn't.'

She shook her head, and her thin, greying hair sat flat and lifeless on her skull.

'It'll toughen her up,' he tried.

'Sometimes I don't understand you, Onni.'

Truth be told, neither did he. But at the time it had seemed important, crucial even, that Riitta do it.

Driving across the bay bridge early on Monday morning, before making the turn inland, Onni saw the oyster farmers slowly moving about on the steaming river. Once, not too long ago, he had considered buying an oyster lease, and he almost did, but the construction of the Parliament House was starting up, and he thought he might be part of something. Of history-making. Day to day, on the ground, it didn't feel much like that. It felt like work in a way that crayfishing never had.

Riitta had woken early that morning, pulling herself out of bed to have breakfast with him in the hour before sunrise.

'Keep sleeping,' he'd suggested, but she stubbornly sat herself down at the kitchen table with him, her nightdress loose across her small shoulders. Her eyes, struggling to peel open, and the morning scent of her. Children were especially soft and innocent in the morning. Onni dolloped some watery porridge into a bowl for her.

'Have some fruit,' he said, roughly chopping some strawberries. 'Eat them all.' And he offered her the cinnamon shaker as an added treat.

It was easier to show his affection in this way.

Once he had packed his bag, Riitta helped him load his tools into the back of the Land Cruiser.

The following weekend, Onni did not return to the coast on Friday. He and Jouko had gone in on a dredge pump together. That Saturday, they lifted it onto a trailer and took it down to Little Snowball Creek. There had been a small rush down there in the late eighteen hundreds—real likely country, they called it, with some heavy nuggets and slugs to be got for those with the right amount of energy and perseverance. Weekend prospectors still visited the area, looking for leftovers. The seasonal waterway was currently more of a rivulet, shallow and muddy and dried up in parts. The alluvial soils, Onni knew, were made up of shale, fine-grained sandstone and quartzite.

'This will do,' said Onni.

'Or down there,' suggested Jouko.

'Or perhaps in that bend in the river.'

Who knew?

At last they decided, arbitrarily, on a spot.

As he waded into the shallows of the freshwater stream, Onni was aware of a kernel inside him, from which some hope trickled. Perhaps he could still get lucky?

The growl of the pump and the smell of petrol were welcome accompaniments to the work. He'd missed those sounds. The sounds of industry laced with the gurgle of water.

'Riitta was inconsolable,' said Alva on the phone on Sunday night, 'when she heard you weren't coming.'

He wondered briefly whether Alva was just talking about the girl.

'I'm sure she forgot about it soon enough,' he said.

'Not all that shines is gold, Onni,' said Alva.

On the bench before him sat the repurposed Vegemite jar. A few shards of gold could be seen, glinting among the grit. They were tiny fragments. He was reminded of little Riitta down in the shed. Balancing on the sawhorse in the dappled sunlight.

You won't die soon, will you, Ukki? she'd asked. *Because we still have lots to do.*

Vihta

RIITTA FOLLOWED THE THREE WOMEN into the sauna. It was a procession of bare bottoms, white, fleshy and dimpled. Mummu entered first, followed by Riitta's own mother, and then Helvi, Mummu's best friend, the artist, who was visiting from out west.

'*Naisten vuoro,*' said Helvi, with a wink over her shoulder towards Riitta. Women's turn.

As she sat on the wooden bench, Riitta inhaled the pinewood scent of the small room. Ukki had converted it a few years ago, when Riitta and her mother had finally moved into their own place and all three bedrooms were no longer needed. Ukki wasn't fussed about saunas, but Mummu loved them, and had one every Saturday night.

Now, Riitta's goosepimpled skin welcomed the touch of the dry heat, rising from the hot stones in the *kiuas*. When undressing, she had attempted to hide her pubic hair from view, but now, enveloped in the relative darkness of the sauna, and with Helvi's words on her mind, Riitta found she could relax. She let the muscles in her thighs loosen; she allowed her hands, which had been clasped across her lap, to fall, palms up, at her sides.

Women's turn, she repeated to herself. Was she one of them? Up to now, Riitta had not welcomed the arrival of womanhood, keeping her new self hidden beneath her baggy boy's shirt and shorts. When her period came, she had looked at the blood with resignation. She knew she could not slow this progress any more than she could stop Mummu and Ukki from getting old.

Mummu, Helvi and Mum were arranged along the top rung, while Riitta sat on the middle one. She was only half a Finn, and being in the sauna always reminded her of this. She couldn't handle the heat.

From her place, Riitta stole glances at the two old women. She could just make out the large mounds of hair at their crotches, and their nipples, plum red, standing high and proud on their soft, wide breasts.

'*Kato minkälainen pyöreä pulla minustakin on tullut,*' said Mummu to Helvi, gripping the loose skin at her waist. Look at what a round *pulla* I've become.

'*Ja minä kans, Laurin arpi piilossa läskikasassa,*' replied Helvi.

She was pulling taut the layers of flesh below her own navel. Riitta had only partly understood Helvi's comment: something was hiding under the fat. In the dim light she thought she saw the suggestion of a scar, like a small snake below the skin.

The two of them chuckled.

They hadn't seen each other in a long time. Mummu had marked the day of Helvi's arrival on the calendar with an X, and had been checking off the days as the visit drew closer. Ukki had made fun of her: '*Niinkö morsian olis tulossa,*' he teased. '*Kato,*

Mummu on niin jännittynyt että vapisee kuin haavan lehti.' It's as if her bride were on the way. Look, Mummu's so excited she's trembling like an aspen leaf.

Riitta had joined her grandmother to look silently through the old black and white photographs from the islands. Mummu had stared a long time at the one of her and Helvi gutting fish by the water, scarves tied around their heads, framing their younger faces. Riitta knew the place as though she had been there herself. She thought about how she might have been an island child—but was not.

Three types of sweets had been prepared and arranged on the coffee table before they left to collect Helvi from the airport. Mum didn't come. 'You two have a lot of catching up to do,' she'd said, in a detached tone. She was right; on the way home, Mummu talked and talked. She seemed livelier, a woman, rather than a grandmother. Helvi brought news of their old friends and acquaintances, running through a string of Finnish surnames, some familiar, some not. Someone had been married; someone else had been divorced; a man called Esko had died, which was a sad state of affairs, but meant their friend Petra was finally free. Riitta, dozing in the back as they navigated the mountain bends, could have listened to their voices go on forever.

'What's a *laurinarpi*?' Riitta asked. She had almost swallowed the question, but somehow it felt right to join the conversation there in the sauna.

'My Lauri scar,' translated Helvi, and Riitta realised she had rolled the two words together. She could follow most, but not all, of Helvi's singsong Finnish.

'When I was giving birth to Lauri,' said Helvi, 'he got stuck, and at the very last they decided to cut me open and bring him out this way. So now I have scars in both places. Here, and down there.' She pointed to the place between her thighs. 'One from each boy.'

'Oh.'

'When I was younger, I thought it was best not to know what awaited you,' said Helvi, 'but I've changed my mind. We don't talk enough about it, about what happens to our bodies during childbirth, or afterwards, for that matter.'

'*Totta, pissakin menee housuihin,*' said Mummu. That's true, you even piddle your pants.

'*Hyi, Mummu,*' laughed Riitta. But it seemed it was no laughing matter.

'You recover,' said Helvi, 'of course you do. It is the toughest of all body parts.' She pointed, again, down there. 'But you are scarred.'

'At that moment,' added Mum, 'you don't care. It's like collateral damage. All you want is for your baby to be all right.'

Riitta wondered about the injuries she might have inflicted on her way into the world.

'You want them to be perfect,' said Helvi. 'Lauri came out hollering, and he didn't stop, do you remember, Alva? He hollered for a year. I've since thought it would have been easier if I were the deaf one.'

There was a moment of quiet. The temperature was slowly increasing, but it was still manageable.

'Was Lauri born deaf?' asked Riitta.

At first Helvi didn't answer. The stones in the *kiuas* sizzled and groaned.

'He began to lose his hearing at around the age of five,' said Helvi.

Riitta could hardly fathom it, not hearing. 'Poor Lauri,' she said.

To her right, Mum shifted on the timber bench. She reached for the ladle and tossed a small amount of water on the stones. The vapour rose, clouding the room, and the temperature climbed a notch or two. A bead of sweat trickled from Riitta's hairline, between her eyebrows and onto the tip of her nose, where it hung, poised. Now it was really getting hot, and Riitta had to fight the urge to move down to the lowest bench, the children's seat. She was reminded of a recent science class. They had been learning about thermal energy and how it worked. A rise in temperature, she had copied down into her notebook, causes atoms and molecules to move faster and collide with one another.

'*Minulla on kuuma, menen ulos vilvoittelemaan,*' said Mum. I'm hot, I'm going out to cool off.

It wasn't like her—Mum usually lasted the longest.

Riitta savoured the rush of cold air as the heavy door was momentarily opened. Helvi countered the intrusion by tossing another ladle of water on the *kiuas*. Letting out a sigh, she returned to the subject of Lauri.

'I've come to believe that in life things have a tendency towards equilibrium. Something is taken from you, and another thing given,' she said.

Riitta waited.

'Lauri lost his hearing in part, yes,' continued Helvi, 'but he gained something in all that. A secret sense. He is more aware of the world around him than anyone I know. For a while, I wanted to fix him. I thought it was his vision that might sharpen, to compensate, but now I think he learned to listen with his body in a way that the rest of us don't know how.'

'It was your vision that sharpened,' said Mummu.

'When you're a mum,' said Helvi, 'it's hard to accept that your child is different. And you want to blame someone, anyone.' Her serious eyes locked with Mummu's. 'Then you find the fault in yourself.'

'When we were little, we were taught that everything happens because of a sin, but as you get older you can't believe that anymore,' said Mummu.

'*Tulee aivan omia sanojani rouvan suusta,*' Helvi quipped. Sounds like my very own words coming out of madam's mouth.

'You're not guilty in this,' said Mummu, keeping her sombre tone.

'No, but I've behaved badly at times.'

'As have I.'

They both let out a long, loud exhale, as if to exorcise from their bodies some unwanted thing.

'*Joka vanhoja muistelee sitä tikulla silmään,*' said Helvi. A poke in the eye for one who dwells on the past.

The conversation had turned a corner into a more adult place, and Riitta felt left behind. The heat, she noticed now, had reached an agonising level. How the two women remained on the top bench Riitta didn't know. She felt separate to them, on her low rung.

'Honey,' said Helvi, 'go and fill up the bucket with cold water and bring that mother of yours back in here with you.'

Riitta left the sauna and went through the washroom. She found her mother sitting naked on the cooling bench outside, her shoulders hunched. If only she wouldn't sit like that.

'What are you doing, Mum?'

'Just getting some air.'

Riitta sat beside her, her back straight, as if to counteract her mum's pose. Vapour rose from Riitta's skin in the frosty evening; she felt the heat swiftly leaving her body.

'Aren't you cold yet?'

'Getting there.'

'Helvi said we have to fill this bucket with water and then go back in.'

Mum complied. They returned through the washroom, pausing to fill the bucket to the brim. Riitta heaved it across the threshold and into the sauna.

'*Hyvät tytöt,*' said Helvi. Good girls.

She threw two full ladles of water onto the *kiuas*, and a great amount of steam rose from the hot stones. The temperature soared.

'*Kuka on ensimmäinen?*' asked Helvi. Who's first?

In her hand she held the *vihta*, a bundle of silver birch branches that she and Riitta had prepared earlier. Mummu didn't usually bother with a *vihta* in the sauna, but Helvi insisted. To begin with she had made the twine, taking a thin metre-long branch and peeling the bark away using Riitta's special pocketknife. Helvi had been sitting on a tree stump in the yard, while Riitta sat cross-legged at her feet. She watched Helvi's small, creased hands twist the branch this way and that, to make it flexible, she explained.

'Finns weren't easy to convert to Christianity,' Helvi had told her as she worked the branch. 'Paganism was in our blood. We were dogged by nature, and fought tooth and nail to keep our own language. Other traditions persisted too, like *Juhannus*. It used to be called the celebration of Ukko, the god of thunder.'

Riitta loved building the *Juhannus kokko* with Ukki each year. They'd scour the bush, collecting logs and branches, then they'd raid the shed, pulling out old timber cuttings and broken furniture. It was the hurling of the wood onto the pile of tinder that was most fun. And then the whoosh and roar when the fire was lit.

'They used to say the more liquor consumed over *Juhannus*, the better the harvest would be that coming season.' Helvi grinned. 'They certainly had some excuses for it.'

This year, Ukki had allowed Riitta half a glass of beer. They'd sat in folding chairs by the raging flames, sharing a fat sausage he'd cooked in foil on the coals, and sipping on their beers. '*Hölökyn kölökyn*,' Ukki had said, raising his glass. It was gibberish, but it kind of meant 'Cheers'.

Once the twine was ready, Helvi placed it on the grass beside her and stood. She circled the birch tree, selecting several young limbs and snapping them off in an easy, proficient motion. Together they removed the lower leaves of each branch.

'In the end,' Helvi continued, 'the missionaries relented, and paganism was incorporated into the Christian tradition.' She took the collection of branches and bundled them together, tying them off using the bark twine.

'And we went to church, like good Christians, and then we went home and practised our rituals. Like this one.'

The branches, now bound tightly together, resembled a squat broom.

'Maybe that's what taught us to be diplomatic,' she said. 'Stubborn, but in the end aiming for compromise.'

Before Helvi had arrived, Riitta had asked Mummu what she was like.

'She's the smartest person I know,' Mummu had said, 'and if she'd stayed in Finland, she probably would have been a professor.'

Riitta had asked her mum too.

'She's Mummu's favourite person in the whole world.'

Back in the sauna, Helvi instructed: 'Head down, Hilda.'

Mum bowed her head. Helvi dipped the *vihta* into the bucket of water and brought it down on Mum's back. She beat her gently at first, sending droplets of water flying in all directions. The sweet, woody scent of birch filled the room, and with it, Riitta felt her airways expand. Soon the beating at her side became more vigorous. Up and down the *vihta* went, the leaves slapping Mum's skin with increasing violence.

'*Riittääkö?*' asked Helvi. Enough?

'*Ei,*' replied Mum, '*lisää.*' More.

After some time, they swapped places, and Hilda began to beat Helvi with the *vihta*.

'*Kunnolla, tyttö,*' said Helvi. Properly, girl.

So Mum did it harder, and Riitta noticed small red welts beginning to form on Helvi's back.

When her mother began to beat Mummu with the *vihta*, Riitta averted her eyes. Whatever was happening here, she wished it to be over.

At last, Mum dropped the bundle of branches and Mummu straightened up. There was a moment of quiet.

'Riitta's turn,' said Helvi.

Riitta bowed her head. For her, Helvi did it softly, and it wasn't the same. While the branches were brought down on her back, Riitta recalled something a boy had said to her back in primary school: 'I heard the Finns like to get naked in the sauna and whip each other with branches.' She'd given him her annoyed look. 'No, they don't,' she'd lied.

With each gentle hit, Riitta's thoughts dissipated. Then it was just the rhythmic beating of the branches against her spine. Thwack, thwack, thwack. When she raised her head, leaning back against the warm timber wall, she was aware only of the blood pumping through her veins, of the hot and cold sensations mingling on her exposed skin.

'*Tyttö, tänne akkojen kans*,' said Helvi. Girl, up here with the hags.

She wouldn't have done it if it was just her mum and mummu, but she had to, because it was Helvi.

'*Nyt otetaan kunnon löylyt*.' Now let's take the hard heat.

Helvi threw several ladles onto the stones, and the heat rose thick and fast. Riitta flexed her nostrils with each in-breath, but the air was too dense. She opened her mouth and gulped the heat into her lungs. She couldn't stand another minute.

'*No niin*,' said Helvi. Okay, it's time.

Helvi lifted the bucket with two hands. She groaned with the effort of it.

'*Painaa kuin synti*,' she said. It weighs like sin.

She doused each of them in turn, including herself. When the cold struck Riitta's skin the relief was sudden and immense. Helvi,

Mummu and Mum had begun to shriek and laugh, and Riitta, with her wet hair dripping into her eyes, could only join them.

'At higher temperatures, particles have more energy,' Riitta's teacher had said. 'When they meet, hotter particles collide with cooler ones, transferring their energy across until a balance is reached.' Riitta had pictured a frenzy of bumping and clashing, ahead of a stillness. Thermal equilibrium, he had called it.

Swimmer

EACH MORNING WHEN ALVA WALKED the short white curve of the Cove, she stopped for a few moments to watch a swimmer. She noticed the long clean arcs of the woman's overarm stroke. The feet kicking endlessly behind, like a small motor pushing the vessel onwards. She was a graceful swimmer, and Alva felt a yearning of sorts. What for, exactly? Not the woman, no. It was something about the simple dynamics of movement. The lovely, gliding-forward motion.

Alva had missed out on swimming.

And it was only now, in her seventies, that it hit her.

To think: a fisherman's wife who couldn't swim! But it was not so uncommon, all things considered. Back on the islands, there were many migrant fishermen who never learned to swim. It was not in their blood. Hilda and the other kids, they'd learned to swim as they learned to walk, just as they had learned English together with their mother tongue. The kids became Australian in a way their parents never would. They, the children, inhabited a separate world from the halfway place she and Onni and the other migrants occupied.

This is what Alva thought, as she stood and watched the swimmer.

Mind you, Alva was no stranger to the sea. She went in the water every day, right through the winter months. Oh, how she loved it: how it cleared her mind and calmed her nerves. In the water, even her hands stopped shaking. And the feeling of salt, dried crusty on her back and shoulders afterwards. Ah yes, this was the best gift that Australia offered: the wide blue ocean. It was in a league of its own compared with the ashen Gulf of Finland. Strange, thought Alva, that in a country so vast and brown, all bush and desert, it was the thin margin of coast that held the most appeal for her. But although she loved the water, Alva always remained in the shallows, walking her arms along the sea floor like a fat, sluggish cray. She envied, now, the self-assured way that woman moved through the water. She wanted to swim too.

But she was an old woman. It was too late for silly fancies like that.

Some days her daughter joined her on her morning walk. They stopped briefly at the far corner of the beach, about to turn and loop back the way they had come. The Cove, like a white brushstroke at the northern edge of the town, was sheltered from the southerly wind. It was almost always calm there. Compared to the Abrolhos, this was a tame place.

Alva paused, observing the swimmer again.

'I would've liked to do that,' she confided.

Hilda followed her gaze.

'It's not too late, Mum. You're not dead yet, you know.'

Alva grimaced. No, but it wouldn't be long now, she was sure. Alva feared, had always feared, the coming of the illness that had killed her mother. She could hardly believe she'd grown old. Death was always circling, a dark shadow that lurked just out of view.

'I could teach you,' said Hilda then.

The thought made Alva embarrassed. 'No, no, I wouldn't put you through that.'

They entered the water, the idea playing on Alva's mind. *Yes, she wanted to say now. Yes, yes, please teach me.* But Hilda had better things to do. She had her work, Riitta, and that bloke. Alva hoped this one would be a grown-up. Hilda had a way of picking them, these half-baked men, beginning with the first one, Randle. She remembered it clearly: the day Hilda told her about the baby. All that had passed between them but was not said. In Hilda's eyes, a stubbornness, a wilful rebellion, but also pity. Pity for her ignorant migrant mother who didn't know about her world. It was true, Alva hadn't known about anything. She'd felt like a fool here from the beginning, and the feeling had never gone away. She'd watched as Hilda learned English. It had been as if they were on two separate trains running side by side, and Hilda's train had sped ahead while Alva's had chugged at walking pace along the tracks.

Now, Alva waded into the water, goosebumps spreading out across her thighs. The landscape of her skin, changing from smooth to bumpy, reminded her of the sea's ruffled surface as a southerly buster made its way up the coast. The immediacy of the change always surprised her. How different the world felt from one moment to the next. She thought of it as a rearranging of the elements.

When the waterline reached her thighs, Alva lay down into it, while Hilda waded on into deeper water. After some time, without words or gestures, Hilda returned to her mother and took her hands, pulling her out, just a few strides. And in that way it was decided.

'I'm going to teach Mum to swim,' said Hilda.

They were sitting on the front verandah, Onni on his folding chair, legs crossed at the ankles. He was bald, with deep-set eyes that had kept their oceanic sheen despite his advancing years. Onni looked up from the *Telegraph*, his gaze skipping from daughter to wife.

'*Onkohan se jätetty liian myöhään?*' he said. Haven't you left it a bit late? Then, in English: 'Like Aussie say. Old dog no learn the new trick.'

'*Niin, ehkä.*' Sure, perhaps.

Alva resigned herself to it briefly, until Hilda came to her defence.

'*Mutta, kyllähan se Äiti yrittää saa,*' she said. Mum can try.

The sun was warm for April.

Alva wore her floral bathers and a swim cap. She was happy. How lovely it would be, to share these mornings with her daughter. It had been some time since they'd done something together, just the two of them. As she pulled the rubber of the swim cap over her ears she looked up and caught something in Hilda's expression. Her half-smile as she stole a glance at her ageing mother. Was it a sympathetic look?

'What?'

'Nothing. You look sweet. And a bit daggy.'

Alva laughed it off, but she felt diminished. The radiant feeling slipped away, and she padded uneasily towards the water.

The first task was to get her feeling comfortable a little further out, Hilda said. She had to learn to tread water, to swim on the spot. Her daughter coaxed her onwards, until the waterline cut across her chest and underarms. Following Hilda's commands, Alva lifted her feet tentatively off the sea floor and practised doing circles with her legs. She did the movements as instructed, but while Hilda's body seemed made of air, hers was as heavy as rock. Alva's head began to slip lower and lower, and in a sudden panic, she froze. Her eyes bulged, clinging to the vision of the sky above. The sky, the sky. Blue and cloudless and life-giving. She sucked in air, then water. There was the feeling of being lifted. Strong hands, securing her beneath her underarms and hoisting her upwards. Orange sunlight colouring her vision as she broke the surface and looked through watery eyes at Hilda. Like a terrified child, Alva clung to her daughter's shoulder.

'You can still touch here, Mum,' Hilda said, laughing. 'Just put your feet on the ground if you start sinking.'

Once recovered, Alva stood with her arms hanging limply at her sides. She was a wet rag, a useless thing.

'Äiti never learn,' she said, shaking her head left to right.

She'd started saying it years ago, about the time that Hilda's English had surpassed her own. She'd say it in a self-mocking tone, if she misused a word or pronounced it incorrectly, which often happened. It was said in jest, of course, but many insecurities were buried within those words. She battled an ever-increasing sense of her own foolishness.

'Äiti never learn,' she repeated.

'Mum, you'll learn. It'll just take time.'

Onni was on his way out when they got back. The two women brushed the sand from their feet on the lawn. Alva was disappointed in her efforts. She hoped Onni would not ask how it had gone. He paused briefly at the front door.

'I took the old esky apart,' he said, looking at Hilda rather than Alva. 'I left the foam lid on the back deck. She can use it as a kickboard. Get her feet going.'

Then he was off, and Alva had to hide her smile.

Holding the esky lid out in front, Alva attempted the motion of kicking. She remembered the woman who swam the length of the Cove each morning, how the water boiled around her feet like an outboard motor. A constant driving force. But the back half of Alva's body did not want to stay afloat. As though her feet were tied with sinkers, she remained in an L-shape. A ridiculous hunchbacked swimmer. It was then that Hilda put her arms underneath her mother's belly, palms up, as though carrying a load of wood or a sleeping child. Alva was sheepish. Aware of her round belly resting on her daughter's long, slim arms. The physical closeness was disconcerting, strange yet familiar. They had not touched in this way for many years. Alva thought of putting a stop to it, but a minute or so passed and the awkwardness dissolved. Her feet magically rose up. The blue skin of ocean stretched out before her; a gull squawked overhead; the sun shone and the water bubbled at her feet.

For Alva, the world seemed to shift. Suddenly, the sea was on top, and the sky under.

A rearranging of the elements.

Slowly, slowly, Alva learned to keep her body afloat. With her arms outstretched, holding firm to Onni's bit of foam, she made her body a straight line. Then she learned to dog paddle, pushing the water around in small scoops. Cupping her hands like paddles or oars, she spurred herself forwards. You had to keep moving, that was the key. But not in any old way, no; you couldn't just flail around out there. You had to use your body to your advantage. You had to make your body flat and taut, so the water would hold you like a hull, and keep your feet long and pointed and moving in unison, like a propeller. Soon, Alva's dog paddles became the wide sweeping motions of breaststroke. Her movements were no longer those of the grounded, scuttling cray, but those of a swimmer, broad and flowing.

Success.

It was a shared victory, and that made it all the more sweet.

Alva sat with Onni on the verandah, looking out at the quiet street. Nothing moved. She had grown fond of Sunpatch over the years. It was a good place, and they'd found some other Finns in the region.

Onni closed his eyes and let his head tilt back against the white bricks of his house. He'd begun to slow down recently, sitting for long periods, taking pleasure in small sensations, like the winter sun warm on his eyelids. Onni didn't seem bothered by the idea of getting old. He didn't seem to be afraid of dying, like she was.

Now, Alva noticed a few coral-coloured flowers on the Geraldton wax, and her mind went to the west.

'I'd like to go back,' she said, after a moment.

Onni slowly opened his eyes, adjusting to the brightness. '*Suomi?*' Finland?

'No, to the islands.'

'Why now, Alva?'

'Now that I'm a swimmer.' She declared it proudly.

'What's the difference, swimming here, swimming there?'

'I'd have liked to swim there. In the lagoon off Leo's Island.'

'We've had our time there. No need to go back. You're always looking back.'

It was true. Alva had spent her life looking back, wondering whether each decision to move on had been the right one. Didn't all migrants feel like this, at least a little? Once untethered from your mooring, you somehow always remained adrift.

Alva and Hilda swam in line. They made their way slowly from one end of the Cove to the other. A secret smile unfurling on both faces. Eventually Hilda took off, in overarm—she wanted to do a few final laps at speed. Alva watched her daughter surge onwards. A thin, wilful woman, with a grown child of her own. Hilda was forever rushing from one thing to the next. But perhaps she and Onni had been that way too, when they were younger. For a short while now, thought Alva, they might swim side by side, mother and daughter, but then Hilda would go on ahead. It was the natural order of things. Alva had already noticed the way Hilda was taking control. Organising this and that. Making the appointment with Dr Singh. Hilda had reassured her that he would be patient. That she could interpret if need be. That he wouldn't mind her tremor. Alva thought all of this with a mixture of pride and regret. Had so many years really passed?

It was on a winter's morning, when steam rose from the sea—now warmer than the June air—and hung suspended above it, that two things happened. Alva made it, alone and swimming in overarm, to the end of the Cove and back again without stopping. A full lap. By herself. Out where she couldn't touch the sea floor. Moving freely through water, Alva had recalled the feel of the *potkukelkka* from so many years ago, when, after begging for firewood, her old aunt had let the sled gain speed, gliding down the hill to home. Elated, her heart swelling, she waded back to shore, and there, as she dried herself with her towel and looked out over the rising mist, she felt the first real pains.

Ash

IT HAD TAKEN A LOT of coaxing to get the old man to make the journey. In the end it had been their fight that had done it. Hilda could still feel the tension between them, and knew it mostly came from her. Onni had a baffled look stuck on his face, but he would accept her anger quietly, let it run its course. This was not the time to be irritated, she knew. Not now, and not because of a tree. But he shouldn't have done it, her mind insisted.

She looked across at her father. He looked so small and ordinary in his plain t-shirt and baggy shorts, his cheap but comfortable shoes. She wanted to take his hand. Hilda had once heard someone say that you didn't become an adult until you'd lost a parent, but she felt childlike now, lost, confused. She looked down at the stump of her missing finger. You never really got used to it. An amputation. The phantom limb was always there. A reminder that you were not whole, and would never be whole again.

The ashes were above them, in the luggage compartment. Hilda had had to transfer them from the urn to a container to adhere to the airline's weight restrictions. They were in a Tupperware container with a purple lid, which was better than one of those cheap plastic boxes you got from the local takeaway place, Hilda figured. She imagined her mother's essence mingling with the memory of food in the container. The last thing she'd used it for was the leftover spaghetti. But Alva wasn't fancy and she had liked spaghetti.

Hilda sat uneasily, watching Onni's hands in the seat beside her. The skin was dry, blotched an earthy brown. They rested on his knees, and every now and again he would rearrange them. Hilda wondered if he was afraid, like she was. She thought about what she would say to her dad if the plane suddenly plummeted from the sky. She was worried her mind would go blank, and she'd have nothing meaningful to tell him in their last moments. And he'd die thinking she was still cross at him, which she was.

As the plane began its descent over Geraldton, Hilda noticed Onni studying the landscape from his window seat. He had said he was not interested in going back. But there he was, drinking in the layout of the town.

They landed at the regional airport. The same airport from which people were ferried across to the islands in small six-seater planes. Hilda had flown that route many times, when Onni had stayed on the island alone and she and her mother had returned to Geraldton in time for the start of the school term.

Helvi and Risto stood waiting at the gate. Helvi had grown more matronly over the years, but retained a certain elegance. She moved swiftly towards Hilda, embracing her, and this, Hilda realised, brought a flood of relief. The last time they had seen one another was when Riitta was fourteen years old and Helvi had come to visit Alva at Sunpatch.

'Let me see you.' Helvi cupped Hilda's face in her hands and checked her with fierce eyes. 'Alva's girl.'

Hilda watched her father shake hands with Risto. A strong, almost violent handshake that seemed to go on and on. Perhaps something passed between them, too.

They drove along a wide, well-kept highway, passing a sign that read *Welcome to Geraldton*. Long greenhouses lined the sides of the road, and Risto explained that they grew cucumbers there now. Before it had been the Italians who were the growers, now it was the Vietnamese.

The car bumped softly into the driveway at Sunset Beach, where Helvi and Risto now lived.

'So you'll take her out there?' Helvi looked over her shoulder as they made their way along a garden path.

Hilda nodded.

'It's true that she loved the islands,' Helvi said to her own reflection as she pulled open the sliding door, though Hilda sensed some reservation.

Helvi and Risto had done well. Theirs was a two-storey red-brick place a few streets back from the beach. Hilda noticed a speedboat on a trailer parked out the front of the double garage. Inside, some touches of the old country: a *raanu* wall-hanging in the rusty colours of autumn; a rag mat on the kitchen floor; and of course, downstairs, a pinewood-lined sauna.

Hilda's breath caught on seeing the painting in the living room. A grey-blue island scene. The rambling *kivi kämppä* with an old throwaway cot out the front. And in the foreground the ghostly shadow of a woman. The figure was discernible even in its ambiguity.

They started slowly, sipping black coffee and tearing apart pieces of Helvi's *pulla*. The cardamom hijacked Hilda's senses, so that her mother returned to her in a brief flash. At first they talked about grandchildren, about Riitta, who was back home looking after the dog.

'She's a good girl,' Hilda heard her father say.

Yes, she was much more sensible than Hilda had been when she was younger. All of a sudden Hilda felt like apologising to her father. A huge, sweeping apology. But then there was the hard, treeless space that had spread out between them since the episode with the birch. And just as quickly, the feeling was replaced with something else: a thought that he should apologise to her.

The room where they sat had two lounges facing one another, with a low timber coffee table between them. A tall bookshelf covered the far wall, filled with English and Finnish books. Hilda noticed two huge and ancient volumes of *The Kalevala*. The telly was in a different room altogether, and Hilda thought that this—the sitting room—might be what distinguished their lives, Helvi and Risto's, from the lives of her own parents. They'd stayed, and it had turned out to be a good move. Their boys had taken over the cray lease. Ismo and Lauri were still fishing—some of the only Finns left on Little Rat now, Risto told them.

'How are the boys?' asked Hilda.

'They're good,' answered Helvi, touching Hilda's forearm lightly. 'They get along, even after all these years working the boat together. And Lauri's oldest helps now too.'

Hilda desperately wanted to tell Helvi that she'd found the letter, stashed in a shoebox under Alva's bed, but it wasn't the right time.

Risto interrupted: 'A lot of the small guys are selling up. It's all going big.'

'I've heard that Greenough's a place for millionaires now,' Onni said. He was talking about the suburb south of Geraldton. Hilda wondered how much the houses here in Sunset were worth.

'Sure is,' said Risto, 'and it seems we might have built those camps for the sea lions after all.'

The two men launched into reminiscence.

'You remember, Onni? Back then you were allowed two hundred pots per man, whatever the size of your boat.'

'There was a limit on the size of your pot,' added Onni. 'Can't remember what it was.'

Neither could Risto.

'You'd lay them about every three feet.'

Both men had been crayfishermen, so Hilda didn't know why they needed to explain the trade to one another now.

'Remember someone tried super pots?'

'They weren't much good.'

'Not so many crayfish in the water these days, the boys tell me.'

'No?' asked Onni.

'Remember the water was teeming with them?' said Risto. 'You could walk out the door of your camp at night, stick your hand in the water and pull up a crayfish.'

Onni laughed. 'It wasn't that easy.'

'Maybe not.'

'I had two boats for a while there, after I bought the new one,' said Onni. 'That was about as glorious as it got for me.'

Hilda saw her father's life's work, assembled beside Risto's for all to see.

'No matter. A man gets old regardless, and there's no glory in that,' Onni said next. 'Whatever you've got, you have to give it up. That's what it's like. When you're young you're on the go, and better not to know the ending.'

The decades, thought Hilda, like sandpaper, had worn down the edges of her father's wanting, of his ambition, of thinking, *I'll go there, I'll do this.* Worn it down to an armchair, with nowhere to go but there.

'You regret giving it up?' asked Risto. 'The lease, I mean?'

'Well, I might've been a rich man.'

'No one would've predicted it. The scale of the boom.'

'No, but the girls wanted to stay.'

'Because you were all happy there,' Helvi interjected.

'But I thought there was money to be made elsewhere,' said Onni, 'and my back was giving me a lot of trouble by then.'

Hilda sensed there was more to it.

'Men worry about the end of the forest,' said Onni. 'Women worry about the end of the world.'

Was it a sort of admission? Hilda watched her dad, his kind face. He'd always been prone to philosophical statements, but more so in his older age.

After a moment, Helvi added: 'That one island was almost ours, wasn't it?'

And they all sat there, remembering, until Helvi said, '*Lauletaan.*' Let's sing.

Their voices started out like lone shadows, dancing separately around the dim room, until they came together, became one being.

Ei kultainen nuoruus
Jää unholaan
Vaan muistoissain jälleen
Sen luoksein saan.

My golden youth
Shall not be forgotten
When in my memories
It remains.

Later, Hilda helped Helvi clear up.

'I wonder why you're taking her all the way back there,' said Helvi, as she loaded the coffee cups and saucers into the dish-washer. 'Your lives are in the east now.'

'She loved it there,' said Hilda. 'Those were her best years.'

Moving about the kitchen with her mother's best friend, Hilda felt a sense of calm settle over her. No one else understood like Helvi. Only they knew. It was a conspiratorial thing, because Alva had kept her inner life hidden from all but a select few.

'I remember your mum had a set of beautiful glasses from Finland. *Riihimäen lasit*. A wedding gift, I think. Probably the nicest thing she owned back then. She had them sent over a few years after they migrated. But she never unpacked them. They stayed in the box all those years at the house in Bluff Point. You made the move over to the east coast, and finally, there, she unpacked them.'

Hilda smiled; she knew the set of glasses Helvi described. They were kept in the cluttered kitchen cupboard at her parents' place, with all the other mismatched kitchenware. There was a chip on the rim of one of the glasses, she remembered. They used them every day.

'I don't know if that's because she felt settled,' said Hilda, 'or because she knew she never really would.'

'You know, Hilda, back in Finland we had a saying: *Rapakon takana*. If someone went away, went out into the world, we used to say they'd gone to find out what was beyond the swamp. To think of your mum, coming all the way out here. All the cards were stacked against her. They were poor. I mean, *really* poor, Hilda. I saw it with my own eyes when I visited her home village. But she did it. That little girl from Toholampi, from that tiny falling-down cottage where all they had to eat through the winter were potatoes. She was brave enough to venture beyond the swamp.'

Hilda smiled. She was proud of her mum, but she also knew how much Alva had struggled.

'Those who stayed, they always knew where home was. Mum got a bit lost, I think.'

'Maybe so.'

'But like you said before, on the islands we were all happy.'

'There's just so much water out there,' said Helvi, returning to the matter of the ashes.

'Yes,' said Hilda, 'but she learned to swim just last year.'

Hilda wanted to remember this version of her mother. Alva dripping wet, an exultant smile on her face, her chest puffed out ever so slightly. But the image that returned more often was that of Alva in the weeks before her death. On their last outing to the Cove. A tall, thin ghost of a woman, long limbs folded into the wheelchair. To look at her was almost frightening. They'd had to settle themselves down on the grass overlooking the beach, because Alva was confined to the chair by then and it was too difficult to bring her down onto the sand. She'd made an odd comment that day, as her watering eyes looked out at the inevitable sea. 'It wasn't your fault,' she'd said, curling her dry hand around the stump of Hilda's missing finger. 'I shouldn't have let you punish yourself for it.' But Alva had become confused in those last weeks and you couldn't be sure what she meant by the things she said. Hilda remembered speaking to her after a rare dust storm had come through from the west, colouring everything an apocalyptic orange. 'The dust,' her mother had said, 'has covered everything in white. *Tulee kylmä, pitäis hakea puita.*' The cold is coming, we should collect some wood.

That night Hilda lay in the single bed in one of the guest rooms. She thought about her mum and her glassware. Didn't we all do that with our most cherished possessions? Keep them carefully wrapped and stored, saving them for a better day?

Helvi knocked on the door on her way down the hall. She sat beside Hilda, looking like she might tuck her into bed. Hilda would not have minded.

'Mum never told me,' she blurted. 'I found the letter you wrote her back when Lauri first got his diagnosis.'

Hilda had been going through Alva's things, sorting them for Dad, she told herself, when she came across the collection of letters. She had struggled through Helvi's scrawling longhand, decoding the revelation:

Dearest Alva,

It's been a good year out here again. There seems no stopping the hunger for crays. Ismo is working the boat with Risto, and Lauri joins them as often as school will allow. Petra and Esko have sold up (or sold what was left) and followed their boys north to Darwin. I hope things work out for them there. Geraldton is windy today, as usual. I've been going to Northampton to paint the wind pushing through the long yellow grass. You remember how beautiful it is out there? Those singular colours, the yellow, the blue, and those majestic gums.

I should have written sooner, but I have been ruminating on the past, wondering if things might have turned out differently. They know more about Lauri's problem now. The doctor says it's hereditary. It comes from the mother's side. That was hard to hear. But there is also some relief in turning the accusation on myself.

I think about all the lost years. I am proud of our friend-ship, Alva, which found a way, despite everything. There is still

time, of course, only now we are separated by a continent, rather
than a sea of unsaid things. Give my love to your girl. The boys
still miss her. And I miss you.

Your friend, Helvi

Hilda had gone over and over it in the subsequent weeks: the
reasons for Alva's silence, why it mattered, why it didn't.

Helvi, in her dressing-gown, studied Hilda's face, as if compre-
hending it all. She stroked her hair as Hilda blinked away tears.
'Sometimes I think we're hardest on those we love best.'

Helvi kissed her on the forehead and left the room.

It wasn't completely true, what Hilda had said just now. Her
mother had told her, in her stubborn way, that afternoon at
the Cove.

Hilda had booked them onto a boat. It only took half an hour
to fly from the mainland to Big Rat, but Hilda wanted to get
her dad back on the water. He was in his seventies now, and had
not been on the sea for over two decades. He had only thrown
his line in from the beach. He reckoned it didn't matter, but it
wasn't right.

The boat would leave the next day, so they had time to look
around Geraldton.

Borrowing Risto's car, they followed the coast road into town.
The railway station was closed—that was where they had the
Sunday market now, Helvi had said. They did a lap of Marine
Parade. The waterfront was new and shiny and manicured.

Well-trimmed grass bordered a bike path that snaked along the foreshore, and kids squealed as they followed each other down the slippery dip at a giant modern playground. Four rock walls reached into the harbour at intervals, and a pontoon floated in the middle.

'No, *onhan siellä täällä tuttuja paikkoja*,' said Onni. Well, here and there, there's some familiar places.

They reached the port. A huge ocean liner was on its way out; it signalled its departure with a long, low belch. Hilda pulled onto the side of the road so that Onni could watch. He was an industry man at heart, after all. Once the vessel neared the outer reaches of the harbour, they continued their tour. The wheat silos were still there, towering above everything, and further along, the fishermen's wharves and the cooperative.

Ahead, the road passed over the railway line and into Port Moore.

Hilda slowed the car as they came upon the red-and-white-striped lighthouse, and that spot where she had lost her virginity. Tufts of saltbush, like sparse pubic hair, lay flattened on the dunes. Beyond them the sea stretched out, wild and white-capped.

'Let's go see our place,' suggested Hilda.

Inside the car, they seemed to inhabit their own spaces, the invisible thing butting up against them.

'No need.'

Onni was not sentimental about the past, or at least he pretended not to be. Hilda thought again of the birch tree. Was her reaction so unreasonable? But it had felt like she'd had to suffer Alva's death twice. She'd been furious when she saw her father's handiwork: a hollow space by the fence line and, in a pile next to the trailer, the corpse of the birch tree, its broken

limbs the colour of ash. In the weeks that followed her mother's
death, Hilda had begun to think of the tree as an embodiment
of Alva herself: a quiet, pale thing that had struggled through
all those years on foreign soil. Drinking up the meagre water
given, needing more, but enduring, only to be hacked down so
unceremoniously. Hilda had damaged the tree herself before
Onni had had his way with it, though she kept that private.
After finding the letter, she'd made her way into the backyard
and broken three of its outer limbs. Then she'd lowered herself
onto the grass and cried.

For Onni, though, things touched or nurtured by Alva did not
carry the spirit of Alva now that she was gone. He laid concrete
over the site of the too-thirsty birch—it seemed he delighted
in concrete—and Hilda stopped talking to him, until at last he
relented. He called to say he would return to the islands with
her to scatter the ashes.

Now, dismissing her dad's reply, Hilda started off towards
their old place. She still knew the way, even after so long. She
took Chapman Road, turned left into Hosken and then right
into Harrison. She brought the car to a stop by the kerb and
felt disorientated as she looked out the window at the spot where
the house used to be. Was this it? Or had she got it wrong after
all? It was just a big empty block, except for a large shed down
the back.

Her father's boatshed.

They were in the right place.

Hilda opened the door and stepped out of the car. She stood
at the edge of the property, the long, dry grass waving hello
in the breeze. The property was a blank slate on which she

conjured their old cottage, and, off to the side, the sleep-out, which was later converted into a sauna. Her mind sketched in her cubbyhouse, built of corrugated iron like an island shack, and covered over in Alva's grapevine. Behind that, her mother's small but successful orchard, and the chook pen adjoining the far end of the boatshed.

She felt the presence of her dad beside her.

'Well, not much left of that,' he said at last.

Hilda noticed small plumes of smoke puffing from gaps between the gutters and the roofsheets of the boatshed.

'What's that smoke about?'

Had they arrived just in time to witness it burn? The only remaining proof of their lives here, of what they had built? Suddenly Hilda began to feel desperate. Not the boatshed—not that, too.

She strode across the vacant block. Behind her, Onni's footsteps were slow and careful as he picked his way over weeds and pig melons. Prickles roughed their ankles.

At the side entrance to the shed, Hilda peered through the opening and saw a feeble campfire that had been lit directly on concrete, billowing an unworthy amount of white smoke, and a figure hunched over it. A mangy fox terrier lunged at them from a short rope nearby. Its incessant yapping echoed through the shed. The man's eyes watered as he called out in a choked-up voice: 'Shut up, Idget.'

The man had the same knotted mane as the dog. He had a brief coughing episode, then staggered towards them and out into the light. Hilda looked into his dark eyes, framed by a sooty face. She guessed he was younger than he looked.

'We used to live here,' she ventured. 'My dad here built this shed.'

The man grunted as he gathered more sticks. It wasn't important to him. He said he'd come on hard times. That's how he and Idget found themselves here.

Idget: not just a term of endearment, apparently. The dog's name.

'She gave herself that title.' He paused and straightened up, but not completely. 'One night she did something really smart and then she did something really dumb. I was shit-faced and I woke up and said, *You idget!*' His beard cracked open, revealing a satisfied smile. 'And that's how she got her name.'

As he spoke, Hilda had been gazing into the boatshed. She saw Onni working on the cray boat—his arms strong and sinewy and sun-darkened—while she, a little girl, sat on a sawhorse watching him. She remembered him finding a task for her. He'd bring her several nails and two pieces of timber, so that she might practise her technique with the hammer. A fleck of ash floated past her and settled on her father's shirt before disintegrating.

It was hard to know how to respond to the man's story. Instead, she took stock once more of the shed.

'Don't die of smoke inhalation now,' she warned, but he didn't seem worried about that.

Afterwards, they sat in the car quietly, each studying their own hands.

'*Kyllä sillä sisua oli,*' Onni said. '*Lähti tännekin. Yritti tehdä jotain tästä.*' She sure had *sisu*. Came here even. Tried to make something of this.

His eyes danced across the vacant block.

Alva's absence was all around them, but there was something else too, the foretelling of a future with no mark of theirs in it. Why had she insisted on it, on defeating him with this? Hilda felt a welling in her throat, a hot wave of regret creeping up her body.

'*Se on elämää*,' he said. That's life.

Onni reached for her hand then, briefly, and Hilda realised that it was he who comforted her, not the other way around. His calm eyes said that he had accepted life's impermanence in a way she had not. But being there at the property, witnessing the land's return to its former self, she saw that nothing was solid. She saw the spectre of their lives dancing before them: the house that Onni built; the shed encasing their old cray boat; the gardens Alva had tended. Everything you made was eventually undone by time or the elements or by those who came after you. The birch is gone, she told herself, and soon this boatshed will come down too. Beside her, her old dad persisted, a leftover thing. The skin of his hand, which had reassured her a moment ago, was ashen and brittle, paper-thin. But blood courses through it yet, she told herself.

'*Mennään, Isä.*' Let's go, Dad.

The man now stood at the entrance of the boatshed, his little yapping dog by his side. He waved goodbye with a toothless grin. Behind him, at the blurred boundary between this property and the next, there was a lone, straggly tree, bowed from a lifetime of southerly winds. It must have been one of old Mr Vella's olives.

Tinnie

RIITTA WAS NAMED AFTER A BOAT.

It usually happened the other way around. The thing was, there was never any boat. It was the boat of Mum's imaginings, of her hopes and dreams. Sometimes Riitta wondered if Mum would've preferred the boat.

This was what Riitta thought as she watched Mum and Ukki drive off, headed back to the islands. Mum's first love affair, and the boat the baby that never was. Riitta was the child of a second union, with the civilised east.

'Well,' she said to the German shepherd at her heel, 'it's just you and me, mate.'

Down at the Cove, Riitta threw a stick and watched the dog hurtle towards it, a flurry of nut-brown fur. Steam escaped her mouth with each out-breath. She crossed her arms and jumped up and down a few times.

'Bloody cold!' she called to a passing walker.

The sea was grey and uninviting. It was still autumn, but winter was baring its teeth. Ukki had asked if she wanted to scatter some of the ashes here. She'd thought about it. This was where Mummu had learned to swim, after all. In the end, she'd decided it wasn't right, to divide someone up like that, half here, half there. Mum said Mummu had always lived like that anyway, it was her condition. But Riitta didn't think that made it right. Let her be whole in death, then.

The service was held at the All Saints' Anglican Church, because there was no Lutheran congregation on the south coast; Mummu's proper church was in the capital, two hundred k away. But it was arranged that the minister, a pious man in his seventies, would drive down to give the liturgy. Ukki had been reluctant to speak to the priest in the first place, and refused many of the traditional components of the service. They'd met with him a few days before the funeral to talk over their plans, Riitta's mum addressing him with over-the-top reverence. She'd set out three types of cake for him, as though his disapproval meant the disapproval of God. Mum, who claimed she was an atheist. The priest offered four hymns, suggesting seven verses of each. Even in the home his inflexion rose and fell with the dramatic and dignified feel of a sermon. The long, drawn-out silences. So that Riitta felt her body slouching beneath the boredom of it all—and this wasn't even the actual event. Ukki was mostly quiet, shifting uncomfortably with each suggestion. And when Mum indulged the man with yet another question about his liturgy,

Riitta felt Ukki's foot swing past her under the table, kicking at her mother. She had to hide her smile.

The minister had mostly ignored her grandfather's wishes, though, and on the day he gave his sermon in the usual way, speaking at the same maddeningly slow pace. Riitta was aware of Ukki's rising impatience.

The service went on and on.

Helvi, who was not able to be there because she was in Finland for an exhibition, had travelled to Mummu's hometown of Toholampi, as a way of saying goodbye, and sent a note to be read at the funeral. She described the tiny cottage, the rocking chair in its place by the window, and the sauna down the back.

It was while sitting on the cold hardwood pew that Riitta felt the arrival of an awful, nameless fear. She looked across at her mother and saw the wrinkles on her neck spreading out like tidelines in the sand, and her breath caught in her throat. Mum must've thought she was upset about Mummu, and grabbed at her, pulling her into a forceful embrace. Those wrinkles evoked a unique terror in Riitta. Looking from the photo of Mummu on the memorial card to Mum's neckline, she felt time speeding away from them. Mummu's death meant that Mum was next, and after that, Riitta herself. It was getting hard to breathe; there wasn't enough oxygen. Life, thought Riitta, is a gasp of air in an eternity of not breathing.

Back at the house, the Finnish women had made pastries and sandwiches, and laid out the food on white linen tablecloths. As if on cue, that very week the Geraldton wax had blossomed in the yard, and Riitta and her mother had arranged sprigs of the delicate pink flowers in vases ahead of the wake.

After the wake, she went back to Shin's house. In bed, she pulled him to her with an uncharacteristic urgency, surprising them both. Shin approached it slowly, thinking that perhaps the moment called for tenderness, but Riitta hurried him along. She put her hand on his as he reached for the condom, but he found it regardless. Afterwards, they sat in bed and there was an awkwardness in the air that had to do with her desire. It had been out of place, after the wake. She wasn't usually like that with him.

Riitta picked up her copy of *The Grapes of Wrath* from the bedside table. She hoped he wouldn't mention it, but he did.

'What was that about?' he asked.

'What? Nothing. It just feels better.' Though she knew it wasn't that. It'd come from somewhere else. It was something to do with Mummu, with Mum. With saying goodbye. It had to do with being around death, she thought now. It made you want life.

Walking with the dog back from the Cove through the flat grid of streets, Riitta snuck a look into the houses she passed. The night was drawing down, and the townsfolk had switched on their lights but were yet to pull their curtains closed. There was the glow of televisions here and there. Two silhouettes moving about a kitchen. Riitta liked glimpsing these houses, their living rooms, as if she might yet figure something out about life, about family. What was hidden behind the windowpanes? What dislocations, lost brothers, disappointments and teen pregnancies? She passed the junk pile out the front of number twenty-three. The place was a dump. There was a scattered collection of pre-loved items for sale in the yard. The skeleton of a lawnmower, two rusty children's bikes with flat tyres, a banged-up tinnie. The boat was laid upside down on the unkempt grass. Boats were in her family once, but that was in another time—before her. In wobbly handwriting a sign read: *All items in very good working order. Offers welcome.*

What a joke.

Riitta thought about all the things that were accumulated and left behind by each of us. She felt sorry for the children of number twenty-three, who would inherit that mess. Luckily for Riitta and her mother, Ukki was the type who wanted to get rid of everything, even the sentimental stuff. She thought briefly of the other side of her family—Dad's side. All those old Holdens decaying in the paddock. A car graveyard, Nan had said, when Riitta visited last summer.

That night, she sat in Ukki's armchair—she claimed it as soon as he was out the door—reading her novel. Had she read them a few months ago, Ma's words might have meant less, but now, Riitta felt a vague recognition:

> They was the time when we was on the lan'. They was a boundary
> to us then. Ol' folks died off, an' little fellas come, an' we was
> always one thing—we was the fambly—kinda whole and clear.
> An' now we ain't clear no more. I can't get straight. They ain't
> nothin' keeps us clear.

She skimmed Ma's words a second time, groping at their meaning. She was still wondering about her urgency after the funeral, still feeling a bit sheepish around Shin.

'Thought you didn't want to do what she did?' he'd said later that night.

'What?' She'd flushed pink. She didn't, she'd said. Did she?

Next day, she was in Mummu and Ukki's bedroom, rifling through Mummu's wardrobe. Her grandmother's one-piece swimsuit dangled from a coathanger in prime position among the winter jackets and dresses. She could almost see the proud ghost of Alva within it. It had been a collective family triumph, when Mummu learned to swim.

Riitta took a long, sheer dress from the rack, the chiffon fabric almost like tissue paper. It was the dress Alva had worn on the ship from Finland on the day it docked at Fremantle Harbour. Her mum had told her the story. Mummu had saved her best item of clothing for that day. Now Alva Saari's only granddaughter pulled the dress over her head, the light fabric falling across her breasts. Gathering up the skirt, she examined herself in the mirror. Shafts of light shone through the lacework, suggestive of the figure beneath. She didn't recall ever seeing Mummu wearing it. Couldn't really imagine it. But once upon a time, her grandmother must have looked something like this. Riitta let her hand fall across the brittle material. How could it be that this dress survived intact while the solid, flesh-and-bones person who had once worn it was now gone completely?

She rummaged through the drawers next, but there was nothing of any significance. What she was looking for she was not quite sure. Riitta got down on her hands and knees and peered under the bed. There was a shoebox at the far end, and she had to get onto her belly and wriggle halfway under to reach it. She sat cross-legged on the floor, Mummu's dress collecting in folds around her. Riitta removed the lid of the shoebox and peered inside.

Letters.

All of them written in Finnish, in the almost indecipherable longhand of Mummu's era.

A cloud of disappointment settled over her, but she sifted through the fragile pages anyway. Some of the letters were from Finland. From Mummu's siblings, Pentti and Aino. But the majority of the letters were from Helvi.

She was returning the papers to the shoebox when a faded photograph slipped free from the stack. It was a photo of her mum, of Hilda as a girl. Maybe fifteen. She was on a boat, her jacket ballooning in the wind, and her hair all over the place. On the back of the photograph was scrawled: *Viimeinen päivä Pikku Rotalla: 12/6/1975*. Last day on Little Rat. Riitta turned the photograph over again and looked into her mother's pale blue eyes. That same girl was pregnant with Riitta not a year later. It didn't seem right. Why didn't Ukki just let her take over the lease? Then she wouldn't have needed that. Wouldn't have needed to have *her*. But studying the photo Riitta did not see her mother, not really. She saw herself. She saw herself in that same boat, hand on the wheel, going one way or another.

Riitta mulled it over for a few days. Took the hound to the beach in the mornings and the evenings. Every time she passed number twenty-three she stole a glance at the pile of saleable items, each apparently in very good working order. On her fourth evening alone at the house, she found Helvi and Risto's number in the little black address book by the phone and dialled. Helvi answered, and Riitta spoke to her in her Australian version of Finnish. 'No, not Mum,' she said. 'I want to talk to Ukki.'

'*Mitäs tyttö?*' Ukki's voice reached her like a gentle pat on the head.

She told him about her plan. 'Reckon it's worth a hundred and fifty dollars?'

'*Joka ostaa hevosen, ostaa taakan,*' Ukki said. Who buys a horse buys a burden.

She didn't care for his sayings right then. 'But is it worth it?'

'It's worth what it's worth.'

She didn't know what he was saying, but he wasn't saying no.

Riitta was passing the notes over and shaking the man's hand before there was time to second-guess herself. No pulling out now. She'd made Shin go with her, and they stumbled beneath the weight of the tinnie. A few small steps at a time. A minute's rest. It was a laborious delivery, and they were huffing and puffing accordingly. It took half an hour to carry the boat around the block to Ukki's place.

'You don't even have a trailer,' said Shin.

'I'll get one.'

'You don't have a boat licence.'

'I'll get one of those too.'

'It's just kind of come out of nowhere.'

'Don't be a naysayer like Ukki,' she told him.

'So Onni agrees that it's a dumb idea?'

'You can't always listen to old people,' Riitta said. 'They're too cautious.'

Ukki was becoming more cautious with age. He used to chuck her in the back of his rattly old Land Cruiser, no belts or proper seating back there, and they'd smash along the sandy track for several kilometres until they came to the deserted tract of beach. They'd spend the late afternoon fishing for flathead. You'd go down right on dusk, when there was a sharp chill in the air and the tide was full. Once you were on the beach, it was a serious, solemn affair. The flathead would be running in the troughs, and when the bottoms of your pants got wet and your toes went numb, you didn't complain.

She remembered when he used to take her down for a swim when she was smaller still. How he sat on the beach watching her. He'd scan the horizon, his hands formed into pretend binoculars, and when she emerged from the water he'd say, *'Ei ollut haikalaa.'* No sharks. And somehow it made her feel safe, comforted by his fisherman's eye. But these days, when Riitta told Ukki she was off to the beach, he would warn her from his sheepskin-lined chair on the front porch: *You've left it too late. Wind's up. Too much swell today. No good.* Mum reckoned it was some kind of ploy. But what for?

A good chunk of Ukki's day was now spent in that chair. Occasionally, Mr Palermo came over from next door and they sat side by side on the porch, watching the quiet, empty street. You couldn't call it conversing. They both spoke broken English, their sentences like badly aimed arrows, never quite connecting with the target. But it didn't seem to matter.

Onni would come around, she thought now, surveying her grand purchase. He always did.

'We need this,' she told Shin. 'Mum and Ukki too.' The fambly needs it, she thought.

'Your grandpa needs a shitty old tinnie to decay in his yard?'

'Just help me carry it over there.' Riitta was pointing to the bare patch of yard where the birch tree used to be. The concrete reached right up to the fence line now. That was Ukki's doing.

They flipped the boat over, leaning it at an angle against the timber palings.

Riitta laid down the final stroke of paint with a satisfying flick of the brush. She'd written the boat's name in cursive along the side of the weather-beaten hull: *Alva*. Ukki always said that boats shouldn't have names, but he didn't get to decide this time. It was only right, considering how Mummu had finally mastered the water. Riitta knew now that it was continuity she was after, a line going forwards. A boat was a child of sorts, she reasoned. Riitta stepped back to survey the tinnie in all its glory. She couldn't wait to show Mum.

Crayfish (red)

ONNI SAARI SEESAWED HIS WAY along the wharf, his daughter herding his old bones onto a boat 'one last time'. He had seen enough of the open sea, enough coral outcrops for one lifetime, he'd told her, but she wasn't discouraged. As the boat left the harbour they stood in silence at her bow, watching the vessel plough through the white-capped water. Salt air rushed his hard-ened cheeks and he secretly gulped it in, turning only when he heard the booming words of the tour guide. A young man in boardshorts and a *Shipwreck Tours* cap stood on the deck with a microphone. Onni strained to make out his speech.

'. . . more beautiful and untouched than the Great Barrier Reef . . . the Abrolhos Islands abound in natural wonders . . . spine-chilling history of shipwreck and mutiny!'

Well then, a tourist boat for an old seadog.

The commotion died down as passengers settled into booths in the cabin. But Onni stayed where he was, wiry hands planted on the railing. He looked ahead, hearing once again the language of water, feeling the ebb and sway of the sea in his rickety joints. A three-hour journey saw them across the line these days. He thought of his wife Alva back in the early sixties making the eight-hour trip across with the tiny baby Hilda. How the swell rocked the carrier boat and Hilda shrieked, a bucket for a dunny and a few craggy, tangle-haired fishermen for company. Ah, but they had been young then, full of quiet spirit and ambition. Onni the old man turned to look east, to gauge their distance from the mainland. He took note of the landmarks he had once used to navigate his way back to Champion Bay: the flat tops of the Moresby Ranges, and the closest of the rises, Mount Fairfax. He waited until the long strip of red-brown country fell below the horizon. It was at that point, they had always agreed, that you entered into another universe. For the Abrolhos was unlike any other place he'd known before or after the precious years he'd spent there, fishing for crays.

Nearing the Easter Group, Onni perceived the pale shallows of the reefs. From a distance, the islands resembled illusory villages floating on water, the ribbons of land beneath the corrugated-iron shacks so low and brief. Beyond them, a free-spirited cray boat skirted the outer reef.

As the boat came through the Eastern Passage, Onni watched dozens of sooty black shearwaters take to the air from Campbell Island, soaring on the updraft of the south-westerly. Seabirds prospered here, where the push of a strong wind helped them launch into flight. They were ugly, shabby creatures, those mutton birds, but they moved with the elements rather than against them. They could teach a man a thing or two. That was island life for you—the fishermen learned the motions of the sea, the wind; they learned to move with both and predict their changing moods. And yet, after all those years, all those mornings spent on the water, the sea could still catch you off guard.

They had reached the home reef now. The boat sidled in to dock at a jetty and the crew fastened the vessel in place, making the same knots and loops he had once tied with his own deft young hands.

First stop, Little Rat.

Onni lumbered along the uneven slats of the timber jetty, his daughter offering an elbow for stability, clearly worried he might fall in. He had come full circle—it used to be the little children they worried about, playing absent-mindedly on the jetties. He waved her away.

'*Minä pärjään, ei tarvi koko ajan vahtia.*' No need to watch me all the time.

The brittle and rocky ground welcomed his unsure feet, bound in shoes this time around. The land was familiar—bone-dry and bleached white from the sun. The wind-bent saltbush a dull and muted shade of green. Many of the slab-and-tin huts they had built back in the early days were still standing, sandwiched between shiny new Colorbond roofs. But in all honesty, the place could never be fancy. Power still came from generators and water had to be carted out on the carrier boat.

The tour group was allocated a couple of hours for snorkelling, but Onni seldom swam these days. He and Hilda used the time instead to take a stroll around Little Rat. Slowly, they picked their way along the rubble path. Up ahead, a door banged rhythmically in the wind. He squinted. Yes, there it was. The little corri hut that his brother had started and Onni had completed. The hut that had cradled his small family against the blustering south wind all those years ago. Hilda quickened her step. She had been fifteen when they'd left, old enough to carry this place with her wherever she went afterwards. She pushed open the paint-stripped door and peered inside.

'*Tyhjä möki.*' Empty camp.

Ripped and faded curtains hung like rags on the window frames, and a rusted fridge lay on its side in the small kitchen. A few ceramic mugs were stacked in the open cabinet, the door of which had come off its hinges, and a cooking pot stood on the stove as if in readiness for the next meal. At the far end of the room, an old wire cot, rusted through, was leaning against the wall. It was as though the place had been left behind and later raided, like houses in wartime. The colours were of another era, washed-out mustard yellows and dung browns, pastel pinks and olive greens. Onni could see Alva here in his mind's eye. She wore a simple cotton dress that hung down to her ankles, her strong bare arms sun-kissed, her short, straight hair framing her round face and deep-set eyes. She mixed up Sunshine powdered milk, whisking it to froth for the gang of kids that ran amok outside the hut.

Through the next doorway they found Alva's sauna. The stove rusted through, a tin bucket and ladle on the floor next to it. Onni swallowed to rid himself of the lump in his throat. Hilda squeezed his shoulder and left him a moment, continuing along the island path, so that it was just Onni standing there in the tin camp with the ghost of Alva, his old heart aching.

They ambled further, to the south edge of the island, where an old street sign had been erected: *Ocean Drive*. But it only emphasised their distance from civilisation. Beyond that, a pot-bellied sea lion sunbathed at the entrance to what was once Latvian Igor's camp. Onni understood now what Risto had meant. This camp, too, was completely neglected, and the sea lions had taken up residence here. Igor's old camp still stood, but bent sideways somehow, his jetty crumbling. The sea lion barked and skidded away as they approached. The door to this camp was open too, and inside, a similar shambles. Onni watched as Hilda picked her way hesitantly through the single room. Igor had built a basic camp—enough space only for one. He had led a solitary existence, but eventually it had come to light that there'd been a wife once, a child too. Now Hilda stood before a jury-rigged shelf—a piece of timber that had been fixed to the wall. Igor's mantlepiece. She studied an object.

'What is it?' Onni peered over his daughter's shoulder. A small piece of porcelain lay on the shelf. 'What's that?' he asked again.

'It came from the Wallabis,' Hilda said. 'From the wreck.'

Onni studied the shard. A blue-brown pattern on a dusky yellowed background. It was something between them—Igor and Hilda—that did not include him. Onni had watched as Hilda attempted to befriend Igor all those years ago. He had always believed the taciturn Latvian to have a good heart, and so he'd let it run its course.

'I remember sitting on his jetty after the cyclone,' said Hilda, 'waiting for him to come back.'

'Yes,' said Onni. 'Until the sun went down and we called you in.'

He recalled her furrowed brow when he told her that Igor had disappeared. Maybe he'd gone out on a fishing expedition that night, they all said. Gone out on some crazy whim, looking for the catch of his life. And it was easier to think these thoughts than the alternative. But then Igor returned. Something had shifted in his daughter on seeing the Latvian's boat draw in beside the jetty, and Onni felt strangely thankful to him for weathering the storm.

Lunch was served back on the boat. Beef casserole, coleslaw and potato salad from a bain-marie. Onni and Hilda ate while the tour guide spoke about the marine life of the Abrolhos. He described the long migratory path taken by the crays. How the larvae drift up to a thousand kilometres offshore, where they grow and develop, before being swept back towards the continental shelf by winds and currents. Only after a series of moults and long treks across the seafloor do they reach full maturity, developing their hard, red outer shells. Many would die before they made it back to the offshore reefs.

Not for the first time, Onni was struck by the similarities between the crays and the migrant men who had fished for them. He thought of his brother, and wished suddenly to look out towards Disappearing Island, to where Nalle had gone down all those years ago. Leaving the cabin mid-presentation, he hobbled along the deck until he came to the stern. He gazed out to the south-west, to where waves crashed in scribbles of white foam around a low sandy island, flat as a pancake. Hilda had come after him, and stood a little way off. Onni remembered how he had jumped into the water there, had flailed, alone, in that same spot. It was on that day, as he motored back to Little Rat half drowned and drank in the view of the island, that he thought he understood, for a short while, what the elusive Sampo really was. That mystical gizmo from the Finnish epic *The Kalevala*. In the folktale it took the form of a mill that ground out flour and salt and money, and anything else its owner wished for. But in reality, it was something else altogether, something much less tangible. And it was fitting, thought Onni now, that in those ancient verses, the Sampo was lost at sea.

A member of the crew approached them on the deck.

'Better get Dad inside,' Onni heard him say to Hilda. 'We're moving on. Gets a bit blustery out here on the deck for the oldies.'

Hilda came to stand next to him.

'Man is a curious creature,' he said to her. 'He'll find a place like this, and then leave it behind. Spend years looking for it somewhere else.'

But they both knew it hadn't been that simple.

In the afternoon, they went north to the Wallabis. The boat skirted Morning Reef, the site of the *Batavia* wreck, and the guide told the three-hundred-year-old story of mutiny and murder. The name *abrolhos*, given to the islands by a seafarer during the spice trade period, for a long time was thought to mean, 'keep your eyes open'. It was now believed to mean 'spiked obstructions'. Either served as a fitting warning to early ships. Onni thought about all those wrecked boats, all those waterlogged bodies that scattered the reefs of the Abrolhos at one time or another. The flesh falling from bones and being taken up by reef-dwelling and pelagic fish.

That evening, the sea thrummed and the wind whistled and moaned outside the cabin window. Nesting birds let out shrill and tortured shrieks. Those noises used to frighten people; they took the shape of the angry and tormented ghosts of the *Batavia* saga. But Onni listened out for them. How he had missed the sound of the islands in his ears at night!

In the morning, the boat crossed the reef, headed for Leo Island, where a sandy cove awaited the tourists, aqua blue and crystalline. This was the spot. The place where Alva had imagined herself swimming only weeks before the cancer took hold. Onni remembered how she'd declared it so proudly when he'd asked her why she needed to go back: *Because I'm a swimmer now.* He'd dismissed it. And then she was gone. Leo Island was beautiful, he thought now. A lone camp was set back a small distance from the cove, from where a fishing family watched the tourists funnelling onto the beach.

Their beach.

Though no fisherman owned land out here. They leased their camps and came and went with the seasons. It was the islands that owned them, really.

Hilda stripped down to her bathers and waited for him.

'Let's take her out.' Hilda was holding on to the plastic container with the ashes inside.

Could they really be the ashes of Alva? Onni imagined the man from the crematorium scraping them up with his iron spade, like clearing out a fireplace. His thoughts became muddled, his stomach jittery. Onni thought himself unsentimental in regard to all this. He planned to donate his own corpse to the Australian National University's medical school. 'I finally got into university,' he'd said to Alva, when the letter came thanking him in advance for his generous contribution to science. Alva could hardly abide the thought of it. But Onni did not believe that the spirit remained with the physical body, or that the spirit carried on at all, for that matter. Except now, all of a sudden, when Onni didn't want to let Alva's ashes go. The moment had snuck up on him.

He shook his head. 'Too cold. You do it.'

'*Isä*,' Hilda said, '*tule, mennään. Tämä on Äitille.*' Dad, come. Let's go. This is for Mum.

He saw her as a little girl, with matted white hair and a brown, brown face, coaxing him in, coaxing them both in—him and Alva.

Onni stripped down to his shorts and followed his daughter to the water.

'*Oisinhan voinnut opettaa häntä uimaan*,' he said. '*Mutta sinä sen sitten teit.*' I wish I had thought to teach her to swim. But then you did it.

He saw the smile on Hilda's face and knew she'd been waiting for it. To hear him say it.

As they waded deeper into the lagoon, Onni caught Hilda looking at his old, ragged body, rough as salt cod. Her eyes went to the sagging folds of his stomach and drooping pectorals. He knew it pained her, now more than ever, to see his ageing plain like this. He lowered himself in and, like a hug from an old friend, the sea swamped him.

They slowly pushed out into deeper water, away from the tourists who paddled in the shallows. Along with the container, Hilda held two dried sprigs of Geraldton wax.

'What are those for?'

'We'll toss them out along with her.'

When they were far enough away from the chitter-chatter of other swimmers, Hilda stopped and passed one of the sprigs to Onni.

Now he wanted to get it done. He didn't want to dwell on it. Make a big thing out of it. But he took the sprig and waited for further instructions. He had to be cautious with Hilda, after the episode with the birch tree. Still, he stood by his act. The birch had to go. But he would keep this to himself.

Hilda began to sing then. The classic Finnish folksong about the girl from the small cottage who travels a long way from home.

Sä kasvoit neito kaunoinen
isäsi majassa,
kuin kukka kaunis suloinen
vihreellä nurmella.

You grew up, young girl,
In your father's cottage
Like a pretty flower
In a green field.

As she entered the second verse, she began to falter. She didn't know the song as well as the old people did. Onni heard his voice come from deep inside his abdomen, its low and tuneless timbre reaching out to catch the stumbling thread of Hilda's before the song fell over.

> *Maailma sitten vieroitti*
> *pois meidät toisistaan,*
> *vaan sua armas iäti*
> *mä muistan ainiaan.*

> The world took us
> Away from one another,
> But you, my love,
> I remember for eternity.

Hilda threw the ashes from the container, followed by her sprig of Geraldton wax. Onni followed suit, and they watched as parts of Alva slowly sank and disintegrated into the water.

The final tour activity was to meet the carrier boat, the *Irus II*, as it docked at Little Rat to deliver goods to the fishing families and collect the last few days' worth of cray hauls. Onni stood to the side, watching the familiar routine of mornings on the islands.

He turned when he heard his name called.

'Saarisen Onni?'

A middle-aged fisherman stood on an impressive jet boat. Onni squinted, studied the man's face. Yes, he knew those eyes. It was Ismo. Risto's boy.

'Ismo. *Mitäs poika?*' What do you know, son?

The two men shook hands and Onni waved Hilda over. They had been such good friends, Ismo and Hilda, and Onni watched as they struggled to reacquaint themselves with the older version of the other. Ismo's smile was awkward and out of place, and for some reason Onni thought of a helpless fish at the end of a line. They did a strange dance: one reaching out a hand, the other leaning in; the first withdrawing their hand and leaning in, the other now pulling back.

They laughed, abandoning both methods of greeting.

'Hang on,' said Ismo. 'I'll get Lauri.'

The other fisherman was shifting boxes on the *Irus II*, his head down, until Ismo intercepted him. Lauri looked across at Onni and Hilda before jumping nimbly over the side of the carrier boat and making his way towards them. He shook Onni's hand first and then turned to Hilda with a wide grin.

The brothers looked like islanders. Scruffy, unkempt. A few small holes, like round lagoons, in Lauri's paper-thin t-shirt.

The rosy colour in Hilda's cheeks had begun to fade. She asked about the camps, their disuse and decay.

'The industry's changing,' said Ismo. Each sentence was punctuated with a gesture, Onni noticed. 'Bigger fishers want to lease the cray licences off of the little guys to get a bigger quota. But they don't need the camps. Some of the camps haven't been used for years. Your old camp's empty.'

Hilda nodded.

'Bit of a shame. S'pose people thought they might come back—you know, maybe next year or the year after. So they left their stuff. But they never got back, for one reason or another. There are fewer families every year.'

Hilda and the boys had always turned to English, so Onni joined them. 'You only Finns left here?' he asked.

'Almost. There's just us, and the folks over on Leo's.'

'Things always changing. Never staying the same,' said Onni, nodding to himself.

'Mate. Big time. The shiny bums back on the mainland. Fisheries. They sit there, polishing their arses on their office chairs, makin' changes out here just to justify their jobs. They want to make this place a tourist destination. Throw us cray-fishermen out.

Onni shrank a little. Questioned himself—the tourist.

'The fishing's changing a lot too,' said Ismo. 'All our crays get shipped to Asia, to Taiwan and China. That's where the market is, see. We run by the Chinese calendar these days. Chinese lucky days, those are our lucky days too.'

'You guys love what you do?' asked Hilda.

'It's in our blood,' said Ismo. 'Crayfishing is all we know.' He looked to his brother. 'Lauri's most at home when he's here. Wants to die out here, don't you, Lauri?' Ismo looked around as he said *here*.

Lauri grinned, nodding towards the end of the jetty as he spoke, but Onni could only catch a word here and there. He noticed the hearing aids snug inside the man's ears. Like his.

Ismo repeated it, for Onni's sake most likely. 'Jokes with his kids about getting old and batty. He says that when he loses his marbles and he's no good to anyone anymore, they gotta bring him down here to this jetty and tell him to keep on walking.'

The four of them laughed. Onni wondered if Hilda was thinking about the accident. Then Lauri said something else.

'Yeah, Onni,' said Ismo. 'What was it that made you leave?'

'Ah, my back go bad,' he replied, because it was the easiest thing to say. Like many migrants, he was an industrious man at heart, with a mind to make a small fortune, but he had fallen short of his aspirations. As he got older, he'd begun to accept the past, seeing that chance blew you about like the variable north wind. But it had been that one morning on the sea that had made him leave, really.

Luckily, Alva and Hilda had gone earlier, on the charter plane which by that stage flew between the islands and the mainland. Onni had failed to notice the small warning signs of a rising sea. Now, he remembered the *Kalevala* verse that Sulo used to recite, and wished he'd paid closer attention:

> *Katsaise etinen ilma,*
> *tarkkoa takainen taivas,*
> *onko selvät ilman rannat,*
> *onko selvät vai sekavat!*

> Look before you into ether,
> look behind you at the heavens,
> well examine the horizon,
> whether clear or filled with trouble!

Not that it had ended in disaster. And that made it harder to bear, in a way. It was one wave that haunted him afterwards. He remembered how the dark water had risen up in front of him, and he had thought of joining his brother in that moment. For the first time, he had understood that death would come to him, too.

Onni had never found his rhythm on the sea again. The fear stayed with him, and when his back began to nag he welcomed the injury with some sense of relief. He and Sulo had talked a little at that time. Sulo had said the ocean could do that to you. Make you think you knew her, then turn on you. She was not a loyal friend, he'd said. And yet you couldn't turn your back on her, thought Onni. Throughout his whole life, he was happiest when he was by the sea. Even in recent years, as he fished from the beach at the north side of Sunpatch, hunched and struggling with an empty hook, he was happy.

Back on the jetty, Ismo asked Hilda what she did for a living.

'A nurse.'

'You'd be good at that. You always had a sure hand.'

'Yeah, and I never minded the blood and guts.'

They laughed. Lauri was grinning, looking sideways at his brother as he gestured a reply. Ismo shook his head.

'Yeah, yeah. Lauri's giving me shit because I always put my hand over the eyes of my catch.' He turned his palms out, his mouth cracking into a sheepish smile. 'I met a Greek fisherman years ago. He was fishing off Roma. Used to do it. Reckoned it eased their panic.'

Ismo had been a sensitive kid, Onni remembered now, and in some ways he was surprised that he'd stuck it out on the islands. But it looked as though he'd found a place here with his brother. They complemented one another, one man making up for what was lacking in the other.

'So, you like what you do then, Hilda?' asked Ismo, returning Hilda's earlier question.

'Sure, it's fine. Nothing like this, though. This is the life, hey, Dad?'

Onni smiled, taking in the surrounding islands.

'You can come decky for us next season,' offered Ismo, and Lauri nodded.

Hilda laughed. 'I think that boat has sailed.'

'You could do it,' Onni heard himself say. 'Why not? Riitta's already off living her own life.' He knew it came too late. She'd needed the permission years ago, not now. She would have made a fine skipper.

'Well, if you change your mind . . .' Ismo told Hilda.

Onni the old man shook hands with both fishermen.

'You got the good life,' he told them. 'If I be a young man again, and I can choose what to do with my life, I choose the fishing.'

The tourist boat headed back east, and Onni watched the islands dip below the horizon. He'd learned many years ago that the Sampo couldn't be kept.

It was a feeling.

A moment.

A shard of island that may disappear at any time in the waters of a rising sea.

Author's Note

THE ISLANDS IS A WORK OF FICTION, however, my imaginings have been informed by my family's experiences living and working on the Abrolhos Islands between 1959 and 1972. I have not had the pleasure of calling the Abrolhos home, but the islands have held a place in my family's collective memory for many years. I hope I have gone some way to depicting the beauty and wildness of this unique landscape and way of life. Any errors are entirely my own.

My work has also been informed by talks with crayfishers and their families, and several works of fiction and non-fiction. *Abrolhos Islands Conversations*, compiled by Alison Wright, with artwork by Victor France and Larry Mitchell, offers wonderful insights into island life in the twentieth century. *Islands of Angry Ghosts* by Hugh Edwards presents a thorough account of the Batavia shipwreck and mutiny, and the eventual discovery of the wreckage in the 1960s. Hat tip to Thea Astley and Elizabeth Strout, whose brilliant novels, *Drylands* and *Olive Kitterage*, inspired the novel-in-stories form I have used here.

Acknowledgements

THE STORIES IN *THE ISLANDS* take place on the unceded lands of the Yamatji and Yuin peoples, and were written on Bundjalung and Yuin country. I acknowledge the First Nations peoples as the original custodians and storytellers of those regions.

This book began while staying in a fishing shack on Little Rat Island in 2016. I am indebted to the fishing families of the Abrolhos. Among them, I wish to thank the Laine family—Tapio, Jenny and Harry—for inviting my mother and I to the islands and for sharing your stories with me. To the wider Laine family, thank you for welcoming us to Geraldton with such open arms, and especially to Lisa and Kari for reading the book in manuscript form. A heartfelt thank you to Elina and Uuno Tolonen for welcoming me to Perth as one of your own, and for sharing with me your memories of my grandparents and the early days in Western Australia.

Cheers to fishermen Jim Nedwich and Ben McDonald for your guidance on all things boating and fishing.

A big thanks to Geraldton-based poet Nola Gregory for helping me to shape the character of Woolly. Nola is a descendant of the Gija and Bard peoples of the East and West Kimberley. Also to Kizzy Nye, Walbanga woman of the Yuin people, for your sound advice on the beach haul fishermen of the NSW south coast.

To my Year 12 English teacher Francesca Harmey, thank you for instilling in me a love of literature and giving me confidence in my ability to write. Since then, I have had several great teachers and mentors, including the wonderful lecturers at UTS, Lynda Hawryluk at SCU and Byron Writers Festival's Marele Day. Thank you for your wise council. Thanks also to everyone at Byron Writers Festival for your ongoing support and encouragement.

It has been a privilege to work with the team at Allen & Unwin. Thanks to Annette Barlow for having faith in *The Islands* from the outset and providing the framework needed to grow this book to maturity. To Ali Lavau, for your hawk eye and genuine care for the story. What a pleasure it was to receive your correspondence. A special thank you to Courtney Lick for going the distance with me, to graphic designer Alissa Dinallo for the beautiful cover art and to proofreader Clara Finlay for the expert and thorough review. I'm grateful to all those behind The Australian/Vogel's Literary Award, for which my manuscript was shortlisted in 2020, and to Varuna Writers House and the exceptional writers I met during my stay.

Love and gratitude to all those who read early drafts of *The Islands*—my dear friends, various members of the Mad Crew, my cousins, brother, family friends, colleagues and family-'in-law'—thank you for showing an interest in the project. In doing so, you helped me believe in its worth and gave me the courage to continue. Special mentions are owed to: Rachael Ferguson, for nutting things out with me at various times; to Sarah McVeigh and Amy Piddington, for your enthusiastic and whole-hearted engagement with the story; to Sam Rhodes, Garry Hough and, again, Francesca Harmey, for offering your thoughtful feedback and contributing to the development of the novel.

Enormous appreciation to my aunties, Seija and Tuija, for your willingness to share your memories and stories with me, for giving me permission to use them as fodder in fiction and for the hours spent reading and remembering. Also to my family in Finland, for answering my many queries about folklore and Finnish proverbs, for offering assistance when needed and for reading the work along the way.

Thanks Dad, for your unwavering support of everything I do. Deep gratitude to my partner, Josh Vogel, for reading and re-reading, for the endless discussions and insights, for always believing and for backing me in this long-drawn-out creative pursuit.

The biggest thanks of all goes out to my mum, Kaija Talviharju, who tirelessly read and edited every single chapter of *The Islands*, multiple times, over the past six years. Your excellent ideas and understanding of the Finnish character have played an important hand in creating this book and the people within it. *The Islands* would not exist without you. Thank you also for reading to me when I was little and for showing me the magic of stories. How fortunate we are to share a love of books and writing.

And finally, to Mummu and Pappa (Maila and Auno 'Herman' Talviharju), for leading me to the sea. *Kiitos. Johdatit minut merelle.*

Credits

(collection first published in 1946), translation © Herbert Lomas, 1986, in *Books From Finland Issue 4*: https://www.booksfromfinland.fi/1986/12/poems-5/, printed with permission.

Quote on page 128: from the traditional folk song *Isontalon Antti ja Rannanjärvi*, public domain, translation © Kaija Talviharju, 2021.

Quote on page 218: from the Christmas song *Joulupuu on Rakennettu*, public domain, translation © Kaija Talviharju, 2021.

Quote on page 259: from the folk song *Kultainen Nuoruus*, lyrics by Kullervo, © Warner Chappell Music Finland, translation © Kaija Talviharju, 2021, printed with permission.

Quote on page 273: from *The Grapes of Wrath*, by John Steinbeck, published by Penguin Random House in 1992 (first published by Viking Press Inc., 1939), printed with permission.

Quote on page 288–289: from the traditional folk song *Lapsuuden Toverille (Sä kasvoit neito kaunoinen)*, by P.J. Hannikainen, public domain, translation © Kaija Talviharju, 2021.